THE KID FROM RIGA

The weapon in his hands grew hot as he fired at the soldier who advanced towards them in a scuttling crouch. Then he felt Otto's hand on his shoulder shaking him roughly.

'The building,' he shouted above the thunder of the artillery. He started to climb from the trench and a shell exploded to their left. Otto was thrown back by the force of the explosion and Peter could feel the shrapnel humming past his face. His left ear stung as if a wasp had attacked him and he clapped his hand to it. The blood that flowed from the severed lobe felt warm on his hand. Dazed, he looked up and saw why Otto had called the warning.

The whole façade that towered above him seemed to sway gently, then great fissures appeared and it started to lose its shape before gathering momentum and crashing down upon him.

By the same author

MICHAEL MOLLOY

The Kid From Riga

Futura

A Futura Book

First published in Great Britain in 1987
by Hodder & Stoughton Ltd

This edition published in 1989 by Futura Publications,
a Division of Macdonald & Co (Publishers) Ltd
London & Sydney

ISBN 0 7088 4230 5

Reproduced, printed and bound in Great Britain by
Hazell Watson & Viney Limited
Member of BPCC plc
Aylesbury, Bucks, England

Futura Publications
A Division of
Macdonald & Co (Publishers) Ltd
66–73 Shoe Lane
London EC4P 4AB
A member of Maxwell Pergamon Publishing Corporation plc

for Sandy

Into my heart an air that kills
From yon far country blows:
What are those blue remembered hills,
What spires, what farms are those?

That is the land of lost content,
I see it shining plain,
The happy highways where I went
And cannot come again.

A Shropshire Lad
A. E. HOUSMAN

PROLOGUE

Berlin, 29 April, 1945

Peter Holtz roused himself from a dozing, fitful sleep and realised numbly that he could not remember the last time he had taken off his uniform. But he could recall the day he'd first put it on. His leather boots had been buffed to a deep glow and the rough grey wool of his tunic and trousers pressed sharp to the creases.

Now the boots were cracked and his tunic impregnated with dirt and sweat, but it no longer itched where it touched his skin. He wore it now as an animal does its pelt, as much a part of his body as muscle or bone.

His eyes were bloodshot, and the lids red-raw from the yellowish dust that clogged his nose and mouth and rose like mist from the ruins of the city around him.

Once this shattered landscape had formed one of Europe's proudest capitals. Now the elegant buildings lay devastated as if stamped upon by angry giants.

Except for the great edifice that rose above the trench he crouched in, everything else was in ruins or reduced to rubble by the ceaseless bombing that the city had endured; somehow this building had escaped destruction. Despite the pitted shrapnel scars, the scrolls and carvings that decorated its regal façade remained to serve as a testament to the glories of the past.

In the east, the sky began to turn pale green with streaks of orange and red heralding the sun. Ahead in the distance he heard a rumbling sound and the squeal of metal upon metal.

He nudged Otto who lay asleep in the trench beside him, his head, with its stubble of grey hair, resting on the crude anti-tank weapon he cradled in his arms. Otto

9

grunted and rubbed his eyes, spat to clear his throat of the dust and scanned the ruins before them anxiously.

'Tank,' he said in a hoarse voice. 'Here come the Ivans.' He raised the Panzerfauste bazooka to his shoulder. 'Come on, hero,' he said, referring to the Iron Cross Peter Holtz wore at his throat. 'Time to go to work.'

Peter took a magazine, snapped it into his machine-pistol, cocked the weapon and waited.

'Don't fire until I rout them out,' Otto ordered as the noise came closer.

'I know,' Peter replied, his voice steady.

Slowly the muzzle of the Russian T34 nosed around the shell of a building about fifty metres from them. It reminded him of a prehistoric monster sniffing for its prey. They could see the crouching figures accompanying the tank as they darted between the piles of rubble. Despite the bagginess of the brown uniforms Peter could make out that one of them was a woman.

Slowly the tank loomed closer until it seemed to fill his entire field of vision. He could smell oil on hot metal and the shattering cacophony from the engine roared inside his head. Then Otto fired the bazooka and the shell pierced the steel side of the monster and exploded like a great bell being rung. Two of the crew tried to escape. They were so close as they scrambled from the turret that Peter could see the indentations his bullets made as they slapped against the soft black leather of their tank coats.

From the surrounding trenches, the rest of the company began to fire on the retreating troops. Peter saw the woman running and aimed a burst just as she got to cover.

Quickly he changed the empty magazine of his machine-pistol and as he did so, he noticed his hands. They were cracked and ingrained with dirt, the nails jagged and rimmed with filth. He remembered his mother's warning: 'A gentleman is never dirty,' and suddenly his childhood seemed so long ago.

Captain Kahz half raised himself from the trench next to theirs and shouted for attention from the remains of his company. Although his uniform was in tatters, he looked the perfect image of the German fighting man; craggy features, hard, sinewy body, and at his throat the

10

Knight's Cross which he had won before the gates of Moscow.

'This is it, lads,' he shouted in the silence that had descended. 'No more retreating. Our orders are to hold here. Remember to die like soldiers for Germany.'

He slid back into the trench and Otto turned to Peter: 'The Ivans will bring up artillery now.'

Almost as he spoke there was the crack from a Russian self-propelled field gun and a chunk from the corner of the building exploded and showered them with fragments of masonry. Then shells began to hammer down around them and the ground shook violently, as though they were inside a great ship in a storm. Through the yellow dust they could see the misty figures of brown-clad infantry moving on their positions once again.

The weapon in his hands grew hot as he fired at the soldier who advanced towards them in a scuttling crouch. Then he felt Otto's hand on his shoulder shaking him roughly.

'The building,' he shouted above the thunder of the artillery. He started to climb from the trench and a shell exploded to their left. Otto was thrown back by the force of the explosion and Peter could feel the shrapnel humming past his face. His left ear stung as if a wasp had attacked him and he clapped his hand to it. The blood that flowed from the severed lobe felt warm on his hand. Dazed, he looked up and saw why Otto had called the warning.

The whole façade that towered above him seemed to sway gently, then great fissures appeared and it started to lose its shape before gathering momentum and crashing down upon him.

Afterwards, there was silence and the gently drifting yellow dust. Peter was pinned beneath two great chunks of masonry, but he was alive. He could feel the blood soaking into the collar of his tunic. A figure in brown Russian uniform looked down on him. He blinked to focus his eyes and saw it was the woman he had tried to kill. She looked at his dirt-streaked face and the blond, tousled hair.

'Who are you?' she said in German. She had a gentle, cultivated voice similar to his mother's.

11

'Private Peter Holtz,' he said clearly.

'What is your age?'

Peter thought for a moment. 'I am twelve years old,' he said.

'God Save the Queen' we living sing,
From height to height 'tis heard;
And with the rest your voices ring,
Lads of the Fifty-third.

A Shropshire Lad
A. E. HOUSMAN

Chapter One

The rain had stopped but a light breeze blew from the east down Pall Mall which made Lewis Horne shiver as he stood on the top step of the Reform Club and looked up into a bright blue sky.

He was sunburned but not with the even colour that comes from lying beside a swimming pool. The tan was harsh and patchy and the hands that adjusted the collar of his raincoat were calloused with tiny, healing nicks like those of a workman who has been busy at his trade.

Charles Austen Mars and his wife, Sybil, stood on the pavement below looking very grand. Charlie was wearing a black silk top hat tipped forward over his brow and a heavy gold watch-chain hung across the waistcoat of his morning clothes. The top hat and Charlie's tall, bony frame made Sybil appear almost childlike from Lewis's vantage point. The pale cream and rose dress that matched her complexion emphasised her slenderness and the wide-brimmed straw hat that framed her face was trimmed with fresh flowers. He had never seen her looking so good.

Charlie closed the great black umbrella that he carried, shook it free of raindrops and unconsciously let it flap unfurled as he had been taught to do at Eton. They both looked up and smiled at Lewis as he came down the steps.

'Now I can see how you looked on your wedding day,' Lewis said as he joined them. Charlie gave a short, barking laugh.

'You should have seen *her* on our wedding day – seven months pregnant and her nose all red from crying. I almost walked away from the registry office.'

Sybil punched his arm as the three of them turned and started to walk towards St James's Palace. 'He's told that story to the girls so many times that he's started to believe it,' she said. Lewis looked at her and thought, once again, how deceptive women could be. It seemed incredible that the daughters she referred to were now under-graduates.

'Isn't London lovely after the rain?' Sybil said. Charlie nodded.

'Always at its best after a good wash.'

Lewis looked along Pall Mall; the air had a brilliant clarity as the sunshine flashed and sparkled from the gleaming traffic that splashed through the puddles of rainwater. He thought how different it was from the deadening heat and clouds of choking dust he had driven through a few days before.

When they reached Marlborough Road they turned left and started towards The Mall, where groups of people in similar finery strolled towards Buckingham Palace.

Lewis found it slightly odd to keep to the easy step that Sybil set and glanced around at the crowd, relieved to notice that some of the other men wore dark suits as he did. There were a few military uniforms and the oc-casional exotic dignitary in national costume. A slim major in the Scots Guards stalked past them and Sybil turned to Lewis and said: 'Why didn't you wear your uniform?'

'If it comes to that, why aren't you wearing a top hat either?' Charlie spoke in a slightly plaintive voice.

'I've got another appointment later,' Lewis said as he thrust his hands into the pockets of his raincoat. 'Dress uniform or morning coat would be a little obtrusive where I'm going.'

'Oh, yes. I forgot that spies can't afford to stand out in a crowd,' Sybil spoke quietly as she looked up in amuse-ment at Charlie who, in his top hat, was at least a foot and a half taller than anyone else.

Distracted by the greeting called out by an acquaint-ance, Charlie missed the irony in Sybil's voice.

'For God's sake, Syb. We're not spies,' he said, as he nodded in reply to the man who had called to him.

'Secret agents then,' she said, as she grinned at Lewis.

'Security officers is the preferred designation – that's all – nothing melodramatic,' Charlie said in a slightly pompous voice.

16

'Well, it sounds jolly dull. I think it was more glamorous when you were a history don.'

Lewis glanced across to St James's Park as the two of them wrangled amicably. Cars were parked close together on the wide verges to each side of The Mall; most of them were accompanied by chauffeurs but the occasional figure stood in a way that told Lewis he was a bodyguard.

'It is a shame that Hanna couldn't come today,' Sybil said lightly, but Lewis could feel the probe.

'Yes,' he said non-committally and looked away to where a bearded policeman was talking to a stately African in skull-cap and flowing robes.

'I was just saying it's a pity that Hanna couldn't be with us, Charles.' Sybil was trying another tack.

'Mmmm . . .' Charlie answered, obviously preoccupied, then turned to Lewis with sudden attention. 'Where is she by the way?'

'Paris,' Lewis said in the same flat voice. 'At a medical conference, I think; we haven't seen each other for a few weeks.'

Charlie took the hint, raised his eyebrows to Sybil as a warning and changed the subject.

'Where did your father say he'd meet us?'

'By the north bandstand. Wherever that may be.'

'That direction,' Lewis said casually as he pointed without thinking towards Marble Arch. Sybil noticed that he had made the gesture instinctively.

'Can you always tell which point of the compass you're facing, Lewis?' Sybil said with interest. He looked at her in surprise.

'Yes, I thought everyone could.'

'No,' Charlie said. 'It's a bit like whistling – some can, some can't.'

By now they had skirted the roundabout in front of the Palace and crossed Constitution Hill to join the queue waiting to pass through the gate to the right of the great entrance. As they shuffled forward with the crowd Charlie hummed *'They're Changing Guard at Buckingham Palace'*.

'How many times have you seen the guard changed, Lewis?' Sybil said.

17

'I *stood* guard here when I was a subaltern,' he said. 'The song's right. A soldier's life is very hard.'

A policeman examined their blue entrance cards and waved them on towards the quadrangle that lay behind the familiar frontage of the Palace.

'This will destroy thousands of pounds' worth of new shoes,' Sybil said as they crunched across the rough gravel towards the Grand Entrance.

'Imagine what it's like for a guardsman who's been up all night polishing his boots,' a Bishop, resplendent in purple and gaiters said to them as they walked with him into The Marble Hall. Lewis had been inside the Palace before so he hardly bothered to glance around at the paintings and the cases of Chelsea pottery in The Bow Room. But the other guests, who were for the most part on their first visit, gazed with fascination as if hoping to find the odd Royal person lounging about with their feet up on the sofas. Eventually they passed out onto the long terrace that looked over the largest private garden in London before making their way there for the Garden Party proper. It was a splendid sight.

Below, Lewis could see Gentlemen Ushers briefing those people who might be graced with a few moments conversation and hundreds of others forming great avenues that members of the Royal family would pass down in order to reach their own private enclave. A green and pleasant land, he thought as he gazed upon the lawns and the heavy foliage of the trees. For a moment Lewis contrasted it all with the bleak desert landscape he had so recently left. Then they descended the wide steps and turned right on the gravelled pathway to find Sybil's father seated on a shooting stick in front of a bandstand. He was listening to a vigorous rendition of *'Those Daring Young Men In Their Flying Machines'*.

'Hello, Fred,' Charlie said as they stood before him.

'My dears,' Lord Pickford replied warmly and with a rather nice display of manners raised his hat to his daughter.

'You know Captain Horne, I think,' Charlie said.

'Of course. How are you, Lewis? Fit?'

18

'Fine, General,' Lewis answered.

Sybil's father was one of those tough looking aristocrats with great, broad shoulders and a broken nose, who could easily be mistaken for a prize fighter until he spoke with a clipped Edwardian accent.

Lord Pickford stood up and snapped the handles of his shooting stick together. The band began to play *Blaze Away* as he turned to his daughter: 'Sybil, your Aunt Lizzie is over there by the tea tent hoping to get a look at the Princess of Wales. Run along and keep her company, will you?'

Sybil looked at her father with a mixture of exasperation and amusement. 'One day, dad, you will be stoned to death by feminists,' but she did his bidding after a wave to Charlie and Lewis. Lord Pickford watched her go with satisfaction.

'More like her mother every day, Charlie, every day – good lot those Cheevnings. All the girls are stunners. Met a young gel here today, same sort. Says she wants to interview me.'

'What about?' Charlie asked as the three of them began to stroll along the path that ran parallel with Constitution Hill. Pickford thought for a moment. It was an affectation of his to pretend that he was growing a little slow in his old age.

'Writing a book about the control commission in Germany after the war. She'd heard I played some part in that business.'

As they walked beneath the trees that hung over the pathway, the last remnants of the afternoon's rainfall occasionally fell on them from the overhanging foliage. As if to take his revenge upon nature, Lord Pickford jabbed at the grass verge with his shooting stick.

'There's a lot of talk about the House that we've got a traitor in Whitehall,' he said evenly. 'Is that so?'

'Everything seems to point to that conclusion,' Charlie spoke in the same tone as he smiled acknowledgment to a South American Naval attaché.

'What do you call them now? Moles, isn't it?'

'That's the current terminology,' Charlie said.

19

'I prefer the word traitor,' Pickford countered with conviction. 'Mole is too friendly for my vocabulary. Sounds warm and jolly. And there's nothing lovable about betraying your country. Do you think it right to call him a mole, Captain?' he suddenly said.

Lewis considered for a moment. 'He's well dug in and he's ruining the lawn – I think it's a fair description.'

'Which particular lawn is he ruining at the moment?' Pickford asked.

'Quatara,' Lewis said and smiled ruefully as he thought of the few lawns they actually had in that tiny country.

'Refresh me about Quatara,' Pickford said briskly.

'A desert kingdom, or rather, it used to be. Mostly Bedouin,' Charlie said. 'The Royal Family are pro-British as we put them on the throne. Still massive oil revenues despite the recent drop in world prices and they mostly spent it here until the revolution. A small, effective army initially trained by us called the Loyal Legion. Eighteen months ago there was a coup led by a group of Marxist revolutionaries who rather cleverly locked up the Royal Family in the palace while the Legion was out of the capital on exercises and threatened to execute them if the Army tried anything. The Legion crossed into the next state which is friendly to us.'

Pickford looked at Lewis. 'What condition is the Legion in now?'

Lewis looked towards Charlie Mars.

'Come on, young man,' Pickford said. 'You didn't get that suntan at Frinton.'

Charlie nodded. Lewis paused to collect his thoughts, then began: 'The Legion's in fair shape but morale is low. You know how Arabs like action. Meanwhile, the revolutionaries are training up some fair competition. They've got Russian advisers and equipment. From what I saw, I'd say a year and they'll be equal to the Legion.'

Pickford nodded.

'Oh, there's another element as well,' Charlie said. 'The Brotherhood; a group of Shi-ite zealots who want a fundamentalist religious state. They would murder anyone's grandmother, including their own, in the name

of Allah. They hate the Royal Family and the Revolutionaries in equal measure.'

'What is the Royal Family like – are they good people?'
Charlie turned to Lewis again.

'I think *you*'d better answer that. You know that part
of the world better than me.'

Lewis shrugged. 'It's difficult to use the word "good" in
relation to them. They're Arabs, they have their own
values.'

'What do you mean by that?' Pickford said sharply.

Lewis thought for a while as they walked through a
part of the garden that was heavily shaded by trees.

'British people think the whole world wants to emulate
us, with our laws, moral values and institutions. When
they see foreigners here they fondly imagine they've come
to improve themselves; get an education, absorb some
democracy. It isn't like that. Arabs want to stay Arabs. Oh,
they might want to buy a hospital from us, or a racehorse,
or our latest military hardware, but in all essential things
they will remain true to themselves. What might be called
"a good Arab" in Whitehall is capable of the kind of behav-
iour we haven't seen in this country since the Wars of the
Roses. And the Marxist Arabs are the same. Few of them
go in for moderation. It seems to be a racial trait.'

'So you're saying you can't trust any of them?' Lewis
paused again.

'No. Under certain circumstances it is impossible for
an Arab to break his word.'

'That sounds very Irish,' Pickford said as he jabbed with
particular ferocity with his shooting stick. Lewis nodded
in agreement. 'Arabs can be very Irish.'

'So how is the mole affecting things?' Pickford asked.
Charlie waited until they had passed a harried-looking
man in hired morning clothes who was being harangued
by his wife and plump daughter for not arranging an
introduction to the Queen Mother. 'I'm only a bloody
Mayor,' their victim kept saying plaintively in a Black
Country accent. When they had passed, Charlie spoke:
'We had some good people in Quatara. Every time we tried
to organise something to bring back the Royal Family, the
revolutionary government got to hear of it. They may be

Marxists but they cling to some of the old ways – such as public beheading.'

'So you're still hunting the mole?' Pickford said.

'We think of little else,' Charlie replied as they watched a confident girl with ash-blonde hair walk towards them. She was accompanied by a thin, elderly man in a well-pressed, brown suit, who looked vaguely familiar to Lewis.

'Here comes the gel I told you about,' Pickford said.

Lewis watched her with interest: despite Lord Pickford's description she was nothing like Sybil. The girl was slim but with an athlete's body, quite unlike the willowy shape of Charlie's wife. Her face was open with a dusting of freckles across the high cheeks and slightly snub nose. Her straight hair was fringed and cut just above shoulder length. If Sybil was the school Ophelia, Lewis decided, then this girl was Captain of Games.

Despite the low heels she wore, her legs seemed very long and the bare shoulders above her light blue summer dress were finely shaped. He felt a sudden stab of physical attraction and then a moment of regret as Hanna came into his mind. She glanced in his direction as they were introduced.

'Jessica Crossley, Lewis Horne.' Lord Pickford made the introductions and Lewis felt her dry, warm palm press into his. Her blue eyes flickered over him and the large, well-formed mouth twitched into a fleeting smile. Then he was ignored.

'Hello, Jack,' Pickford said to the man in the brown suit.

"Ow are yer, Fred?' he replied in a gruff Cockney accent, and Lewis instantly recognised the boney features of Lord Silver.

'Bit off your beat isn't it, Jack?' Lord Pickford said in a friendly voice.

'I only came 'ere to frighten Tory women,' he said dryly. 'One recognised me a minute ago and made the sign of the cross.'

They all laughed but Lewis knew there was truth in the remark. In the years before he accepted his peerage, Jack Silver had been a considerable figure of dread in the safe Tory shires of England.

22

'You're Austen Mars, the historian,' Jessie said to Charlie.

'I am,' Charlie admitted with a slight, self-mocking bow.

'I've read some of your books. I enjoyed them, although it wasn't my period,' she said in an easy, conversational tone. Lewis was impressed. Charlie could be fairly intimidating to someone of her age.

'What *is* your period, Miss Crossley?' Charlie asked politely.

'Post-World War II Europe. At the moment I'm writing about German women in the aftermath of the war.'

'A rich seam of investigation, and these two gentlemen are helping you?' Charlie said as he gestured towards the two Lords.

'As a member of the control commission and Jack here a trade union delegate, I can't think of two people better qualified,' Pickford said. 'Imagine how you would feel, Charlie, if you could actually speak to a couple of chaps who were in Cromwell's parliament.'

'Quite so, but beware of the pitfalls, Miss Crossley.'

'What would they be, Mr Mars?'

Charlie smiled dryly at the two elderly peers who stood in attendance each side of her. 'Well, the memory can be deceptive and human nature being what it is, most people subconsciously adjust events of the past to show themselves in the best possible light.'

'What do you suggest to avoid that eventuality?' Jessica Crossley said.

'Question them separately about each other,' Charlie said with a grin. 'And then ask a third party who knows them both.'

'Well, you can start with me,' Lord Silver said emphatically. 'I'm dying for a cuppa.' Jessica Crossley hesitated for a moment until Lord Silver took her firmly by the arm and guided her towards the tea tents.

'Wait, I'm coming with you,' Pickford called. 'I don't want that scoundrel telling you a lot of nonsense about me.'

'She'd better look out for Jack Silver,' Charlie said to Lewis as they watched the trio walk away. 'He used to have a considerable reputation as a ladies' man.'

'Really?' Lewis scrutinised the back of the retreating man with renewed interest.

'Oh, yes,' Charlie said. 'There was even a joke about some lady coming out of a lift with him and saying she now knew what a silver lining was.' Lewis chuckled.

'Do you think Miss Crossley is safe with him?'

Charlie nodded. 'Oh, yes. If he tried anything I'm sure Fred would run him through with that shooting stick.'

They turned away and continued to stroll off the pathway through the wet grass.

'Where did Bellingford say he would meet us?' Charlie asked.

'By the lake – near the bridge,' Lewis replied. They walked on in silence for a while, then Charlie spoke: 'I gather things are a little strained between you and Hanna,' he said in a carefully neutral voice. 'Is there anything Sybil and I can do? You know how fond we are of you both.'

Lewis thought for a while. 'Thanks – but no. I'll just have to see how things work out in the next few weeks.'

Before Charlie could question him further they both spotted Jeremy Bellingford, looking the part of the junior minister as he stood talking to a man of medium height.

Bellingford's companion was slightly plump which the superb cut of the morning clothes did much to disguise. His dark features were round and blunt and he had a small, well-trimmed moustache. His cravat was fastened with a huge diamond; it was a solitary hint of flashiness. Next to him Bellingford possessed the fashionplate perfection of a tailor's dummy.

'Ah, gentlemen,' Bellingford said in a hearty voice as they approached, his eyes flickering over Lewis's informal dress with obvious annoyance. 'Mr Ahmed, may I be permitted to introduce Charles Mars and Captain Lewis Horne?'

The Arab nodded haughtily to Lewis and turned to Charlie. 'Mr Bellingford has just been telling me we were at the same school,' he said in an English accent as perfect as the cut of the diamond at his throat.

'Yes,' Charlie said.

24

'What house?'

Charlie told him and they continued to discuss the mystical practices of Eton for a few moments until Mr Ahmed turned to Lewis: 'This must be all rather confusing to an ill-dressed grammar school yobbo like you,' he said in a pleasant voice. Lewis looked him up and down for a moment while the smile froze on Bellingford's face. When Lewis replied, it was in a calm, even tone.

'I knew they let gyppos into Eton but I had no idea that the Palace had become so lax. You may have got that suit at Savile Row but it still looks as if it's stuffed with camel dung.'

The colour which had drained from Bellingford's face rushed back in a deep blush of rage.

'HORNE!' he said in a choking voice. 'How dare you speak to a guest of Her Majesty's Government in that appalling manner. Apologise at once.'

'If you insist, Jeremy,' Lewis said in an innocent voice. He spoke rapidly to Mr Ahmed in Arabic. It seemed to mollify him; at least he bowed slightly to Lewis.

'What did you say?' Charlie asked.

'I told him that under the pretext of running a brothel his father was a receiver of stolen goods.'

Charlie looked impressed. 'That's paraphrasing Johnson, isn't it?'

Lewis nodded. 'I changed mother to father. Arabs feel insults about their fathers with greater keenness.' He turned to Mr Ahmed again. 'Don't you, you sheep-stealing Bedouin bastard?'

Bellingford looked transfixed with horror. He was trying to speak but found that he could only make a curious kind of noise, like water gurgling through old plumbing.

Then Mr Ahmed began to laugh, revealing startling, white teeth. He produced a large silk handkerchief and wiped his eyes.

'My dear fellow, let us put Mr Bellingford out of his misery.'

Horne held out his hand and Ahmed took it in both of his.

'You look well, Lewis. You don't seem to have changed since we were at Sandhurst.' He slapped the plumpness of his stomach. 'How do you like my look of portly grandeur?'

'Very becoming, Ali,' Lewis said.

Suddenly, Mr Ahmed seemed to stand straighter, his expression serious.

'Will you give me a moment with Captain Horne alone, gentlemen?' He spoke with quiet politeness, but there was a barely perceptible note of command in the voice. Bellingford seemed ready to object but Charlie Mars gently guided him away. When they were out of earshot Ahmed clasped his hands behind his back and studied Lewis.

'I think I owe Bellingford an apology,' he said. 'I tricked him into arranging this meeting without telling him that I know you.'

'I rather gathered that,' Lewis said dryly.

Ahmed took his time before speaking again. He gazed around the great sun-dappled garden still sparkling from the rainfall. The band was playing '*Summertime*' and the multitude, in their dignity, crisscrossed the lawn as if taking part in some intricate military tattoo. It was a very English occasion. Ahmed smiled.

'You know, when I am at home I miss this extraordinary country very much.' He looked across the gardens for a few moments more then turned to Lewis again and spoke very briskly. 'You remember my brother, Rashid?'

'Yes,' Lewis answered. It was hard not to remember him as he appeared at least twice a week in the gossip columns. Ahmed held out a card.

'It is a telephone number in Paris,' he explained. 'Please call him there tomorrow night after six o'clock. It is important.'

Lewis nodded and placed the card in his top pocket. Ahmed relaxed again and smiled at him. 'I see from your file you have written a book. Was it successful?'

Lewis shrugged and smiled back. 'It got some friendly reviews, but the English Civil War isn't the stuff best-sellers are made of.' Ahmed nodded slightly in the direction of Bellingford and Charlie Mars.

'What about those two? Are they trustworthy?'

Lewis thrust his hands deep into his raincoat pockets.

'Bellingford is highly ambitious.

'He doesn't know it, but he wants to be Prime Minister of a Britain that vanished in 1914. Charlie Mars is the best friend I have. He taught me at Oxford. I trust him completely.' Ahmed nodded.

'Good. Well, I mustn't keep you any longer. Give my regards to Rashid when you speak to him.'

With that Ahmed strolled over to collect Bellingford, exchanged a few pleasantries and, with a casual wave, was gone.

'Apparently he thinks very highly of you,' Charlie turned to Lewis and they began walking towards the tea pavillions. 'He looked through a lot of files until he found your name.'

'We were good friends at Sandhurst.'

'Did you get anything worthwhile?'

'A telephone number in Paris for his brother Rashid; it may lead to something.' Charlie nodded. After a time they reached the outer fringes of the crowds that clustered around the long row of striped tents where tea was being dispensed. A curious mixture of anxious hysteria and studied politeness emanated from the queues of people as they jostled each other for service.

Charlie turned to Lewis. 'Didn't you say Hanna was in Paris?' he asked gently.

'Yes, at a medical conference,' Lewis said as they walked towards Sybil and Lord Pickford.

'Why don't you pop over there tomorrow? You could buy Hanna lunch and see Rashid at the same time?'

'Thanks. I might take you up on the offer,' Lewis said.

'What offer?' This last question was Sybil's. She had overheard the last part of their conversation as they strolled towards the table in the nearest tent.

'Lewis is going to the Folies Bergères. Strictly in the line of business,' Charlie leaned over the small table and took a tiny strawberry tart from Sybil's plate.

'We got you some,' Pickford said. 'Or rather, Sybil did. She did a fine job in the crush.' Lewis drank the tepid, smoky-flavoured tea and nibbled on a small cake.

'That's interesting,' Charlie muttered to him. Lewis followed Charlie's gaze to where Mr Ahmed stood, a few tables away, talking to Jack Silver and Jessica Crossley.

'Lord Silver is very close to the Israelis, isn't he?' Lewis said quietly. Charlie nodded.

'Very close. Mr Ahmed seems to be an exceptional Arab indeed.' Lewis drained his teacup and stood up.

'Well, I must be going. I'll telephone you later, Charlie. Goodbye, General.'

Sybil leaned towards him and he pecked her on the cheek then set off towards the exit and nodded as he drew level with Ahmed and Lord Silver. Jessica Crossley called out to him as he passed.

'Mr Horne, are you leaving?' Lewis paused.

'Yes.'

She nodded to the others and walked over to him.

'Do you mind if I go with you?'

'I'm going to Green Park Station, Miss Crossley,' he said. 'I don't have a car.'

'That's fine,' she said cheerfully and fell into step beside him. Lewis was now walking at his normal pace and he noticed that she kept up with him easily. Then he remembered the length of her legs. Once they were out of the Palace grounds and into Green Park, Jessica Crossley spoke.

'Lord Pickford told me you are a writer as well.'

'Very part time,' Lewis said carefully. 'Mostly I work for an import and export company.'

'Lewis Horne,' she said aloud, and then 'L. F. Horne.'

'That's right,' Lewis said.

'You see, I've heard of your book.'

'I'm very flattered,' Lewis said.

'What does the F stand for?'

'Fairfax.' They walked on for a few paces and Lewis decided to be more forthcoming. 'General Fairfax was my father's hero. I suppose I wrote it for him.'

'Did he enjoy it?'

'He didn't read it. He was killed.'

'I'm sorry.'

'That's all right,' Lewis said easily. 'It happened a long time ago.'

They were still some distance from Green Park Station when it began to rain heavily once again. Lewis looked around for cover, but there wasn't even a tree nearby. He took off his raincoat and held it over both their heads and they walked as fast as they could for the station. While they were still some distance from the entrance the rain increased in ferocity, bouncing from the pathway and drumming a loud tattoo on the raincoat above their heads. Lewis put his free arm around Jessica's waist and they ran the last few yards to the station. They arrived damp and laughing. The incident had struck a note of intimacy between them. On an impulse, Lewis said to her: 'Would you like to come to a party?'

'When?'

'Right now. It's not a big one. Just some friends celebrating an anniversary. They're holding it in the afternoon because some of the guests have to work in the evening.'

Jessica hesitated for a few moments before answering.

'Yes, I'd like to go,' she said firmly.

A busker with a piano accordion who had been morosely staring at the rain beating down started to play *La Vie en Rose* to them and Lewis smiled ruefully. He suddenly thought of Hanna and Paris.

*

The rain had eased off by the time they got to Covent Garden. The tourists had emerged from cover and once again they packed the wet pavements and walkways.

After a few minutes they reached Snapper's Wine Bar and Lewis rapped sharply on the locked door with a coin. Presently it was opened by a man with a dry shock of tousled hair whose stocky body was clad in a crumpled, baggy, tweed suit. His blunt features were covered in the blush of broken blood vessels that usually signalled a heavy drinker.

He recognised Lewis and opened the door wide to allow them to enter without comment.

'Jessica Crossley, this is Brian Weston,' Lewis said as they walked into the dim interior.

'Delighted to make your acquaintance,' Weston said with a careful bow. Lewis noticed the slight slur to his voice and the bottle of champagne he held by the neck.

He led them through dark shadows across the sawdust-strewn floor to a far corner of the bar where a laughing group of people were settled around a large, candelit table. The light flickered across blow-ups of famous faces that decorated the walls. The group called out greetings to Lewis as he entered the circle of light and then looked expectantly at his companion.

'Jessica, this is Colin and Judy Miller. They're celebrating their first year of marriage,' Lewis said as he waved in the direction of a couple who sat at the head of the table. There was a scattering of hellos, and Jessica smiled at the group of fit young people in their late twenties – they looked a suburban tennis club crowd. Brian Weston put a glass of champagne into her hand and poured more into the glasses on the table. There was a slight deference towards Lewis, an affectionate respect. Like a team would show to a popular captain.

One of the men at the table looked slightly older than the others. He scratched his sun-freckled forehead, ran his hand over thinning red hair and winked at Jessica.

'Nice tea at the Palace, boss?' he said easily to Lewis in a London accent. Lewis gave a sudden, very French shrug which somehow signified the strong bond between the two men. Gradually they resumed the pattern of their conversation and as a newcomer to the group, Jessica stayed silent, obviously listening to the people around the table.

Lewis and Colin Miller spoke with clear, educated, classless accents. The man who had winked at her introduced himself and his wife as Sandy and Jean Patch. She had butter-coloured hair and spoke with a West Country lilt. The man who sat next to her had such a dark complexion that he looked Italian but his voice was pure Clydeside. The girl with him was also a Scot but she spoke in the more genteel tones of Edinburgh.

The couple opposite Jessica were in deep conversation. The young man had wavy, fair hair and Jessica guessed he had grown his moustache to make him look older, but it seemed to emphasise his youth. His companion had short, black hair and when she turned towards Jessica her pale coloured eyes flashed a greeting. More striking than pretty, Jessica had the feeling that they had met before.

'I'm Janet,' the girl said with a grin that revealed two dimples and very white teeth, 'Lewis's sister,' and she nodded to her brother who was listening to Brian Weston.

Jessica laughed as she saw the resemblance. Lewis's hollow-cheeked, slightly battered face and rough black hair had been gently altered to produce the feminine version in Janet.

'Come on then, play the bloody thing. I only got it in for you,' Brian Weston was saying to Lewis in a belligerent voice as he slapped the top of an ancient upright piano.

Lewis bowed to the company and sat down on the dusty, velvet-topped stool, stood up again, adjusted the height, made an elaborate show of flexing his fingers and played a few experimental chords on the chipped keys. Then tenderly he coaxed 'The Nearness of You' from the battle-weary instrument.

At the second verse the dark man with the Scottish accent began to sing. He had a rich tenor and no inhibitions. Lewis continued to play and they all joined in the numbers they knew. Everyone looked relaxed in the glow of the candlelight.

'Strange, how potent cheap music can be,' a voice said close to her in a fair imitation of Noel Coward.

She turned and looked into a smiling face with deep laughter lines around the eyes. The man was slim and even by candlelight she could see he was carefully dressed in a black silk mohair suit. Jessica remembered an expression of her grandmother's – band-box smart. It suited the man.

'Roland Perth,' he said, holding out his hand. 'I'm Janet and Lewis Horne's wicked landlord.' She shook the hand.

'Jessica Crossley. I'm an acquaintance of Mr Horne.'

Roland Perth raised his eyebrows and Jessica realised he was considerably older than the thirty-five she had first taken him for.

'Acquaintance,' he said, 'what a delightfully formal word in this day of instant friendships. You must get to know him better – he's an absolute dear. I shall prise him away from that wretched piano and make him dance with you.'

As Lewis finished the number he was playing, Roland Perth tapped him on the shoulder and took his place at the piano.

'Now, my darlings,' he called out. 'Mr Weston has been gracious enough to put down fresh sawdust for dancing.

31

I shall be awarding the Ann Ziegler and Webster Booth ballroom prize. Do any of you remember them? Of course not, you can hardly remember Twiggy, can you? Anyway, on with the waltz.' And with that he began to play with a skill that easily equalled Lewis's.

The couples did as they were told and Lewis came over and held out his hand to her.

'Can I have this foxtrot?' he said with a smile. His arm encircled her and he could feel the firm contours of her body against his. They stayed close together as they danced. Lewis liked her. He liked the smell and the feel of her, the hint of a lisp as she spoke, her freckles and her long legs but still he couldn't totally relax. Sensing a change she drew away and looked at her watch.

'Time to go,' she said just as Brian Weston called out 'Ten minutes to opening time.' Jessica held out her hand to Lewis.

'Thank you, it's been fun.'

Lewis walked her back through the gloom to the door of the wine bar. Through the glass they could see the rain had started yet again; pounding down in torrents and bouncing from the roofs of the parked cars. They paused and looked at each other, each wanting to say something. Lewis turned and took an umbrella from a coatstand.

'Brian won't miss this,' he said. Jessica nodded gravely to Lewis and walked out into the rain. From the interior came the melancholy sound of *'Body and Soul'*. Lewis watched her as long as she remained in sight. Then he dug into his pocket, took out a coin and began to dial a number on the paybooth telephone next to the door.

'Mars,' a voice said after the second ring.

'Charlie – it's Lewis. I'd like to take you up on the Paris offer.'

'All right. I'll mention it to Jeremy Bellingford. He's here with me.' Lewis could hear a conversation muttered distantly, then Charlie Mars came back on the line.

'Fine. Will you fix it?'

'Yes. I'll call you when I get there.' He hung up the telephone and watched the rain for a while. Paris, whatever else he had to do, still meant Hanna.

Some lads there are, 'tis shame to say,
That only court to thieve,
And once they bear the bloom away
'Tis little enough they leave.
Then keep your heart for men like me
And safe from trustless chaps.
My love is true and all for you.
'Perhaps, young man, perhaps.'

A Shropshire Lad
A. E. HOUSMAN

Chapter Two

The hot morning sun divided the Boulevard St Germain-
des-Près into fragments of light and shadow so that Lewis
had to shade his eyes as he sat at his table outside the
Café Flore. He watched a waiter setting the tables for
lunch in the glass enclosure outside the Brasserie Lipp
on the darker side of the street, and thought how much
he liked this city.

Although the languages spoken around him were German and Swedish the smell unmistakably spelt Paris: a
mixture of fresh coffee, harsh tobacco and traffic fumes.
He had given up trying to read an article on the crisis in
the French microchip industry and now the copy of *Le
Monde* lay discarded next to his empty coffee cup. A
waiter paused for a moment beside him and Lewis tapped
the saucer with his index finger.

'Encore, s'il vous plaît.'

When the bells of churches began to chime twelve
o'clock, he looked among the pedestrians on the packed
pavements for a familiar figure. As the last bell sounded,
Lewis spotted him coming from the left, moving fast
despite the curious, lop-sided gait.

Rene Malle looked immaculate in a navy-blue blazer
and charcoal grey slacks cut in that sharp, angular style
certain expensive French tailors give their clothes. His
left hand, on which he appeared to wear a tight, black
glove, clutched a slim document case. The Frenchman's
gaunt features broke into a warm, smile as they shook
hands.

Lewis took his overnight bag and raincoat from the
other chair and Rene Malle sat down with a grunt. As he
did so he released the document case from his artificial
hand so that it fell on to the table. With his good hand he
raked through the short bristles of his iron-grey hair.

'So – welcome to Paris,' he said in heavily accented

English. Lewis nodded and studied him for a moment. Rene Malle had passed out top of his class at St Cyr Military Academy and seemed set for a career that would lead to a Marshal of France's baton until the man next to him had stood on a landmine in an Algerian vineyard. When they had sewn what was left of him together, Rene refused the offer of a desk job with a training regiment, resigned his commission and enrolled at the Ecole des Beaux Arts. Now he was one of Europe's most accomplished military illustrators and a NATO liaison officer with Lewis's department.

The waiter returned with Lewis's coffee but Rene refused a drink. Instead he reached inside his pocket and produced a packet of American cigarettes and an old Zippo lighter. When he had inhaled and expelled a great lungful of toasted Virgina tobacco he held up his artificial hand for closer inspection. At first glance, Lewis had taken the texture to be fine black leather, but he now saw that it was a matt black plastic.

'What do you think?' Rene said. 'The latest thing. I could have had it done in pink but I think this is sexier.'

Despite, or perhaps because of, his missing left hand, leg and eye Rene had enormous success with women; a phenomenon that he ascribed to the inexhaustible curiosity of the opposite sex.

'What are the advantages?' Lewis asked. Rene shrugged.

'I can eat walnuts and lobsters with consummate ease and I don't need a screwdriver for minor electrical repairs.' He held the hand closer so Lewis could see how it was even finished with fingernails. 'I'm sorry we could not meet at the apartment but I had some errands to run. But if you are ready now?'

Lewis finished his coffee, put three five-franc coins on the table and picked up his bag and coat.

'Ready,' he said as Rene ground out his cigarette. They walked side by side along the wide pavement towards the Boulevard St Michel where Rene lived. This was Lewis's favourite part of Paris; called the Latin Quarter since medieval times because of the common language originally spoken by students who attended the University, there was still an atmosphere of academic purpose about the areas that it put him in mind of Oxford.

'How is Charlie Mars?' Rene asked as they came out of the Rue Serpente and waited to cross the Boulevard St Michel. 'Does he still pine for the quiet comfort of his old college?'

'He's whipping Gower Street into shape,' Lewis shouted above the roar of traffic. 'In fact, he transported his entire study there. There's virtually no difference in the rooms.'

Rene nodded as he took Lewis's arm and pushed him across the road. 'Of course, I forgot you were one of his star pupils. A first class degree, was it not?'

Lewis grinned as they reached the safety of the side-walk.

'That was in history. He taught me infinitely more about jazz.'

They walked on for a few yards more and Rene took a bunch of keys from his pocket and paused before a shabby door.

'I once stayed in an Oxford college,' he said and he closed his eyes as if to shut out a bad memory. 'It was, if I recall correctly, during the month of February. I do not think I have ever been so cold. Even now I shudder at the thought of those icy sheets.'

Lewis nodded in sympathy while Rene unlocked the door and ushered him into a squalid forecourt. It looked as if the scabrous walls of cracked and peeling paint had not been renewed since the previous century. The dark well of the staircase led upwards into an uninviting gloom.

'Who's your decorator down here, Rene?' Lewis said as he started to mount the stair. 'The Phantom of the rue Morgue?' Rene chuckled.

'You know it is not in our nature to be extravagant about things that do not matter,' he said as they climbed to the first landing and stood before a large blackened door that was cracked and scarred where the ancient varnish had blistered away from the wood. But when the door swung open, it revealed an interior that was in astonishing contrast to the grimness of the communal staircase.

Despite the military neatness that Lewis had always liked, there was also a sort of masculine cosiness about the place. The large living room had a high ceiling frosted

37

with plaster decoration and floor length windows with tiny balconies that looked on to the street. Light flooded into the room and reflected from the white walls which were decorated with clusters of military prints and old maps of Europe showing the glorious progress of Napoleon's Grande Armée.

In front of the central of the three large windows was a large draughtsman's desk and stool and next to that a wooden table covered in pots of paint and rows of brushes laid out with mathematical precision. The far left of the room was a living area. There was a long sofa covered in soft green leather, a coffee table and a brass reading lamp. A portable television set stood on the table and the wall behind was lined with bookcases.

Turkish carpets in dark, rich colours were scattered around on the polished wooden floor. Rene walked to the end of the room where the bookcases were and stopped before a huge, ornate safe. On top of it stood a collection of bottles and glasses. He poured two generous whiskies and offered one to Lewis. They both stood by the safe and sipped their drinks in appreciative silence for a few minutes.

'Do you want a gun?' Rene asked in a conversational tone. Lewis was about to refuse when he thought better of it. Paris could be a rough old town.

'What have you got?' he said.

Rene leaned down and dialled the combination of the safe. It was so old Lewis could hear the tumblers clicking into place.

'I've got a sergeant who could open that about as fast as you can,' Lewis said as Rene threw the handle and hauled the great door open.

'A good sergeant is to be prized above rubies,' Rene retorted as he reached into the safe. 'Now let me see – the weather is a trifle warm for carrying a Magnum. Ah, how about a nice little snub-nosed Smith and Wesson .38 with a belt holster?' Lewis took the revolver and a box of ammunition from Rene. He spun the chamber then snapped it open and slid the heavy cartridges into the apertures.

'What's it like?' he said. Rene swung the door shut.

'I don't know. I only got it two days ago so I have not worked on it yet. It should be a trifle heavy on the trigger.'

Lewis held the blue-black barrel up to the light. It was factory new.

'Allow me,' Rene said as he clipped the neat leather holster to Lewis's belt in the small of his back. Lewis slid the revolver into it then picked up his drink from the top of the safe once more.

'Anyone special in town I should look out for?' he said as he glanced along the row of books that were at eye level. Rene shrugged.

'The Russian and the American are as good as gold. There are some funny Poles here organising a photographic exhibition at the Pompidou Centre and our friends from the Middle East are growling at each other as usual. But no, nothing special comes to mind.'

Lewis was aware that Rene was watching him carefully.

'I'm only here to take a message, Rene. No rough stuff.'

The Frenchman finished his drink and poured them both refills from the dimpled bottle.

'Good, I really hate paperwork,' he said with feeling. 'Remember that Irishman and the two Americans in the Bois de Boulogne?'

Lewis nodded.

'God, I thought they had killed you that night.'

'They bloody nearly did,' Lewis said. 'They had Armalites with night sights. They practically chopped down the tree I was hiding behind.'

'But you got them all and with a handgun. Superb!' Rene saluted Lewis with his glass.

Lewis remembered for a moment. The Americans had been rewarded with the trip because they had collected the most money for Noraid at their Boston Irish Club. Two beefy grandfathers in their late sixties whose ancestors had gone to America when Queen Victoria was a young woman. They had smuggled the rifles into France from Italy in the boot of their car.

When Terence Devlin met them in the Champs Elysées they could hardly understand his Londonderry accent. They'd expected someone who sounded like Barry Fitzgerald. Lewis remembered trailing them to the café and their disappointment when Devlin refused a drink. Stone-faced Devlin who sipped orange juice and treated them both with open contempt.

'Will I be able to book a table for lunch at the Brasserie Lipp?' he said as he took a good swallow of the whisky.

'Perhaps not, but I will,' Rene said as he picked up the telephone on the coffee table and dialled. 'What time do you want it?' he said as the number rang.

'One-thirty.'

Rene got the table after some negotiation and Lewis thanked him and took the receiver himself.

'Sorbonne,' a voice said after he had redialled, and Lewis gave the extension he wanted.

'I would like to talk to Doctor Hanna Pearce,' Lewis spoke in careful French. 'I was told there would be a coffee break at this time during the conference.'

'A moment, sir,' an anonymous woman said and after a time Hanna was on the line.

'It's me, Lewis,' he said. 'I'm working over here today. Can you have lunch with me?' There was a fractional pause.

'Yes, providing it's not too far away from the conference.'

'How about the Brasserie Lipp?' Hanna's voice was brisk and business-like.

'That's fine. What time?'

'I've booked a table for one-thirty.'

'I'll see you there.'

Lewis hung up and walked to the draughtsman's table where Rene was looking at a series of his original illustrations. Each showed a soldier from various times in history, dressed in battle order, against a particular type of terrain. The paintings were executed in meticulous detail.

'These are very handsome, Rene. What are they for?' Lewis asked.

'A partwork magazine. They show soldiers who fought in other countries' wars.' He held up an illustration. 'This is a private in one of the Irish regiments who fought for the Union in the American Civil War. You see, they wore regular Federal uniforms except for the green trousers.' He pointed to another of the paintings.

'And this is an NCO in the Spanish Legion who fought

with the *Wermacht* against the Russians.' Lewis picked up another of the paintings that showed an SAS trooper against a tropical background.

'This doesn't look like Borneo,' he said.

'No,' Rene replied in measured tones. 'That is Vietnam.'
Lewis put the drawing down with great care.

'The SAS didn't serve in Vietnam.'

'No,' Rene said with a grim little smile. 'That is entirely a work of imagination.'

Lewis glanced at his watch. 'I think I'll go for a stroll to work up an appetite for lunch.'

Rene held out a pair of keys on a ring to him.

'In that case, we must say our farewells. I am going away for a few days so I must leave you to your own devices. The spare room is made up and you know where everything is in the kitchen.'

Lewis nodded and made for the door.

'Stay out of foreign wars, Rene.'

'Think of the fun I would have missed,' Rene replied as he held up his artificial hand in a farewell salute.

*

At one twenty-nine pm Lewis sat at a small table on the first floor of the Brasserie Lipp and contemplated the glass of Kir that the waiter had just placed before him. Hanna had introduced him to the drink.

To Lewis most dry white wines had a taste akin to sucking a copper coin – and blackcurrant was not a flavour that charged his appetite – but the combination was perfect. He looked for a moment at the glass misted with condensation and the small clear indentations made by the waiter's fingers, then he raised the drink and took a long swallow. As he did so, he saw Hanna Pearce standing before him.

'You drove me to this,' he said sadly and he watched her expression change. A look of softness had altered to amusement at his remark. 'Drink?' he asked, pointing to his glass.

A waiter materialised at the table.

'Encore du Kir,' she said with a smile and the waiter bowed away. Hanna hung her handbag on the back of her chair and folded her hands on the tabletop in a

41

business-like fashion. Lewis sat back and studied the effect she was having on the other patrons of the restaurant. In the months he had known her he had, to some degree, become used to the reactions she produced in other people. He was amused to see that it happened in the Brasserie Lipp; a restaurant that had known generation after generation of truly beautiful women.

'How's the conference?' he asked. She shrugged.

'Fine, nothing special. It's good to see old friends.'

Lewis nodded.

'Charlie and Sybil send their regards. I went to one of the garden parties with them yesterday.'

Hanna looked surprised. She took up the glass the waiter had just delivered.

'That's a bit unusual for you, isn't it?' She shook her head slightly as she put down the glass again. Her blue-black hair, the same colour as the revolver pressing into the small of his back, swung to brush her shoulders. It was enough to regain the attention of the men around her once more and tighten the mouths of the women customers into lines of grim displeasure.

'I missed you,' he said.

'You didn't have to, Lewis,' she said quickly.

He looked at her for a moment.

'It sounded very much like an ultimatum at the end of our last conversation,' he replied evenly. She sighed gently and folded her arms.

'As I remember, what I said was that I couldn't see our relationship going any further as long as you remained in the same line of business.' Lewis drummed on the table top.

'That seems pretty cold-blooded to me. I've heard of emotions being turned on and off like a tap but to have the ability to control the flow from full flood to trickle . . .'

Hanna held her hand to her brow for a moment before she spoke: 'Maybe it's my profession. We see a great deal of pain, you know . . . a lot of suffering we can do nothing about. If we allowed ourselves to be ruled by our emotions they would overwhelm us. I must have some part of my life where I can rest. Surely you can see . . .' She stopped talking to regain her equilibrium. When she spoke again her voice was controlled and matter-of-fact. 'I didn't expect to see you in Paris.'

'I'm only here for the day, something came up at the last minute.' Lewis shifted slightly in his seat and eased the holster in the small of his back a few inches along his belt.

No one else in the restaurant noticed but Hanna was familiar with the gesture. She looked at her menu.

'In that case, I suppose we can expect to see bodies in the streets by nightfall,' she said, caustically. 'A good job there's a medical conference in town. Paris will need all the doctors it can get.'

Lewis was about to reply when the waiter appeared with pencil poised.

'*M'sieur, madame?*' he said like a schoolteacher waiting for a class to recite.

'*Pas d'hors d'oeuvres,*' Hanna said. '*Omelette fromage, salade verte.*'

'*Moi aussi,*' Lewis said, his mind not really on the food. '*Oh, une bouteille du maison blanc.*' He watched the waiter go, then turned to her again.

'Come on, Hanna. I'm just here to talk to someone. You make it sound as if I'm an attack of typhoid.'

She took a piece of crusty white bread from the table while Lewis gazed absently around the restaurant as if seeking solace; he found what he was looking for.

A single man who sat out of earshot watched them both as he consumed his paté and cornichons. When his eyes came in contact with Lewis's, he raised his eyebrows in sympathy and his long expressive face contorted with a smile of camaraderie to reveal vast, ivory-coloured teeth. A man without a woman, but happy in the pleasure that excellent food will always bring to a Frenchman.

Lewis turned back to Hanna and tried a friendly smile. But she remained cool.

'Can you swear to me that you're not carrying a gun at this moment?' She spoke in a low, clear voice. Lewis sat back and said nothing. 'There you are,' she continued, 'what kind of man takes a woman out to lunch while he's carrying a firearm – it's like dating a mobster.'

Lewis always noticed that her American accent, practically non-existent when she was relaxed, was stronger when her voice carried an edge of anger. The waiter remained impassive as he poured wine for Hanna, but he gave Lewis a signal of empathy that was almost identical to the one he had received from the lone diner.

When the waiter had gone Lewis leaned forward.

'Look, it's a tool of my trade. That doesn't mean that I use it all the time.' He thought for an analogy that would appeal to her. 'You carry a stethoscope, don't you?'

'Not to lunch,' she said firmly. 'A knife and fork are all I need.'

Lewis didn't give up.

'Honestly, things are calming down. There are plenty of people with professions more dangerous than mine . . . policemen, pilots . . .'

'Horsefeathers,' Hanna said emphatically. 'Are you familiar with the term? My father uses it instead of the modern equivalent, but it means the same thing. I know what your job is.'

'I'm a security officer,' Lewis said shortly.

'Don't fob me off with that euphemism. You hunt killers, Lewis. Most of them are crazy.' She had lighted a cigarette and her voice seemed calm and reasonable, but there was a sadness to it. 'I know you're good at your job, but you'll always be in terrible danger.'

Lewis kept his eyes on the table before them. His features were hard, impassive. Hanna spoke again.

'Remember the first time Connie met you in New York? She didn't know you but she said you were dangerous; like a pistol? She was right, Lewis. That's what you are, a loaded pistol and I don't want one permanently aimed at me.' She stubbed out the cigarette and took another sip of wine. 'Look, how can I make you understand? I want an ordinary life. Can't you see I'm tired of being different? Do you know why my parents sent me to school in Switzerland? So that I could be with kids that were as rich as I was. Can you imagine? There weren't enough rich kids in New York.

'When I went to grade school there, Vincent used to drive me in the Hispano Suiza. The other children called it the Batmobile. I would have given anything to walk home with them. But I was Cargo Pearce's grand-daughter, the richest little girl in America.' She stopped and looked across the room for a few seconds, then she continued.

'I want a nice, ordinary life. I've had enough of excitement. I wouldn't even mind if it was a little dull.' She held out her hands towards him. 'Think of it Lewis, you could stay home every day, be L. F. Horne all the time. I'm crazy about him – I love the book he wrote. I could be working at the hospital and when I thought of you I wouldn't get a cold feeling here.' She held her hand to cover her abdomen. 'You would be at home in your study, safe, no guns . . . you know an excess of adrenalin is bad for you?'

Lewis's friendly waiter delivered their food and they began to eat in uncomfortable silence.

'Do my words make any sense to you at all?' Hanna said finally. Lewis put down his fork.

'The domestic home is considered to be highly dangerous, Hanna. I've seen the statistics. You'd be amazed at the fatalities that occur in the average kitchen. You think my work is all death; it's not.

'Most of the time I spend reading reports and files; the rest I'm waiting in some damned airport for a delayed flight. You talk about danger. What about hospitals? They're full of diseases, you could catch some fatal bug.'

Hanna's face registered her disappointment.

'I've been inoculated,' she said flatly. 'That's what I need against you.' Lewis's chin came up and she could see a flicker of pain in his eyes.

'Oh Lewis,' she said with a soft smile, and covered his hand with her own. 'Do I really imagine that much and exaggerate the rest?' As she spoke, she caressed his hand with her fingertips. Suddenly she looked down at the tiny callouses: her jawline seemed even firmer.

'You've been somewhere dangerous, haven't you? Those marks on your hands come from handling weapons.'

Once again Lewis remained silent. Hanna pulled her hand away.

'I'm crazy to listen to you. You lie so well, I think you really believe the nonsense you tell me.' She looked around and reached for her handbag. 'I must get back.'

'Have dinner with me tonight,' Lewis said as she got up.

'I can't, I already have an engagement.'

'Can I see you after that?'

She hesitated. 'I don't know . . . give me a call about ten-thirty. I'm staying at the Bristol.'

'Wait for a moment and I'll walk you back.' Lewis half rose from his chair but Hanna held out a hand in protest.

'No, please. I think I'd rather be alone for a little while.'

Lewis watched her go. The Frenchman who had smiled at him in sympathy earlier looked up from his *pot-au-feu* and raised a corner of the napkin that was tucked into his collar to dabble his lips. As he did so he shrugged to Lewis and then returned to his food with ferocious relish. Lewis refused coffee, paid the bill and a few minutes later found himself once again on the Boulevard St Germain with his raincoat slung over his shoulder and his hands thrust deep into his trouser pockets.

For a moment he wanted to run through the crowd that packed the thoroughfare. He wanted to catch her up, tell her he was going to resign his commission, buy a big cardigan from Marks and Spencer, write all the books he had thought of and know the warm security that Hanna's fortune would bring to them both. But he remained where he was, knowing that this would not make him happy.

He looked up at a plane tree that stood against the light, the dark centre of its foliage exploded at the edges where the sun shot through the spiky leaves with emerald brightness. Then he turned and glanced over the street to where he had sat that morning and saw Jessica Crossley walking purposefully across his line of vision.

Without thinking he made for her side of the road and kept about twenty feet behind her. Lewis did not like coincidences in his line of work and if she was in Paris because of him he wanted to know why.

It was an easy job to trail her. There were plenty of people on the streets and she seemed sublimely unaware of Lewis. He kept the ash-blonde head in view and sauntered along with the crowd. They passed along the Boulevard St Michel and half way across the Seine to the island where Notre Dame stood in all its splendour. Jessica mingled for a few minutes with the tourists in the paved area before the cathedral. She gazed up at the medieval façade then turned and led Lewis on in a westerly direction.

Eventually they arrived at Jessica's destination. The Louvre. She walked with determination through the crowds of tourists that milled about outside. Lewis quickened his pace to narrow the gap between them but wasn't quite fast enough. A crocodile of solemn-faced little girls blocked his way while four nuns moved like stately galleons around them, herding their charges towards the turnstile.

Lewis looked beyond them and just saw Jessica disappearing into the crowd. Finally he got to the turnstile and gained entry into the main concourse of the museum.

It was crowded with people standing in packs, buying books and postcards and deciding which part of the palace they would journey to next. Staircases, galleries and corridors led off in every direction. He stood as the multitudes flowed around him like water past an island in a river, and thought what to do next. If she had come to explore some part of the museum she would be here for some time, he reasoned. Therefore a methodical search would probably find her somewhere in the building.

With hardly a glance, Lewis passed by the ancient glories of Sumaria, Babylon and Egypt; the genius of Greece and the treasures of Rome. Through the centuries he hunted Jessica in the great hallways and galleries, studying the crowds who gazed upon the works of Rubens, Bellini, David and Canaletto.

As he continued to search, he was struck by the endless permutations of expression on the faces of the visitors to the museum. They transmitted messages of instant reaction to the treasures that confronted them. Everything was stamped there; enthusiasm, boredom and blank incomprehension. Duty and pleasure obviously meant different things to different people. In the end he called a halt. There was no sign of Jessica Crossley.

He decided to visit another woman. A few minutes' walk brought him before *La Gioconda*, the most famous smile in the world. Lewis stopped and looked back at the *Mona Lisa*, Leonardo da Vinci's compliment to the enigmatic quality of women. Usually the painting attracted a crowd, but on this occasion there were just two other people standing before her, a fair-haired youth in a blue three-piece suit with an open shirt and a dark, pretty girl who glanced down every few seconds at the wedding ring she wore. Lewis could practically see the confetti in their hair.

'I thought it would be bigger,' the boy said after a long period of silence. Lewis could see a look of vague disappointment on the youth's face reflected in the bullet-proof glass that protected the picture.

'*The Last Supper*'s bigger,' the girl said in a consoling voice and she took his arm possessively. The youth nodded as if the information had brought him a degree of comfort and they moved on. Instantly, their places were taken by three tiny, chattering Japanese men, though Lewis continued to think about the young man's remark. To hell with the little twerp; who was he to resent the size of the *Mona Lisa*?

Lewis continued to gaze at the painting for some time until he was aware of someone standing next to him and a lisping voice spoke quietly in his ear:

'What comes to your mind when you look at her, L. F. Horne?'

Lewis kept his eyes on the painting as he replied: 'Are you warm, are you real, *Mona Lisa*, or just a cold and lonely work of art?'

*

They walked through the Tuileries Gardens until they were drawn to the bank of the Seine where they stopped next to a fisherman. He fitted into the landscape so perfectly they felt he could have been placed there to decorate the embankment just for them. He had heavy, handsome features sunburned to a dark Mediterranean tan and thick black eyebrows that almost dominated the face. He wore a small black beret and his barrel-like body and powerful legs were clad in faded '*travail bleu*' – the old time uniform of the French working man. As Jessica and Lewis watched him, he took the stub of a cigar from the corner of his mouth, examined it, then pitched it into the water.

All his movements were executed with great slowness and deliberation which somehow gave them an enormous dignity. His next action was to place the handle of his fishing rod under his right foot so that his hands were free to attend to the food that was spread upon the folding table next to him. It consisted of a long loaf of bread, a wedge of oozing farmhouse cheese and three nobbly tomatoes.

The fisherman munched contentedly for a few minutes then brushed the crumbs from his mouth with a sweeping gesture and said to them '*Êtes-vous Parisiens?*' His voice was deep and pleasant. They shook their heads and Lewis replied in the same tone: '*Nous sommes de Londres.*'

'London, eh?' the fisherman said as he switched effortlessly to English. 'Nice to meet you. I'm from London as well.'

He smiled at their sudden surprise.

'I've been coming to Paris to fish for over thirty years. Are you on holiday?'

They shook their heads again.

'Pity,' he said. 'There's no place like it.' He rummaged in his fishing bag and produced two more tumblers as if he had been expecting their company. 'Would you care to join me in a drink?' He carefully poured two glasses from the dusty bottle and handed them to Jessica and Lewis with enormous care. It reminded Lewis of the way experts handled nitro-glycerine.

'This is supposed to be served at room temperature,' he said and then he looked around with enormous enjoyment. 'Bit difficult out here, eh? Still, I don't think it does anything to the bouquet unless the wind's blowing a bit hard.'

Lewis took the glass and gulped some down. He was greeted with an almost velvety sensation on his taste buds and after he had swallowed he was aware of an after-effect that was both smoky and fruity.

'What is his?' he asked with interest.

'*Château Lafite,*' Jessica said.

'That's right,' the fisherman said with surprise and satisfaction.

'I've never tasted wine like this before,' Lewis said.

'You won't very often,' the man said with a note of real sadness in his voice. 'There's not a lot left in the world. They keep a few bottles for me at the hotel I stay at, but most of it's gone now. As I said to my wife when I put her on the plane to Marbella: "The best thing about the year you were born was the *Château Lafite*."'

'What did she say?' Jessica asked with interest.

'She said "Champagne Cocktails taste the same whatever year you make them."' He joined in their laughter and raised his own glass in salute. When they had finished their drinks he bade them goodbye and they continued their stroll along the embankment. After a while Jessica said: 'Lovers meet along here at night. The pleasure boats on the river shine little searchlights on them.'

'Do you know Paris well?' Lewis asked.

She laughed and shook her head so that her hair whirled in a silver cloud.

'No, I saw it in a film Cary Grant was in once. This is my first visit.'

'What brings you here?' Lewis said as he looked towards the Eiffel Tower. There was a pause for several paces.

'Lord Silver invited me to come with him,' she said in the same light tone that he had used. Lewis remembered the anecdote Charlie Mars had told him of Silver's prowess with women.

'He's a bit old for you, isn't he?' Lewis said carefully, making sure there wasn't a hint of disapproval in the remark.

'How old do you think I am?' Jessica said cheerfully. Lewis stopped and they both rested on the parapet. He thought for a moment then he took her hand.

'A friend once told me you can tell people's ages by studying the backs of their hands.' He looked at hers for a moment. She had long fingers that were square at the tips. The skin was lightly tanned and there were pale blue veins tracing a web of patterns.

'Twenty-four,' he guessed. She laughed again.

'Your friend didn't teach you very well – I'm nearly thirty-one.'

They walked on again and Lewis thought about that remark. It was unusual. Hardly anyone told you how old they were going to be at their next birthday. It was only very young children or those who were proud of their advanced years.

'And now you're thinking "Why isn't she married?"'

50

Jessica said in the same light tone of voice. Lewis
his head.

'Actually, I was trying to guess your inside leg measure-
ment. But you can tell me why you're not married if you
want to.'

'Which piece of information would you prefer?'

'Which is the more interesting?'

She shrugged.

'Thirty-five inches.'

'You must have been good at the high jump,' Lewis said
solemnly.

'I was an all-round athlete.'

'Is that how you won the Lord Silver Memorial Trip to
Paris?'

'No, I got that for my academic prowess. If you really
want to know,' she said, and Lewis could detect a slight
edge in her voice, 'he's a good friend of a friend. He only
had this evening free as he's flying on to other parts of
the world from here and won't be back in England for
some time. He said he would take me out to dinner
tonight and answer the questions I have about the Control
Commission.'

Lewis held up his hands.

'So we've only got this afternoon?'

'For what?' Jessica said in a slightly hostile voice.

He took her by the hand.

'To find a taxi,' Lewis replied. 'You've got a little time.
I'll show you Paris.'

*

Lewis was as good as his word. By keeping the taxi at his
disposal, he managed to show Jessica a collection of parks,
museums, galleries and broad streets full of breathtaking
shops. They visited the Eiffel Tower and finally made
their way along the Champs Elysées to the Tomb of the
Unknown Warrior beneath the Arc de Triomphe.

'Well, what's your verdict?'

Jessica shrugged slowly.

'It's just like Paris.'

Lewis nodded. He knew exactly what she meant.

'No wonder the fisherman comes here every year.' Jes-

51

sica looked at her watch. 'It's quarter to six, I must get back to my hotel.'

'Where are you staying?' Lewis said as they walked towards their taxi.

'Rue Jacob. Is that near? I've lost my bearings.'

'Not far,' Lewis said as he opened the door for her. 'Back over the river to the Latin Quarter.' He gave the address to the patient driver who hammered away into the rush-hour traffic. Eventually Lewis paid him off at the beginning of the Rue Jacob. It was only a few minutes walk for him to get to Rene's apartment. They stood for a moment on the pavement.

'Thank you,' Jessica said. 'That was fun. Perhaps we'll meet again soon.'

'It's a small town,' Lewis said. 'I may bump into you later.'

Jessica looked around the street. 'Yes, I suppose Jack's finished his business by now.'

'What has he been up to?' Lewis asked in a casual manner.

'He had to see a friend of his, a journalist called Khan,' she said.

'Rothman Khan?' Lewis asked.

'Yes, that was his name. Why? Do you know him?'

'I've heard of him, he's a pretty famous journalist.'

'So Jack Silver said.'

'Well, I'd better get on my way.' He walked a few steps away from her and then turned and looked at her legs once again. 'Thirty-five inches, eh!'

'Eighty-nine centimetres if you prefer,' she said.

Lewis shook his head. 'Imperial measurements are better for some things.'

He gave a final wave and set off down the Boulevard St Germain. As he walked, his thoughts were on Rothman Khan. He was a famous journalist. He was also an agent of Mossad – the Israeli secret service – and was normally to be found in Tel Aviv. Suddenly, he thought of Hanna's prediction about bodies on the streets of Paris by nightfall.

Here the truceless armies yet
Trample, rolled in blood and sweat;
They kill and kill and never die;
And I think that each is I.

A Shropshire Lad
A. E. HOUSMAN

Chapter Three

Lewis let himself into Rene Malle's apartment and flopped down on the leather sofa. The revolver dug into the small of his back once again, so he took it from the holster and laid it next to the telephone. Then he dialled the number Ali had given him the day before.

It rang for nearly a minute before a deep voice with a gravelly New York accent answered 'Sam's American Bar.'

'Can I speak to Rashid Ahmed, please?' Lewis said.

'Are you Mr Horne from London?' the deep voice asked in measured tones.

'Yes,' Lewis replied.

'Rashid said to tell you he'll meet you here at nine o'clock – be at the bar.'

'Where are you located?'

'Rue de la Huchette. Do you know it?'

'I do.'

'We're down the end on the left. Watch out, we've only got a little sign.'

Lewis hung up and looked down at the revolver. He could see a tiny reflection of his face in the shiny barrel. He picked it up, snapped open the chamber, knocked the ammunition out on to the table, cocked the empty gun and pulled the trigger to test the action. It was a heavier pull than he had expected.

He glanced at the small digital clock next to the television set. It was ten minutes past six. He had nothing to do but kill time for nearly three hours.

Rene kept a small workshop next to his bedroom. Lewis went in and checked over the tools that were displayed with the same exacting neatness as the paints and brushes in the studio. Satisfied there was everything that he required, Lewis stripped the .38 and set to work on the action until he was sure that the pull on the trigger was to his complete satisfaction.

He looked at the time again; still two hours to go. He found the cupboard where Rene kept his collection of records but they were either chamber music or romantic ballads, and neither suited his present mood. Then he remembered a book he had noticed earlier in the day.

He went to the shelf and took the leather-bound volume back to the sofa. It was the memoirs of Jean St Clair, Coeur du Bois. Lewis knew something of the Coeur de Bois, the name given to the Frenchman who trapped and explored down the Mississippi from Canada and opened up America beyond the Appalachian Mountains.

Lewis skimmed through the book. It told of Jean St Clair's young manhood as a free spirit living with the redmen, the first colonial wars with the British as they pushed further west, then the American War of Independence when he was commissioned as a captain of scouts in Washington's ragbag army of farmers, backwoodsmen and citizen recruits. How he saw despair at Valley Forge and finally, victory as the might of Britain was humbled into capitulation at Yorktown. Lewis reflected wryly that his own regiment had been there to witness and take part in the humiliation. He glanced at the last few chapters and then read the last page with astonishment.

'And so, after these extraordinary adventures I came to New York where I made some success in the shipping business. In the year of 1808 I was introduced to my dear wife Constance by her brother, the prominent banker, Forrest Pearce. The following year we were married and have lived happily ever after.'

Lewis slammed the book shut. Forrest Pearce, Hanna's ancestor. Even when he was trying to put her out of his mind, literature conspired to bring her back to the centre of his consciousness. He suddenly wanted to speak to her again.

Beneath the coffee table was a directory for Paris. He flipped through until he found the number for the Bristol Hotel and dialled the number.

'Doctor Hanna Pearce, please,' he said to the operator and in seconds a man answered.

56

'Hello.' Lewis had not expected anyone but Hanna.

'Can I speak to Doctor Pearce, please?'

'She had to go out for a short time. Can I give her a message?' The voice was confident and educated; East Coast American.

Lewis wanted to know who it was. Instead he said he would call back and he hung up the phone. Then he went to the safe and poured himself a large whisky. More than anything else he wanted to see the man Hanna was going to have dinner with. He thought about what she said at lunchtime.

'Call me later, after eleven.'

If she intended to be back at the hotel by then she must be starting about eight o'clock. He looked at the time again: seven twenty-five. If he hurried he might well get to the hotel before they left. For a moment he contemplated leaving the gun behind. Then he slid it into the holster, picked up his raincoat and made for the street.

*

The taxi got stuck in a traffic jam at the top of the Rue St Honoré. Lewis paid it off and walked the last few yards to where Hanna was staying.

The Bristol looked like an unostentatious, top class hotel with no special entrance to dazzle and impress – until the moment you stepped inside when the privilege closed all around you like a golden mousetrap. Lewis was glad he had worn his best suit and the suntan helped. Only poor people were pale in July. He found a quiet corner of the hushed lobby and waited.

It wasn't long before he saw Hanna pass by with a tall, powerfully-built man. He had dark hair and a very expensive English-cut suit that almost disguised the slabs of muscle across his shoulders.

The features were good and plain, a serious face, Lewis thought. He judged him to be in his late thirties. They stopped for a moment while Hanna handed in her key, and as she walked back to him he smiled at her and she reached up and brushed the hair that had flopped across his forehead. Lewis noted the simple gesture with a stab of jealousy. He knew from experience that women only did that to men they had the deepest affection for. Feeling slightly numb he watched them leave.

'Hello, my boy.' Lewis turned and saw before him a splendid figure. It was the man he had encountered only that afternoon by the banks of the Seine.

Gone were the workman's clothes and the beret. In their place was a designer safari-suit, crocodile-skin shoes, a gold wrist watch and a pale grey silk shirt open at the throat. On his arm was a blonde with a body and a smile that looked as if they had been assembled in a Beverly Hills laboratory.

'Hello,' Lewis said. 'Did you catch anything?'

'No, lad. Sharon makes me throw them back. What are you doing here? Come to try some more of the *Château Lafite*?'

Sharon looked slightly bemused at the conversation. Finally she said: 'Are you going to introduce me to your friend?'

'I'm sorry. This is my daughter, Sharon. My name is Denis Slingsby.' Lewis took the hand which was stronger than he expected.

'Lewis Horne – Slingsby, that's an old Yorkshire name.' The man gave him a sharp look.

'What makes you say that, lad?' Lewis shrugged.

'Slingsby, Bellasis, Wentworth. It's just one of those names that were famous at the time of the Civil War.'

Slingsby nodded. 'That's quite right.'

He looked at Lewis as if he were examining him with a greater interest than he had shown before. Then he clicked his fingers together loudly.

'Horne . . . you're L. F. Horne, aren't you? The one who wrote *The King's Roundhead.*'

Lewis felt a strange mixture of emotions. He had never thought of himself as a person of initials, and now that two people had used that form of his name in everyday speech it gave him a certain pleasure which instantly turned to embarrassment. Slingsby held out his hand and took Lewis's once more and pumped it with even more vigour.

'Well, well. L. F. Horne.' He turned to Sharon who was looking at this exchange with ever-growing bewilder-

58

ment. 'This young man has written a brilliant book, my dear.'

Sharon smiled again at the information.

'Is it a bestseller?' she asked.

'No, I'm afraid not.'

Slingsby squeezed her arm. 'She doesn't read much, do you?'

She gave him a glance of discontent and Lewis could see she had spirit. He realised he had misjudged her. Because she looked like a girl designed for a rich man's yacht, Lewis had assumed she was stupid. He made a mental note about being arrogant.

'Please excuse my father, Mr Horne. He spent thousands of pounds on my education and now does his best to imply to people that I am an imbecile.' She turned to Slingsby. 'Excuse me, daddy, I just want to get something from the suite.'

Lewis watched her walk away and Slingsby took Lewis's arm in a powerful grip.

'Come and have a drink.'

Lewis was about to refuse when he realised there was still some time to go before his appointment at Sam's American Bar. He hesitated.

'Would you mind if it's just a quick one? There's someone I've got to meet.'

Within a few minutes they were seated and drinking large, iced whiskies. Slingsby took a handful of nuts from the bowl before them and munched them ruminatively.

'She's getting to be a handful, that daughter of mine. I brought her here because she's having a bad time with her marriage. I should have brought her bloody husband, he's the one that needs a holiday.' He looked at Lewis mournfully. 'What about you? Are you married?'

Lewis shook his head. Slingsby took some more nuts and an olive.

'You've got the right idea. It makes martyrs out of men and tartars out of women. My father used to say that. I wish I'd paid more bloody attention to him.'

Suddenly, he shook off his melancholy mood and slapped Lewis on the knee. 'So how are you doing at this writing business? Is it a good life?'

59

'Not bad,' Lewis said with a grin. 'My publishers say I might make a couple of thousand out of the book.'

Slingsby sat up in astonishment.

'A couple of thousand for a book like that? How do you live?' Lewis put his drink down.

'I've got another job. I manage.'

'That's the right attitude. Too many people discontented with their lot. That's what's wrong with today's world.'

Lewis and Slingsby sat chatting over their drinks until Sharon reappeared. 'The car's here,' she said.

Lewis, who had stood up at her arrival, held out his hand. 'Thank you for the drink. I must be going now.' Slingsby got up and shook hands.

'Can we drop you anywhere?' he said.

'Not unless you're going past the Rue de la Huchette,' Lewis talked as he pulled on his raincoat.

'We can drop you right there. Come on.'

The three of them walked to the entrance of the hotel where a black Cadillac limousine waited. A bulky driver in a grey suit and mirrored sunglasses stood to open the door.

Sharon dipped down low to enter the padded interior and Slingsby ushered Lewis in before him. As Lewis ducked forward, Slingsby placed his hand lightly in the small of Lewis's back and came into contact with Lewis's revolver. Once all three had settled Slingsby spoke in rapid French to the driver and the car pulled away towards their destination.

*

Lewis thanked Slingsby and smiled his farewell to Sharon; then he watched the car glide away before turning into the narrowness of the Rue de la Huchette. He remembered that Napoleon had lived here while he waited for an appointment from the revolutionary government and as he hurried through the dark shadows to his rendezvous, he wondered how much of the street had changed.

Thanks to the warning he had received on the telephone, Lewis spotted the small green neon sign that spelt 'Sam's American Bar' over a dimly-lit doorway. He walked down a narrow stairway lined with dark red flock wallpaper and turned sharp left into a tiny lobby where there was an unattended lectern and a doorway with a small glass panel that glowed with a soft light from within.

Lewis looked through to a room that was deep in shadow and saw a collection of small, empty tables with white tablecloths, each with a small amber table lamp. He pushed open the door and entered a room that was about forty feet square with a low ceiling. A bar ran along wall to his left, ending in a space housing a grand piano and a set of drums. In front of it was a tiny dance floor, big enough for about six couples if they stood close to each other, with two other doorways leading off from the dance floor.

To his right was a counter and a small area for coats. The walls were crammed with framed photographs but it was too dim to make out the subject matter. At first he thought the room was empty until he saw a huge Negro in a white dinner jacket sitting where the bar turned before the piano. They looked at each other in silence for a moment until the black man said 'Hi, I'm Sam,' in a soft, deep voice that carried across the room. Lewis walked over to him and the man smiled in welcome.

'You must be Mr Horne. Rashid asked me to look after you until he got here. What will you have?' He lifted a section of the bar and squeezed behind it. Lewis hesitated for a moment as he drew in the dank, cellar smell. He could see the walls were stone behind the tightly packed photographs and he remembered that this part of Paris was honeycombed by the medieval cellars that stretched beneath the city.

'A shot of bourbon may help you breathe, the man said in an easy voice. 'We haven't changed the air down here since Hemingway was in last.'

Lewis nodded as he took off his raincoat and sat down on a barstool.

'Hemingway used to come here, eh?'

The man placed the drink before Lewis and curled a massive hand around his own glass.

61

'Man, everyone used to come here.' His eyes roamed around the empty room. 'Everyone except Charles de Gaulle. He didn't go to many clubs.'

Lewis swallowed some of the bourbon.

'What time do you start to get busy?' he asked. Sam shrugged his great shoulders.

'Any time now. You wanna eat? There's someone in the kitchen.'

Lewis shook his head. 'Maybe later.'

'OK,' Sam said and took Lewis's drink and poured a massive shot of extra bourbon into the glass. 'Just shout if there's anything you want.' With that he squeezed from behind the bar again and walked over to one of the swing doors.

'Monique,' he called in a gentle, rumbling voice. 'Tend the bar.'

A small woman with short hair entered the room as he held the swing door open. She had the short voluptuous body that would become heavy with age, but now was at its greatest advantage, displayed as it was in the timeless French uniform of white blouse, tight black skirt and fishnet stockings.

'*Bonsoir, m'sieur,*' she said in a sing-song voice as she took her position behind the bar. Sam sat at the piano and began to tinkle for a few minutes before he made a serious effort to play in a style reminiscent of Errol Garner. Lewis sipped his bourbon and waited.

Gradually the room began to fill. At first a few customers at the bar, then two waiters appeared as more people sat at the tables. Most of the customers seemed fairly old to Lewis and the majority were Americans.

Sam was joined on the bandstand by another Negro who sat at the drums and a saxophonist, bass player and trumpeter who were all elderly and white. They played swing music which was evidently what the clientele wanted to hear judging by the languid enthusiasm with which they called out requests. The room became hazy with cigarette smoke and stuffy from the warmth of close-packed bodies.

The bourbon eased the day's tension from Lewis and a heady muzziness issued the early warning signals that he was on the way to getting drunk. He took a Ricard water carafe from the bar top and filled his glass to the top, and tapped in time to the rhythm of 'One O'clock Jump'. As he glanced up into the glass that backed the bottles lining the bar, he caught the reflection of Rashid standing in the doorway with his arms around two girls who, Lewis could see at a glance, had come straight out of a chorus line. They had that long-legged thrusting posture of showgirls, and their dresses appeared to be made of tiny, shimmering pieces of gold and silver metal. They both wore Egyptian-style headpieces of the same material.

Rashid gave a whoop when he saw Lewis and lurched towards him. He wore a simple pale beige tropical suit, white shirt with an old Etonian tie. More impressively, about five thousand pounds'-worth of jewellery dangled from his thin wrists.

Lewis went to meet them and Rashid took his arms from around the girls' waists and let them dangle over their shoulders as they supported him.

'Lewis, my dear fellow,' he said in a voice as cultivated as his brother's. 'I want you to meet two delightful English girls who are here in Paris to study dancing.' The two girls smiled at him and he could see how young they were despite the heavy make-up they both wore. 'Debbie, Janice, allow me to introduce Mr Lewis Horne who will only add lustre to the evening we are about to enjoy.'

Lewis watched the performance with professional interest. It was a damned good imitation of a drunk. Rashid had managed to capture the nodding and sudden jerky movements correctly, the sharp, pointed features of his face had slackened and his mouth was formed into a sloppy smile. But the eyes remained focused as they darted around the room and they told Lewis how sober Rashid really was.

'Your table is over here, sir,' an anxious waiter said as he steered them to the part of the room that was farthest from the band.

'Champagne,' Rashid said as he slumped into his chair while Lewis and the waiter held the chairbacks for Debbie and Janice. 'Would you girls care for a very good cham-

pagne?' Rashid spoke in a carefully solicitous voice as he
covered each of their hands with one of his own. They
exchanged glances and gave tiny shrugs.

'Sounds lovely,' said the one Lewis took to be Debbie.

'Yes, fine,' Janice agreed.

Almost instantly the waiter reappeared with a magnum
of Bollinger and four tulip-shaped glasses. Janice looked
at them with disappointment.

'Don't they have real champagne glasses, Rashid?'
she said plaintively. He leaned forward and took her
hand.

'My dear, I have some devastating news for you. These
are real champagne glasses. Those silly, wide things you
have seen before are the invention of vulgarians. If you
are ever handed one again, dash it to the floor and think
of me.'

Janice, who had been glancing around the room in a
bored fashion, said: 'Can I have a cigarette, Rash?'

He reached inside his jacket and produced a slim, gold
case which he laid on the table before him.

'You may have this *and* the contents if you promise
never, no matter what the provocation, to call me Rash
again.' She reached out for it and he held her hand. 'Do I
have your promise?'

'Yeah, of course,' she said nonchalantly, and pocketed
the impromptu gift.

'Do I get a present, Rashid?' Debbie asked plaintively.

'Of course, my dear. You may dance with my chum,
Lewis. If he enjoys the experience I will be pleased to
reward you lavishly.'

Debbie looked at Lewis expectantly and he stood up
and led her to the tiny dance floor where other couples
swayed to *'Moonlight Serenade'*. She took him firmly in
her arms and pressed as much of her body to him as she
could manage. As the group were playing in muted tones
it was possible to talk.

'I don't know this,' she said. 'What group made it?'

'Glenn Miller,' Lewis said. She leaned back in his arms
and looked at him.

'You made that up. I've never heard of Glenn Miller.'

Lewis danced on for a while.

64

'He had a band in the Forties.'

Debbie wasn't satisfied.

'The Forties? You can't remember that far back.'

He was saddened by her lack of trust.

'I can't remember Waterloo, but I know what date it was,' he said lightly.

'That's a station,' Debbie said firmly.

'Yes, but the station was named after a battle, like Trafalgar Square.'

'Really?' she said, 'I never realised that. Still, it makes sense. After all, my mum named me after Debbie Reynolds.'

Lewis pondered this piece of logic for a while as Debbie gyrated her body against him. In normal circumstances he would have enjoyed the sensation more, but the knowledge that she was doing it to earn a gift from Rashid blunted his carnal desires.

'Blimey, you're hard to get going, aren't you?' she said and he grinned down at her.

'I've had a hard day. Don't think it's any lack of charm on your part.' They listened to the music for a few more minutes and then she said: 'You two, you aren't poofs, are you?'

'What makes you say that?' Lewis asked with interest.

Debbie became thoughtful for a moment, as if she may have gone too far, then she spoke again.

'Well, there's nothing wrong with it if you are. It's just that Rashid, well he never does anything. He carts us about and buys us presents and things but when it comes to it, he just says goodnight. Mind you, he's always pissed out of his brains so I don't suppose he could do anything even if he wanted to.'

Lewis laughed.

'How old are you, Debbie?'

'Nineteen,' she said as they narrowly avoided colliding with a vigorous elderly couple. 'Same as Janice. Why?'

'Maybe he's waiting until you're twenty-one.'

'Oh, I don't mind,' she said philosophically. 'The way most blokes jump on you over here, it makes a change.'

Another thought occurred to her.

''Ere, are you married?'

65

'No,' Lewis said as the music changed to *String of Pearls*.

'Have you got a girlfriend?' Lewis thought for a moment.

'I'm not sure,' he said truthfully.

'Oh, a bit iffy, is it?' Debbie said. 'Who's to blame, you or her?'

'I suppose I am. She doesn't like my job.'

'What do you do?'

'I'm a deep sea diver,' Lewis said convincingly. 'She thinks it's too dangerous. She'd prefer me to work in an office.'

'Is it dangerous?'

'Not if you're careful.'

Debbie had relaxed now, had stopped trying to work so hard at being erotic. It made her much more attractive. She rested her chin on his shoulder and somehow became softer in his arms.

'If you want my advice, you'll stick to what you're doing,' she said.

'Why do you say that?' Lewis said as her headpiece tinkled in his ear.

'My sister wanted her bloke to give up being a bouncer in a nightclub 'cos he was always having fights. So he took up driving a minicab. Then she gave him up for another bloke. And guess what *he* did for a living?'

'Bouncer in a nightclub,' Lewis said.

'Yeah. How did you know?' she said in a surprised voice.

'I just guessed,' Lewis said.

She ran her finger lightly along his neck.

'There you are, then. If your girlfriend wants a bloke in an office, she'd have found one in the first place, wouldn't she?'

'What you say makes sense,' Lewis said as the music came to an end. Debbie still had her arms around his neck. She leaned forward meaning to kiss him gently, but the effects of the dance and the bourbon made the embrace more passionate than either had really intended.

'Now I can tell you like girls,' she said as they parted and walked back to Rashid's table.

'I have ordered dinner,' Rashid said as they sat down.

66

'Caviare and hamburgers,' Janice said to Debbie with a grimace.

'I think you will agree the hamburgers are exceptional here,' he said as a waiter placed a vast dish of caviare sunk into a bowl of ice before them. Lewis had not eaten a great deal of caviare in his life but remembered it as being enjoyable, and he had only had a light lunch. He ladled a large dollop of the tiny, black, glistening eggs on to a piece of toast and bit into it with relish.

'I think I'll give this a miss,' Debbie said. 'Can I have some more champagne, Rashid?'

'Of course, my dear,' he said and he lifted the magnum bottle from the ice bucket beside him and put it on the table next to her. Immediately a waiter rushed over to them and refilled their glasses.

Debbie drank the contents of her glass very quickly and started on Lewis's which stood untouched by him. When they had consumed enough caviare and Debbie had drunk two more glasses of champagne, Rashid leaned across the table and said in a clear voice: 'I want to go to the boy's room, old man, but I'm not terribly sure I can make it on my own. Be a good chap and give me an arm to lean on.'

Lewis got up and Rashid extended an elbow so Lewis could guide him towards one of the doors beside the band. They passed down a corridor, ignoring the sign for the lavatories and Rashid glanced back to check they were alone. Then he swiftly opened a door marked PRIVATE with a small latch key. Lewis found himself in a tiny room with a desk, telephone, a wall of shelves covered in box files and a pile of cardboard boxes containing lavatory paper. Rashid turned to him: 'Forgive the theatrical effects but I do assure you it is necessary.' Lewis nodded.

'What do you have for me?'

Rashid reached into his waistband in the small of his back and produced a yellow photographic envelope. He handed it to Lewis who opened it and took out a series of colour snapshots of young, rich-looking Arabs. The pictures had been taken at a ski resort. Lewis turned one over. There was a number and a name with a description of height and weight written in fibre-tip pen. He counted them. There were ten in all.

Lewis looked at Rashid expectantly.

'Number five is my man. Please see no harm comes to him.' Lewis turned over the photograph and looked at the face. He had a small beard and a gold earring in the left lobe.

'It was fortunate that you could come in person, Lewis,' Rashid said. 'I learned earlier this evening that those gentlemen will leave the George V hotel tomorrow and make their way to England where they intend to capture the consulate of the People's Republic of Quatara and hold the occupants hostage until thirty of their imprisoned fellow zealots are released from prison in Quatara.'

'When will this happen?' Lewis said as he looked again at the snapshots.

'Very soon. Some time in the next few days. I cannot be more accurate.' Lewis nodded.

'Thank you, Rashid. Incidentally, Ali sends his regards.' The young Arab smiled.

'When you see him tell him it can be extremely tedious to constantly take the part of a playboy.'

They heard a flushing sound from the gentlemen's lavatory next door and Rashid shrugged.

'I suppose I must now resume the mantle of the alcoholic.'

Together they weaved back into the club room and rejoined Debbie and Janice at the table.

It was clear to Lewis at a glance that in the short time he and Rashid had been away, the two girls had become quite drunk.

'The hamburgers were lousy, Rashid,' Janice said in a slurred voice. 'We sent them back.'

Debbie nodded in agreement.

'I think it would be for the best if these girls were allowed to go home,' Rashid said, suddenly acting sober. Lewis nodded.

'Let me get the bill.'

Rashid waved a hand that jingled with gold.

'Don't worry, dear boy. I own the place.' He stood up

and laid his hands on Janice's bare shoulders. 'Come along my sweet thing; time to go.' Lewis watched how both the girls slowly reached for their handbags and placed the straps over their shoulders with enormous care. Just before they stood up he noticed a thickset man with heavy features and a shock of wiry hair look towards them before he walked out of the exit.

The girls started to sway their way to the door with Rashid helping Janice when Lewis remembered his raincoat that was still at the bar.

'Just a moment,' he called, and the three stopped while he picked it up from Monique. He put it on as he walked towards the three and they started to go through the exit door as he caught up with Debbie.

Rashid and Janice turned on to the stairs and Lewis heard a familiar clicking sound. Instinctively he reached out for Debbie to hold her back but he was off balance and at that moment she held on to him as she lurched forward. As the two of them fell he heard the shattering sound of nine millimetre ammunition being fired in an enclosed space.

His mind operated like a camera on automatic as he tumbled in Debbie's embrace into the area at the bottom of the staircase. Each explosion from the guns being fired at them lit the staircase like a flashlight and a series of pin-sharp images seared through Lewis's mind.

With his left hand Rashid clung to the stair rail attached to the wall. Lewis saw the heavy gold face of the Cartier wrist watch he wore explode as a bullet smashed into it. The weight of fire threw Rashid around so that Lewis could see the row of hits like poppies on the light material of his suit before he slowly let go of the rail and collapsed on to Janice who twitched three times as though she had been kicked.

Debbie lay sprawled across him and he could feel her body thrusting against his. Something was odd, he thought. At this range high velocity ammunition should go straight through her body and into his own. Then he remembered the curious metallic dresses the girls were wearing and suddenly realised that Debbie's body was acting as a human flak jacket to protect him.

Although the flash from the three hand guns lit all in front of them, they did not reveal the identities of the people who were actually firing. Then someone behind him in the club itself switched on a light in the stairwell and instantly Lewis could see the three gunmen. The one nearest to him was the man with the shock of wiry hair he had seen leaving the room a few minutes ago.

There was another who was also dressed in a conventional manner but thinner, with receding hair. The third was very young. Lewis caught the glimpse of a black silk handkerchief tied bandit-fashion across a face fringed by long, shiny, light brown hair. He was dressed in a pale, crumpled baggy silk suit with the sleeves pushed back to the elbows, and an open-necked shirt.

Lewis noticed how he held the automatic in his left hand and crouched low to fire. It was a distinctive style. As the bright light flooded them he could see the look of concern on the faces of the two older men. The one with receding hair began to call.

'Come, come,' and he reached out and shook the youth's shoulder as he aimed at Lewis's face. The shot went wide as it ploughed a furrow along the red flock wallpaper and a shower of ancient plaster filled the staircase in a sudden explosion of dust.

Lewis had meanwhile managed to draw the .38 from the holster by thrusting Debbie's body away from him with his knees. An inner voice kept repeating 'Remember you only have five rounds.' He could see that the assassin with the receding hair was behind the youth and the thickset man. The youth was changing magazines. Lewis raised the .38 with both hands and shot the thickset man dead centre. The bullet hit him in the sternum and jerked the heavy body back on to the stairs.

A look of surprise came to the face of the youth and he hesitated, but the man behind him squeezed off two rapid shots as Lewis was moving. He had managed to partially get behind the corner turn that led into the club as the words 'Come, come' were shouted again and he heard the two at the top of the stairs leaving.

He got to his feet and looked down on the carnage before him. Behind him from the club he could hear shouts and screams from the people who had heard the battle on the stairs. He hesitated for a moment, then jumped from behind his cover on to a clear patch of the staircase. No shots came his way.

He ran forward up the staircase expecting at any moment to be fired upon, and burst into the Rue de la Huchette, his adrenalin pumping furiously.

The sound of the battle had cleared the street so Lewis could see the figure in the pale suit thirty-odd yards away about to open the door of a Renault. Lewis took aim with both hands and fired his second shot. It was to the right and shattered the rear window of the car. The youth turned and crouched to the left as he had before and fired two shots.

The bullets kicked around him and Lewis began to run towards the crouching figure. The youth hesitated for a fraction and then failed at the moment of truth. He turned and began to run away. Lewis saw the man with the receding hair take aim. The shot tore through his flapping raincoat and Lewis brought up the gun in his hand. 'Three left' the inner voice told him, and he fired one-handed on the run. It was a lucky shot.

It passed through the shattered rear window and out at an angle, smashing the rear offside passenger's window and into the body of the gunman.

Lewis could hear him grunt as he raced past in pursuit of the youth. He pounded on for a hundred yards or more, twisting through narrow streets until he realised that his quarry had got away. Finally he stopped and leaned against a wall to draw deep draughts of air into his aching lungs.

As he stood with his back to the wall he looked down at his raincoat. Across the narrow street from where he stood was a restaurant where heavy shutters allowed chinks of light into the roadway. The coat was soaked in blood from the bodies on the staircase. And he still held the .38 revolver in his hand. Across the street the door of the restaurant opened as two people, a man and woman, came out talking in the easy tones of friends who had just relaxed over a good meal. Too late, Lewis realised that he was standing in a pool of light from the open doorway.

The woman looked across at him and he could feel the shock she felt at the bloodstained image he presented.

Instinctively he turned and stumbled into the darkness, away from Hanna who had stood opposite him in the doorway with a look of horror on her face.

What thoughts at heart have you and I
We cannot stop to tell;
But dead or living, drunk or dry,
Soldier, I wish you well.

A Shropshire Lad
A. E. HOUSMAN

Chapter Four

The first thing Lewis did when he got back to Rene Malle's apartment was to down a stiff drink. He had stuffed his stained raincoat into a rubbish bin on his way back from the Rue de la Huchette but there was a patch of blood that had almost dried on the knee of his trousers.

He went into the bathroom and sponged it away, then he took his drink to the telephone and called Charlie Mars at his flat in Lincoln's Inn. When Charlie answered, Lewis could hear the sound of Billie Holliday singing 'Crazy He Calls Me' softly in the background.

'How are you?' Charlie asked.

'Bloody, but unbowed,' Lewis answered after taking another pull at the drink. 'It's moving very fast here. I need backup. Do we have anyone in town?'

'Yes. Claude Henderson is there with Lloyd and Walters.'

'Why?' Lewis asked with surprise.

'There was an interesting meeting in the Paris Athene Hotel this lunchtime. One of the parties was Jack Silver. I wanted to keep an eye on the other protagonists. But tell me your problems.'

'There was a gunfight in the Latin Quarter. Rashid is dead and two of theirs, plus a couple of innocent bystanders. Can you call the French off? I'm going to be easy to identify.'

Charlie groaned down the phone. 'God, you know they invented the word bureaucracy. What do you want with Claude?'

'Rashid gave me some stuff. It could be good. But I need reinforcements for surveillance.'

Charlie thought for a few seconds. 'Claude is staying with an old chum at the embassy. I'll call him there and get him to come to you, then I'll see what I can do about Rashid. You'd better let me have some more details.'

75

Lewis gave him a precise account of the events of the day while Charlie made notes.

'You say they could be German?'

'Yes,' Lewis said. 'It could have been "Come" or "Komme" one of them shouted.'

When Charlie rang off, Lewis began his wait for Henderson. He went into Rene's workroom and found a can of gun oil and a rag. He stripped the .38 and cleaned it, which wasn't strictly necessary as modern ammunition fired so clean, but his army training with weapons took precedence. There were only two rounds left in the chamber. He walked back to the safe and stood looking at it for a while. If he had brought Sandy Patch with him, Lewis knew the safe would have been open in minutes.

As it was, he decided to try for a long shot. He dialled a sequence of numbers and got nothing, paused, thought for a moment and then tried another and heard the satisfying sound of tumblers clicking into place. It hadn't been Napoleon's birthdate but the anniversary of his death that Rene had gone for.

Lewis pulled open the door and took out the box of .38 ammunition. He replaced the used cartridges and then after a moment put another five rounds in his jacket pocket. Then he remembered his raincoat lying with the rubbish and decided to see if his host had anything in his wardrobe that would suit him, as they were approximately the same size.

He opened the fitted cupboard in Rene's bedroom and marvelled at the rows of neatly pressed suits and shirts. Below, ten pairs of shoes, each fitted with shoe trees, stood in ranks. Lewis found three raincoats. He considered that the sign of a dandy. After a moment's hesitation he took a dark blue model and glanced at the label. It was from Bloomingdales in New York. Lewis judged it to be about his price range. He took it into the spare room and threw it on to the bed.

Just then there was the sound of a buzzer from the street door. He pressed the release button and then opened the front door so that he could watch the portly figure of Claude Henderson puffing up the stairs.

As Charlie Mars's official number two it was unusual

76

for him to be away from Gower Street where their department was located. Lewis guessed the chance of a trip to
Paris had lured him into menial duties. Furthermore,
Lewis could see that he was not pleased to be summoned
at this late hour. His round face was set in a displeased
expression, so that he looked a little like a grumpy baby.
He was also wearing a dinner jacket.

'Really, Horne. This is too bad,' he said in a plaintive
voice. 'You've quite spoilt my evening.'

'I apologise, Claude, but it's serious business.'

Mollified by Lewis's unusual courtesy, he accepted a
glass of Vermouth and studied the snapshots that Lewis
had laid out on the drawing desk.

'They're staying at the George V Hotel right now,'
Lewis said, 'but they could move to London at any time.'

Claude was quite businesslike. He shuffled the pictures
together. 'Right, I'll get these copied and post watchers
at the hotel. What are your plans?'

Lewis glanced down at the knee of his trousers where
the bloodstain had been.

'I'm going back to Gower Street in the morning.'

Claude nodded.

'I should try and get some sleep, old man. You look
done in. Incidentally, what were you doing at The Bristol
earlier?'

'Having a drink with a man called Slingsby. How did
you know I was there?'

Claude gave a self-satisfied smile.

'We were watching the man you were with.'

'Why? Who is he really?'

Claude ran a hand over his carefully barbered hair. 'An
arms dealer called Max Ernhart. He, Lord Silver, an
Israeli representative and two chaps from your Mr Ahmed
have been having discussions of a friendly nature.'

'That's an unlikely combination,' Lewis said. 'Do we
know what could have brought them together?'

'It could be that Israel is prepared to give a hand at
restoring the Royal Family and if there is any chance of
a rapprochement between Israel and Quatara, a lot of
people will be for or against it.'

Lewis nodded then gazed abstractedly at the delicate

moulding on the ceiling. He was trying to remember if he or Jessica Crossley had suggested the route they had taken from the Louvre that afternoon.

Claude decided to go. He patted his pockets in a fussy manner to make sure he had everything before leaving. After showing him to the door Lewis sat down and looked at the telephone for a while. He was tired but the adrenalin still flowed through his body, making him feel jumpy and on edge.

After a few minutes' thought, he dialled the Bristol Hotel. The switchboard connected him with Hanna's suite and once again the same man answered the call.

'I would like to talk to Doctor Pearce, please,' Lewis said.

'Hold on,' the man said and there was a brief pause. 'I'm sorry, Mr Horne, Miss Pearce doesn't wish to speak to you.'

Lewis hung up and looked at his watch. It was nearly one o'clock. He wanted another drink and the whisky bottle was empty. He decided to see if the Café Flore was still open. The air was gentle as he walked slowly towards the light that showed the existence of others like him who could not sleep.

Exhaustion and shock were making him work almost on remote control as he arrived at the café and scanned the tables. There was one large, laughing group of students from the Academie de Musique cluttering the café with their black-cased instruments and a couple of middle-aged tourists to his right. But one figure engaged his attention more sharply than all the others. She sat alone with a cashmere sweater draped over her shoulders with a large cup of coffee before her.

Lewis stood at her table and as she looked up at him he could see that she was in a mood that matched his own.

'How was your evening?' he asked. Jessica looked up into the clear, starry sky and sighed: 'Fine, until the end. I found there was life in the old dog yet.' Lewis smiled.

'So that's why you're out taking the night air.'

Jessica spread her hands on the table.

'I thought I'd give him some time to get to sleep.'

Lewis sat down and ordered a large cognac and a small black coffee from the same waiter who had served him that morning. Jessica looked at him intently for a while.

'You seem low,' she said and he nodded.

'The gal I love's in love with somebody else.'

'How do you know all those old songs?' she asked. 'That is an old song, isn't it?'

Lewis nodded again. Suddenly he wanted to tell her something of his life.

'When I was a boy my parents were out of the country; my father was in the Army. They had some close friends, schoolteachers who didn't have any children. I lived with them for a couple of years. They had a record collection of old 78s going back to the Twenties. They used to play them all the time. I didn't watch much television but I can do a great imitation of Al Bowlly.'

'Who was Al Bowlly?' Jessica said with a half smile.

'A crooner, almost as famous as Bing Crosby. He was killed in an air-raid early in the war.' Jessica nodded. There was a small leather-covered tape recorder on the table. She pressed a button and the voice of Jack Silver came to them.

'. . . We thought we 'ad it bad in the Blitz, blimey you should've seen what we did to Germany. We knocked 'ell out of it. Mind you, they bloody well deserved it . . .'

She switched it off, her point nicely made, and they sat in silence for a while. The student musicians had moved off and the café was almost deserted.

The waiter stood near them impassively gazing out on to the quiet boulevard. Lewis folded his arms.

'You're lonely, aren't you?'

'Why do you ask?' she said and she toyed with the tape recorder without looking at him. He shrugged.

'Just a feeling.'

She looked up at him and he could see she wanted to tell him something.

'For the last three years I've lived on weekdays with a married man.' She paused and looked up into the sky once again. 'A few weeks ago he was told he only had a short time to live. He decided to spend that time with his wife. Since then, yes, I've been very lonely.'

Lewis finished his brandy in one swallow and turned the glass upside down on the table. 'Do you remember this quotation "... a man hurrying to a great deed who knocks down a child ... out of unfeeling carelessness commits a crime?"' Lewis asked.

'Yes,' Jessica said.

'Who said it?'

'Rosa Luxemburg.' Lewis nodded.

'They killed her too.'

Lewis leaned forward: 'I don't want to spend the night alone, do you?'

Jessica slowly shook her head as she looked down at the table then she held out her hand and he took it in his own.

*

Through a narrow gap in the shutters at his bedroom windows Lewis could see the first streaks of morning light in a cloudless sky. Jessica stirred slightly and he looked down at her as she rested her head in the crook of his arm. A wisp of ash-blonde hair lay across her cheek and she moved again in her sleep to shake it away. The only thing that covered them was a single sheet so he could see the shape of her long body as it nestled against his own.

In the studio he could hear the telephone ringing. Moving as easily as he could, he slipped away from her and pulled on the blue trench coat that lay on a chair next to the bed. Quietly he opened the bedroom door and padded in bare feet to the large room.

'Horne? Henderson here,' Claude said in a brisk voice.

'Yes, Claude,' Lewis replied as he shifted his empty glass from the night before and sat on the coffee table.

'The watchers have done well. Your Arab friends are booked on British Airways Flight 301 from Charles de Gaulle at 7.55 this morning and they have booked into the Hilton Hotel for one night. What does that suggest?'

'It sounds very much as if they're going to start their little games today.' Lewis scratched an unshaven cheek.

'Precisely,' Henderson said. 'I've booked you on the same flight, and told the night shift at Gower Street to have a couple of people at the airport to check them in and make sure they go straight to the hotel.'

'Fine. I'll be on my way. See you later.' Lewis rang off and looked at his watch. It was twenty to six. He walked back towards the bedroom and heard the rushing sound of the shower in the bathroom, so he changed direction and made for the small kitchen at the other end of the flat. By the time he had made two cups of filtered coffee Jessica had emerged dressed and brushing her hair.

Lewis was impressed that any woman could be ready so quickly. He handed her one of the mugs and noticed that in his bare feet she was as tall as he was.

'Hello,' she said shyly and he leaned forward and kissed her on the nose. 'Who was on the telephone?' she asked casually. Lewis sipped some coffee.

'Head office. I've got to get back to London for a sales conference this morning.'

She looked around the room; it was still gloomy as the shutters cut out the early light. 'I like this flat,' she said. Lewis walked over to the desk and picked up a pencil.

'What's your address?' he asked and he wrote the information down carefully. 'Prince of Wales Drive. That's the long row of flats in Battersea, isn't it?'

She nodded and put down her mug of coffee.

'I'd better be getting back to my hotel.'

'Do you mind if I don't come with you?' Lewis said. 'I'm afraid I've got a bit of a rush on.'

'Of course not.'

Lewis walked over to her as he stuffed the piece of paper with her address into the pocket of the trenchcoat. 'I'll see you in London,' he said.

She looked at him for a moment, then leaned forward and kissed him firmly on the lips. 'Put some shoes on or you'll catch your death of cold.' Moments later she was gone.

Lewis walked over to the windows and opened one of the shutters. Light flooded into the room. He stood for a few minutes on the tiny balcony and listened to the early traffic. He could see Jessica pause for a moment across the street to buy a newspaper before she disappeared among the morning pedestrians. He went back to the

81

telephone and called Charlie Mars's London number. Lewis told him of the latest developments and could almost hear Charlie grow thoughtful.

'We'd better to keep as many people away from the consulate as possible. I think I'll put someone in there applying for an import licence for Quataran basketwork or something. That should keep him in there all day.'

'What time will you be in your office?' Lewis asked.

'About ten o'clock. I'm going to get Mr Ahmed to come along to Gower Street. I think he could be of some use to us. See you later.' Lewis could hear Charlie yawn before he rang off.

Lewis showered and then stood in front of the mirror in the bathroom to shave. Written in soap on the glass were the words: THANKS FOR THE MEMORY (old song sung by Bob Hope – I think). He washed them away with a face flannel and smiled.

*

The Arabs disembarked just ahead of Lewis. He held back and glanced at them occasionally as they trudged through the seemingly endless corridors that eventually led to Passport Control. As they stood in separate queues Lewis allowed himself a few flickering glances in their direction. He could see they were tense and jumpy. None of them talked to each other. Instead they shot looks around the hall as they shuffled towards the immigration official. They were all dressed conservatively and each carried a small piece of hand luggage: nothing about them merited a second glance. None of them had brought a suitcase so Lewis was expecting a fast exit when they had walked through customs.

As a British citizen, Lewis came through Passport Control before the others so he had time to glance around the baggage reclamation area and spot Charlie's man by the customs exit. He was holding a piece of card with the name 'Hardman' lettered crudely in black crayon.

'They're right behind,' Lewis muttered to him. 'The only Arabs on the plane.' The young man nodded and fiddled with the zip on his leather jacket without looking at Lewis, who made off in the direction of the Underground to catch the Piccadilly line to Holborn. An hour later, he came out of the station and started a brisk walk towards Gower Street. He had gone only a few yards when a small, red, open sports car drew up alongside him. He looked down at an elegant woman in her early thirties. She was wearing a silk headscarf.

Mary Romanoff Brown turned to him as he lowered himself into the passenger seat and felt for the seat belt. 'That's a dashing new raincoat, Captain Horne.'

'I stole it in Paris,' Lewis said as Mary tried to ease herself back into the traffic.

'I thought it was a bit grand for your modest salary.'

'It's only from Bloomingdales,' Lewis said as the acceleration forced him back into the bucket seat. Mary smiled.

'It may have been bought in Bloomies, darling, but it's very posh. I know, I was going to buy one for Nico on the occasion of his fortieth birthday.'

Lewis peered inside at the label again. 'So five hundred francs wouldn't be a fair compensation?' he said. Mary laughed.

'About five times that would be about right.'

He sat and composed a letter of apology to Rene for the rest of the journey. Presently, Mary stopped outside their headquarters and let Lewis out.

'Tell Sergeant Major Watts I'm just parking, darling,' she said as she hustled off. Lewis called out the message as he crossed the hallway and began to climb the stairs towards Charlie Mars's rooms. He rapped lightly on the secretary's door and entered. A startled girl peered at him through wire-framed spectacles. At first, Lewis took her to be in her early teens but then he saw she was older. It was her slimness and the loose way she wore her light brown hair.

'Hello,' he said. 'My name is Horne. Is Sergeant Hillary about?' He could see she had a roll of plans that she was holding in some apprehension.

'No. I'm afraid he was sent on his new posting yesterday. I came from the Curzon Street pool this morning, sir.'

Lewis leaned against one of the filing cabinets and stuck his hands in his pockets. 'Call me Lewis. We don't go in for much formality over here. What's your name?' She laid the roll of plans down on a trestle table.

'Penny Rose.'

'Any relation to Air Vice Marshal Rose?' Lewis said in a friendly voice.

'Yes,' she said eagerly. 'He's my father. Do you know him?'

'I've met him a couple of times. He's a friend of Charlie's.'

'Mr Mars. Yes, I know. What's he like?'

'Who, Charlie? An absolute lamb, just wait and see.'

At that moment a roaring voice came from the corridor outside. 'Where the bloody hell is the key to my door?'

Penny Rose shot Lewis a look of reproach but at that moment the door burst open and the tall, rangy figure of Charlie Mars suddenly filled the frame. Penny looked up at him, her face transfixed with fear. When he saw her, he immediately became conciliatory.

'Hello, my dear, you must be Penny.'

'Yyyess,' she stammered.

'Well, have you seen the key to my office?'

She looked anxiously around the office and picked up a key ring. 'Are these they?'

'They seem to be,' Charlie said and took them from her.

'Oh, these plans arrived for you, Mr Mars.' Penny held out the roll and Charlie took it. Then he gestured around the room.

'This all looks a bit spartan at the moment, my dear. Your predecessor, Sergeant Hillary, thought the role of secretary effeminate. In consequence he made this room as bleak as he knew how in case visitors might doubt his manhood. I'm sure you will find ways of making it delightful. Just ask Mr Fuller in the stores for anything you may need and I'll sign the requisition form.

'However, I must ask you to leave my room exactly as it is. I cannot bear change. If you have any questions about procedure just ask Mr Henderson's secretary, Kate. She's been here for longer than any of us and knows everything. Now, if you can bring Captain Horne and me some coffee, please . . .'

Penny nodded and looked around the office again. Charlie smiled and pointed towards the corridor.

'Just ask Kate.' He turned away and then turned back again. 'That dress you're wearing?'

She glanced down at it in surprise. 'Yes?'

'It's a Laura Ashley, isn't it?'

'Yes, it is,' she said.

'I thought so,' Charlie said with a certain amount of pleasure in his voice. 'My daughters have similar clothes. Don't forget the coffee,' he said over his shoulder as he and Lewis went next door.

Lewis glanced around the familiar surroundings as he followed Charlie into his room.

The books, the battered furniture and the old rugs had once graced Charlie's study at Oxford and Lewis had first known them as an undergraduate. So similar was the effect that Lewis sometimes imagined he was there to read Charlie an essay or listen to one of the stack of records now piled into a cupboard under the bookshelves next to the marble fireplace.

Charlie walked to a large table at the far end of the room and switched on a large Anglepoise lamp. He spread the plans and weighed down the corners with books, then thrust his hands into the pockets of the cardigan he wore beneath his tweed suit.

'I thought you were bringing Ali with you?' Lewis said as they looked down at the blueprints.

The door opened and Penny entered with two cups on a tray. She looked around the room; every surface seemed to be covered with books and files.

'Just put it down anywhere and ask Captain Meredith to join us, please.'

Penny placed both the cups on the floor next to the chesterfield that stood before the fireplace. Charlie walked over from the table, picked up his cup and sat down next to the book-laden coffee table while Lewis leaned against the mantelpiece and nursed his cup with both hands.

Neither man spoke and Gordon Meredith found them both in the same positions when he arrived a few moments later.

They both glanced up at him and Gordon stroked his fair moustache uneasily as he waited to hear an explanation for his summons.

'Take a seat, Gordon,' Charlie said. 'Coffee?'

Meredith sat in a red leather chair next to the chesterfield.

'Er, no thanks, I've just had one.' Gordon glanced at each of them in turn and Charlie eventually cleared his throat.

'Ten men are in London to capture the Quataran Consulate and hold the representatives there for hostages in the hope it will bring about the release of prisoners in Quatara. What do you think of the situation, Captain?'

'Where are they now?' Meredith asked.

'In the Hilton Hotel.'

'Are they armed yet?'

Charlie downed his coffee cup before he answered. 'We imagine so.'

Meredith shrugged. 'It's best to hit them now before they get out onto the streets.'

'What if we wait until they get to the consulate?'

'You could ambush them. It would be tricky but it could be done.'

Charlie stared into his cup.

'Suppose we let them take the consulate?'

Meredith looked at them both again.

'Then you'd have a classic siege situation. The terrorists would probably kill one of the hostages to show they meant business and then set a time limit for the release of their friends in Quatara.'

'Exactly,' Charlie said. 'And what would be the reaction of the revolutionary government of Quatara, Lewis?'

Lewis thought for a moment before replying.

'Issue a statement saying the British Government was responsible for the lives of the hostages and fly someone in, probably from Paris, to negotiate.'

Charlie nodded again.

'But if we considered that the lives of the hostages were in too much danger to wait for that eventuality or if the lives of British citizens were similarly in danger, we would be justified under international law in going ahead and storming the building, would we not?'

'Yes,' Lewis said. 'There's been plenty of precedence for such action, the Iranian Embassy siege being a case in point.'

Charlie shifted his feet on the coffee table and a pile of books slid gently to the floor. The effect did not make the room look noticeably untidier.

'Who's your best safe-cracker?' he said.

'Sandy Patch,' Lewis replied without hesitation.

Charlie nodded. 'Well, the usual anti-terrorist team is standing by so we can only await developments. I think we had all better stay around the building until we see what transpires.'

When Lewis and Gordon left Charlie's room Lewis made for the library. Gower Street had recently installed a computer for paperwork but photographs were still filed in metal cabinets and cross-referenced to the information in the electronic system. It was a nuisance that staff constantly complained about but Lewis quite enjoyed browsing through the old library when he had the time.

The section was housed in an unrenovated part of the basement next to the computer room where Mary Romanoff Brown ruled her pin-sharp, dust-free modern empire. Lewis pushed open the door to the old library and stood at a counter. A rotund figure with thick, pebble-lensed glasses, called Phil Piper, glanced up from the newspaper crossword he was studying and tugged at his droopy moustache.

'A six-letter word, "Take your cue from Napoleon's beautiful daughter",' he said and chewed the end of his ballpoint pen.

'Cannon,' Lewis said.

'Cannon?' Piper repeated dubiously.

'That's what Napoleon called his artillery – my beautiful daughters.'

Piper laboriously lettered in the word. '"When lefties do it wrong", two words, four and six, beginning with C.'

Lewis looked at him.

'If I do this for you, will you do something for me?'

'Sure, Lew,' Piper said. 'You know our only desire is to serve.'

'Cack-handed.'

'Who is?' Piper asked.

'That's the answer to your clue.'

'Oh.' He lettered the words in and laid down the pen. 'Now, how can I return the favour, my good fellow?'

'Two men were killed in Paris last night; both professional gunmen. Do you have anything on them?'

'Sure.' Piper passed him a wire tray that was normally housed on a shelf below the counter. 'Both about to go in the dead file.'

Lewis picked up the two photographs. The heavier man had been pictured quite recently in Amsterdam. The other photograph was much older. The features were recognisable but here the assassin had a full head of hair. Lewis turned them over and read the captions on the back. Klaus Gottlieb and Heinrich Klenze, both East German, known to work for the Russian Berlin station. Not known for sophisticated methods; simple executions their speciality. Lewis held up the pictures to show Piper.

'Could you cross-check them? I'm looking for a young man, early twenties, long hair, looks like a pop star. Shoots with the left.'

'Cack-handed you mean,' Piper said and set about his search.

Lewis took a seat on the stool on his side of the counter, picked up the phone next to his elbow and dialled an internal number. Penny Rose answered and Lewis told her where he was. While Phil Piper painstakingly combed through the filing cabinets, Lewis completed the crossword.

Eventually he returned with a half dozen pictures. They were all of young men with a variety of complexions and wearing expressions of insolence or ferocity, but none of them seemed to match the youth Lewis had seen on the stairs. He handed them back to Piper along with his thanks and left the musty room for Mary's headquarters.

Just along the passageway Lewis entered a totally different world. Bright, even light from a diffused source in the ceiling created a shadowless room decorated in bold, primary colours.

Young women sat at modern desks breathing the air-conditioned smoke-free atmosphere that computers demanded before they would function at maximum efficiency. Mary sat at a wide curved desk that was set at an angle so she could sweep the entire room at a glance.

As Lewis approached her she was talking to a young woman who was making notes on a clipboard. He stood nearby while she finished.

'All right, Jacquie,' she said finally. 'If they can't come up with the programmes by next Wednesday I shall have to tell the Head of Operations we are unable to complete his request because of lack of co-operation from other areas, so don't worry any more. Just get on with what you can.'

Mary looked up at him and smiled.

'Yes, Captain.'

Lewis was aware that the girls in the room were glancing in his direction and he found it slightly disconcerting.

'Come and sit down,' Mary said and indicated a seat next to hers behind her command console. He took the chair gratefully and watched the rows of female heads return to their work. 'What can we do for you?' Mary asked with the tone of voice an old family doctor would use on a young patient.

'Check a name for me, Mary.' Lewis leaned forward and wrote JESSICA CROSSLEY on a pad next to Mary's display console.

'Any other information?' she asked.

Lewis shrugged. 'No, not really. She's a historian.'

'Every little helps.' Mary tapped away at the keyboard of her display terminal.

'No. I'm sorry Lewis. Nothing at all,' she said after a few moments.

'Could you try something else for me?'

'You'll have to get a move on.'

'I want to trace a young man; very young, he looks like a pop singer and he's a skilful killer, left-handed, wears expensive clothes.'

'What nationality?'

'I don't know. I've given you all I have on him. He may have a connection with the Middle East or perhaps he's just a contract killer.'

Mary looked at her machine for a while and then turned to Lewis. 'I'll play with this for a bit, and call you if I get anything.'

'OK,' Lewis said. 'I'll be in my room.'

He quickly climbed the flight of stairs from the basement, glad to leave the antiseptic surroundings, and met Claude Henderson in the main entrance hall.

'By God, your name is mud at the Embassy,' Claude said. 'You've generated enough paperwork to guarantee employment for a filing clerk until the turn of the century.'

'I suppose it would have been easier on everyone if I'd just let them kill me as well, eh Claude?' Lewis said as he made for the attic room he shared with Gordon Meredith. 'After all, it would save the need for all those memos.'

The rooms were smaller and the corridor narrower when Lewis reached their floor. It had been the servants' quarters long ago when the house had belonged to a merchant in the Baltic trade. The gas mantles in the narrow passageway still worked and the slightly damp smell served to remind the occasional visitor where the poor part of the house started.

Lewis entered his offices and found Gordon Meredith lying full length on his latest acquisition: a tatty chaise longue covered in faded purple silk. One corner had frayed so the horsehair stuffing poked through. Since they had first occupied the room Gordon had set about feathering the nest until it now bore a close resemblance to an Edwardian public schoolboy's study.

'I'm going to be an uncle again.' Gordon looked up from the letter he was reading.

'How many times is that now?'

'This will be the fourth.'

Lewis sat down at the tiny desk they shared.

'There won't be any shortage of Merediths on the border in years to come. How is the farm?'

'Everything seems to be growing in a satisfactory manner, including my sister-in-law. They won a prize at the agricultural show last year for their bull and they're trying for it again. Egg production is up eight per cent

90

and they're expecting a bumper crop of barley. I don't know how they cope with the excitement.'

Lewis sat back in his chair and looked around at Meredith's collection of photographs, books, trunks and old sporting kit.

'Maybe they're right,' he said and Meredith looked at him in surprise. 'Perhaps we're the ones who have got it wrong. I saw Hanna yesterday. She wants me to pack in and write for a living.'

Gordon sat up and folded his letter.

'I can't see it, old boy,' he said after a moment. 'Horses for courses. My brother is a natural farmer. You're a natural at what we do. That's all there is to it.'

Lewis laced his fingers together behind his head and sighed. 'I never thought of it like that before,' he said. Gordon nodded.

'My Aunt Lucy always used to say: "If wishes were horses, beggars would ride."'

'Why did she?' Lewis asked.

'Why did she what?'

'Say that.'

'Because she was the cliché queen of St John's Wood. My brother and I once counted seventy-eight in one day when we were boys.'

'Everything you've just said is totally irrelevant.'

'Yes, old boy, most things in life are. That's why we choose to do what we do.'

Lewis smiled. 'That's fairly intelligent. I may allow you to continue seeing my sister.'

As he spoke, the telephone rang; it was a rather breathless Penny Rose. 'Mr Mars says if you're free could you and Captain Meredith spare him a moment?' Which meant sooner rather than later.

*

Charlie stood by the fireplace and clasped his hands behind his back.

'They've started to move,' he said as they entered.

'All of them?' Lewis said. Charlie nodded.

'All ten and carrying hand luggage.'

'We'd better get our act together,' Lewis said.

91

'Claude Henderson is liaising with the anti-terrorist squad,' Charlie said. 'Bellingford is on his way here, so is Mr Ahmed.'

The telephone rang. Charlie answered and held it out to Lewis. 'It's for you. Mary Brown.'

'Yes, Mary.'

'I've got something you might want to look at.'

'What is it?'

'I'm not sure. Perhaps it will make sense to you.'

'OK. I'll be down in a minute. Thanks.'

Lewis turned to Gordon Meredith. 'Get hold of Sandy Patch. He's probably in the duty room. Tell him to stand by, call Tony Cole and tell him there's a job on.'

Gordon departed and Lewis was left alone with Charlie. He could tell that the older man was keyed up by the situation. The frustration they had suffered in recent weeks ebbed away at the prospect of action.

'I'm just going down to see Mary Brown,' Lewis said.

Charlie thrust his hands deep into his cardigan pockets and stared down at the tatty Persian rug. 'I'll call you when the others get here.' He spoke without raising his head.

Lewis watched the rows of girls look up at him once again as he approached Mary's desk. He sat beside her once more and she tapped out a command on the display unit.

'I conducted a search for your nameless youth by going through the recent Middle East material and didn't have much joy, but this is interesting.' She keyed in another command and moments later the text of a conversation appeared on the screen.

'What is this?' Lewis said.

'The Americans gave this to us forty-eight hours ago. It's a snippet of conversation recorded with a directional microphone in Washington three days ago.

'The two men talking were Nikolai Vashilov, one of the cultural attachés, and Dimitri Markov, who was there with a trade mission. Both of them are KGB colonels and old friends. They're both with the Russian Middle East section.'

Lewis looked at the screen.

VASHILOV: So we've still got them pinned down
MARKOV: (Laughter) Every way, my dear friend, and you know how proud the British are about their expertise with Arabs.
VASHILOV: Still, it would not do to underestimate them. They have been at this game a long time and they can be very nasty.
MARKOV: They can be as nasty as they like. We've got the kid from Riga.

Lewis stared at the last sentence for a long time.

And you will list the bugle
That blows in lands of morn,
And make the foes of England
Be sorry you were born.

                    A Shropshire Lad
                    A. E. HOUSMAN

Chapter Five

The solitary figure of George Ward was speaking on one of the four telephones before him when Lewis entered the Operations Room. As Duty Officer, Ward sat at a high podium facing rows of empty desks which created the effect of an old-fashioned schoolroom. To add to the atmosphere there was a blackboard behind George and, on the wall facing him, a massive map of the world mounted on heavy canvas. The surface was coated with yellowed, cracked varnish and great areas were coloured in red to show the lost Empire of King George VI. One previous Christmas, someone had lettered 'WHAT WE ARE FIGHTING FOR' next to Australia. Lewis walked over to the map and let his gaze dwell on northern waters while George continued with his conversation. 'Is she? ... You're sure? ... So what happened next?' There was a pause, then: 'No ... him too? ... Well, you'd never believe it to look at her. Right, thanks for the tip. I'll be in touch.'

As he hung up, Sandy Patch came into the room carrying two plastic cups and handed one to Ward who was now fiddling with the large spotted bow tie he always wore. His sharp features were alight with freshly received gossip as he took the thin plastic container from Sandy and winced at the heat cf the coffee.

'I say,' he said, running bony fingers through the long, fair hair that curled over the collar of his shirt. 'That new secretary of Charlie's is hot stuff according to Daisy Wicker at Curzon Street.'

'Thinking of going on holiday, boss?' Sandy said, pointedly ignoring Ward's chatter. Lewis nodded and traced his finger up the Gulf of Finland to a town on the map south of Leningrad. Sandy peered forward to where Lewis's finger pointed.

'Rygur,' he said and Lewis shook his head.

'It's pronounced "Reega".'

'Very nasty in winter,' George Ward said huffily. 'Very cold indeed – Riga. Why are you going there?'

'I'm more interested in what comes from there at the moment,' Lewis said in a lighter tone. 'Tell me,' he said in a more serious voice, 'did you equip Colin Miller this morning?'

George nodded.

'What with?' Lewis asked.

Ward walked back to his desk, picked up a clipboard and flipped over a couple of sheets. 'A Morse pen.'

'Is that all?'

George looked down at the sheet again. 'Yeah. Why?'

Lewis nodded, but gave nothing away.

Then, before he could be questioned further one of the telephones rang on the duty desk and George picked it up.

'Hello, yes. Hang on a moment.' He cupped his hand over the mouthpiece. 'Charlie Mars wants you two.'

As they made for the door George kept talking. 'Hello, you don't know me but we have some friends in common at Curzon Street. How about . . .?'

Sandy turned to Lewis as they started up the stairs. 'Are you OK, boss?' he said in a conversational voice, but Lewis could detect a slight edge of concern. He looked at him and grinned.

'Why do you ask?' Sandy shrugged.

'You seem to have a lot on your mind . . . Christ, you know what I mean.'

They climbed in silence for another two flights when Lewis answered belatedly, 'I'm fine, really. But if I need somewhere to lean, I'll let you know, all right?'

Sandy nodded as they approached Charlie's door. When they entered, Charlie was standing at the table studying the plan of the Quataran Embassy. He looked up after a moment and said: 'Bellingford and Mr Ahmed should be here any moment. I've sent for Meredith.' He handed Sandy a sheet of paper without saying anything and Sandy looked down at the series of numbers that were typed there. 'Can you guess what that is?' he said with a wry smile.

Sandy paused for a few moments. 'Possible combinations for a safe?'

'Good man,' Charlie said with approval. 'Those are the key numbers in the life of Muktar Elam, the Comrade Secretary of the Quataran Revolutionary Diplomatic Mission. Birthdays, anniversaries – that sort of thing. I had Mary Brown's department run the analysis.'

Sandy looked at the list dubiously. 'I think I'd better take some plastic along as well,' he said and at that moment Penny Rose entered the room.

'Mr Ahmed and Mr Bellingford are on their way up, sir,' she said and Charlie nodded an acknowledgment. As she stood at the doorway, Meredith hovered behind her and she made way so he could get into the room. He held a slip of paper in his hand.

'This is just off the Press Association wire.'

Charlie took the piece of paper, read it and handed it to Lewis. It was a single sentence from a wire machine printed out in red:

P. A. FLASH . . . Terrorists are believed to have seized
the Quataran Diplomatic Mission's headquarters
in New Cavendish Street.

The flash was timed 12.20 pm. He looked up from the message and saw Jeremy Bellingford and Mr Ahmed had joined them.

'How would you like to be introduced, Ali?' Lewis said.

'I think we can drop the charade now,' Ahmed said and Lewis turned to Meredith and Sandy.

'Gentlemen.'

At that word they both came to attention and Charlie Mars saw a curious impassive look come to their faces. It was the eternal expression of the soldier called to duty.

'I have the honour to present His Royal Highness, General Prince Ali ben Nazzan, Colonel-in-Chief of the Loyal Legion of Quatara. Sir, Captain Meredith and Sergeant Patch.'

Prince Ali held out his hand and Gordon shook it as he gave a curt nod of the head. Sandy did likewise.

'Gentlemen, I am delighted to make your acquaintance.'

'Can I express my deepest condolences with regard to the death of Prince Rashid,' Lewis said formally. Prince Nazzan answered in the same tone:

'Thank you, Captain. He will be remembered.' Charlie Mars handed the newsflash to Bellingford who then passed it to Prince Nazzan.

'What do you intend to do?' Bellingford said.

Charlie thrust one hand deep into his cardigan pocket and scratched his jaw with a long, bony finger.

'I don't want to get our hopes too high but this might get us somewhere. As you know, in recent months all our attempts to influence events in Quatara have come to nothing because the Revolutionary Government have known exactly what we were up to and have been able to kill our agents or block any diplomatic efforts by calling on the Soviets to intervene. It is obvious that we have a high-level mole working for the Russians, someone who has access to every decision Her Majesty's Government makes about Quatara.'

'Why do you say the agent is working for the Russians?' Prince Nazzan asked. 'Couldn't he just be someone sympathetic to the rebels in Quatara?'

Bellingford shot Charlie Mars a warning glance but it was unnecessary. Charlie was quite capable of the correct diplomatic reply.

'No, sir. The scale of the operation and scope of planning suggests this is being orchestrated by Moscow Centre. It is a highly sophisticated piece of work. Only the Russians are capable of this degree of expertise.'

Prince Nazzan smiled grimly.

'What you are saying, Mr Mars, is that if it were some Whitehall Arabist who likes our Marxist rebels he would have been caught immediately.' Charlie nodded and returned the smile.

'Exactly, your Highness.'

Prince Nazzan nodded. 'Thank you. Forgive my interruption. Please continue.'

Charlie paused for a moment to regain the thread of his narrative, then continued slowly.

'If the Soviets have been running the show it is pretty

100

certain they have been doing it through the Revolutionary Diplomatic Mission. Our theory is that the mole deals with the Russians who process the information and then give instructions to the revolutionaries via the London Embassy.'

'So how do you intend to exploit the current situation?' Bellingford asked.

Charlie looked at him in surprise. It was clear that he thought the plan was obvious. Carefully, as one would speak to a difficult child, Charlie explained: 'We intend to storm the Embassy to release the captive diplomats and under cover of the siege examine the contents of the safe to see if there are any clues to the identity of the mole.'

There was a pause as Jeremy Bellingford absorbed the information. In the ensuing silence, Lewis watched as Prince Nazzan looked around at the chaotic scruffiness of Charlie's office. He wondered what was going through Ali's mind until he remembered that he too was an old Etonian. Perhaps they all keep rooms like this, Lewis thought, and he imagined a similar disorder in a Bedouin tent. As he began to elaborate this fantasy with dancing girls, Penny Rose entered the room.

Charlie took the piece of paper she carried and cursed involuntarily as he read the message. 'Dear God.'

The others looked at him anxiously.

'This is a further Press Association report. It appears the terrorists have already shot one of the Embassy staff and dumped the body outside. They've also snatched a party of schoolchildren who were outside in New Cavendish Street and taken them into the Embassy.'

'I think it's time we moved,' Lewis said.

*

Jeremy Bellingford insisted that he go by car to New Cavendish Street. For reasons of protocol Charlie Mars and Prince Nazzan accompanied him, but Lewis, Gordon and Sandy decided to take a faster route and walk. Already the siege had spread its effects through the streets of London and a massive traffic jam had snarled the surface of the city to a nerve-jangling crawl.

At every junction the police redirected those motorists who wished to pass through the affected streets. At the same time crowds of sightseers were drawn, like iron filings, to the magnet of the besieged building. It was a plain, white, stone-clad building of four floors. A large black front door with a Georgian-style fan light above it. Two large windows flanked the doorway and were repeated on the floors above. Smaller windows rose above the doorway.

The three pedestrians from Gower Street passed through the fringe of the crowd at the police barriers to where the anti-terrorist squad had set up their mobile headquarters in Great Titchfield Street. Lewis saw the heavy figure of Commander Brian Lear talking to a youthful-looking man by the door of one of the caravans.

As he got closer, Lewis could see that the man with Lear was older than he had first thought.

'Hello, Lew,' Commander Lear said.

'How are you, Brian?' Lewis asked as he joined them.

'Let me introduce Paul Renfrew of the Foreign Office. He's come along to give us any advice we may need about our Arab friends. Paul Renfrew, Lewis Horne from Charlie Mars's group at Gower Street.'

The two shook hands and Renfrew said with a self-deprecating smile: 'I'm sure Captain Horne doesn't need my advice about Arabs.'

Lewis looked at him keenly. 'You have the advantage, Mr Renfrew.'

The pale man smiled again. 'I'm sorry. I'm with Jeremy Bellingford's section. We've been co-ordinating this business. For the Cabinet.'

'I didn't realise Jeremy had so many demanding duties,' Lewis said carefully.

Renfrew laughed and his features took on an engaging expression. Lines crinkled around his eyes and mouth. He had one of those clear pinkish complexions and well-cut, prematurely white hair that somehow made him seem quite young.

'We let Jeremy carry the papers, that's all.' Renfrew looked over Lewis's shoulder. 'But here he comes now, and in very exalted company.'

Lewis looked around and saw Bellingford usher-
ing Prince Nazzan from his car. Charlie Mars was
first to reach the group. He shook hands warmly with
Renfrew.

'Paul. Good to see you, even here.'

'How are Sybil and the girls?' Renfrew asked.

'All well,' Charlie said.

Lewis noted that crisis was not allowed to interfere
with the ritual greetings of the mandarins who ran the
country.

'Shall we go inside?' Commander Lear said as Jeremy
and Prince Nazzan arrived. They all crowded into the
caravan that was rigged as a communications centre.
Rows of television monitoring screens lined one wall and
a group of shirt-sleeved technicians wearing earphones
fiddled with recording equipment. 'This way,' Commander
Lear said and he took them to the far end of the trailer
where a large-scale map of the area was laid out beneath
a layer of Perspex on a table. The blueprints of the house
were pinned to a cork-lined board, and Lewis noticed that
Charlie Mars had brought his own rolled-up copies of the
same blueprints with him.

'This is the situation,' Commander Lear said. 'We have
marksmen here, here, here and here.' He pointed to
crosses on the map marked in wax crayon on the Perspex.
'We have spotters with radios and binoculars in these
surrounding streets. The back of the Embassy can be
covered by just one of their men. We've plugged in listening posts to the buildings each side and within the hour
we'll have a couple connected through the sewers. They've
got radios turned up loudly, so they clearly have no idea
how sophisticated our equipment is.'

'Where do you think they're holding the hostages?'
Bellingford asked.

It was surprising that he had kept quiet for so long,
and there was something else about him which Lewis
thought odd, though it took a moment before he realised
what it was. Bellingford always wore a dark blue overcoat
when he was in town but now he had on a military-style
anorak despite the comparative warmth of the day. It was
clear that if there were any Press photographers about,

the junior Minister would present the correct image of command.

Lear shrugged as he loosened the top button of his shirt. Taking time to answer, he removed his jacket and hung it carefully over the back of a chair. He took a ballpoint pen from the inside pocket of the jacket and pointed to the front elevation of the Embassy.

'There are only three logical places to hold hostages in there. The two main reception rooms on the ground floor and the Ambassador's old office which is now used by the Comrade Secretary. The room to the left on the ground floor is used for receptions and only has a minimum amount of furniture. That would seem to be a better bet than the other ground floor room which is packed with office equipment and wouldn't give you a clear field of fire to a couple of people guarding a lot of captives. The same applies to the Ambassador's room.'

Charlie Mars looked at the plan for a few moments.

'What are communications with them like?'

Lear lit a small cigar and exhaled streams of blue smoke through his nose.

'The telephone is still connected but at the moment they're only speaking to the Press Association. They've refused to take any calls from us. They've asked for the release of thirty prisoners in Quatara and they've given until midnight tonight before they begin to bump other people off. The first was just to show they mean business. So far they haven't said what they want in exchange for the schoolchildren.'

'Do we know who they are?' Lewis asked.

'Yes,' Lear answered. 'We found out a few minutes ago. They're from The Christ The Saviour Foundation School, six of them and a teacher. The boys are eleven. They wear those seventeenth-century uniforms, long green coats, white stockings and buckled shoes.'

'That must add a nice touch of surrealism to the scene inside,' Charlie Mars said with no hint of humour in his voice. He turned to Paul Renfrew. 'What's your opinion of the situation, Paul?'

Renfrew glanced to Bellingford who inclined his head

in assent and Renfrew put his hands in his jacket pockets and raised his shoulders before speaking.

'Captain Horne knows as much as I do about the attitudes our friends have. The men with the guns in there . . .' he gestured in the direction of the Embassy, 'are religious fanatics. They believe, with total conviction, that they act in the name of Allah and will be rewarded at death with an instant place in Paradise. I don't think the Revolutionary Government in Quatara will accede to their demands, therefore death for the captives would appear inevitable. My advice would be to storm the building immediately. Most sieges go on for some time before there is any activity. The only advantage we have over them is a surprise move now.'

Charlie looked at Lewis who nodded. He was surprised and a little impressed by Renfrew's remarks. It was the first time he had ever heard a civil servant speak without qualifying his remarks with a general caveat.

'Everything Mr Renfrew says is true. My opinion is the same.'

Charlie drummed his fingers on the Perspex top of the table.

'How many of the diplomatic staff are in there, Brian?'

Commander Lear consulted a list pinned to the wall.

'Fifteen; all of them men,' he said after a moment. Charlie looked around the crowded caravan as if he were suddenly aware of his surroundings.

'Where are our quarters?' he said.

'The next trailer along,' Lear replied. 'The SAS anti-terrorist group have their own arrangements next to you.'

Just then one of the switchboard operators called out: 'Call for Mr Bellingford.'

'Who is it?' Bellingford bellowed. The operator asked the question and a moment later said: 'The Cabinet Office, sir.'

'Right,' Bellingford said, trying to sound as casual as possible. He took the phone, listened for a short while and hung up.

'I have to go and give the Prime Minister a personal briefing on the situation,' he said. Then he turned to Renfrew. 'You must come too, Paul.'

Renfrew shrugged at Charlie Mars and they all started to leave the trailer together.

'Strange, isn't it?' Commander Lear said to Bellingford as they stood in the street once more.

'What is?' he replied.

'The quiet. Like a Sunday morning.'

Lewis looked to where a policeman in a flak jacket moved warily across the roof of the building that rose above him. His group stood for a moment on the pavement and said their goodbyes to Bellingford and Renfrew before letting themselves into their own trailer. Inside, George Ward was setting up a radio receiver. There was a certain amount of bobbing about as Prince Nazzan was re-introduced until he asked that they forget protocol.

They sat on benches that ran along the length of the caravan. George Ward had a seat at a table with the receiver before him. Charlie spread his copy of the blue-print of the house and then he took a metal container about the size of a soda syphon out of a cupboard above their heads.

'Captain Meredith, do you know Beethoven's 5th Symphony?' he said.

'Vaguely, sir,' Gordon said.

'Could you manage the first three bars on this?'

'What is it?' Gordon asked as he took the cylinder from Charlie.

'It's an aerosol fog horn,' Charlie said with a smile. 'You can get them at any ship's chandlers. I want you to go to the corner of the street and blow a V for Victory sign at our religious friends.'

'If you say so, sir,' Gordon said in the tone of voice Lewis imagined the soldiers who took part in the Charge of the Light Brigade used to speak to Lord Cardigan.

He left the caravan and the rest watched him approach the end of the street through an observation panel. When he reached his position he waved cheerily and blew three short blasts and one slightly longer one. It sounded very loud in the comparative quiet. Then he turned around and began to walk back to them. As he did so they saw several agitated figures in plain clothes and police uniforms run up to him.

Gordon pointed to the caravan they were in and walked manfully on. He re-entered, and without saying anything handed the cylinder back to Charlie. At that moment, there was a banging on the front door. Charlie opened it and a police sergeant stood to attention and said in a voice heavy with sarcasm: 'Commander Lear's compliments, sir. He says what the bleeding hell was that in aid of?'

'Tell him it's a new form of psychological warfare I promised to try out.'

Apparently satisfied with the reply, the sergeant smiled and Charlie banged the door closed. Almost immediately a Morse signal started on George Ward's radio equipment. Lewis, Sandy and Gordon could all send and receive up to a certain speed. This was far in excess of that. Ward began to write rapidly on a large pad of paper. He tore off the first sheet and handed it to Charlie Mars without turning round.

Charlie put it down on a ledge so they could all see the message. It read:

Foxtrot to Tango – Foxtrot to Tango. Am in first floor room, thirty foot square. Teacher, children, me held here. No others, two guards. One doorway, description from door . . .

The receiver kept chattering and George Ward passed sheet after sheet of paper so that a picture of the scene in the room gradually built up for them. Finally, the flow of information came to a stop and Charlie made a rough sketch of the interior of the room they had identified as the Ambassador's old office. As far as they could gather the lay-out was unchanged from the time Prince Nazzan remembered it.

'Is there any chance it could have been someone else sending the message?' Prince Nazzan asked. George Ward shook his head.

'No, sir. That's Colin Miller. Signallers leave their style on the key with as much individuality as fingerprints. That's Miller for certain; I'd know his touch anywhere.'

'What do you think?' Charlie asked Lewis who stood looking at the blueprint of the Embassy. Lewis shrugged.

'There's nothing subtle we can do . . . we'll just have to hit them quick and hard and hope they concentrate on us and not on shooting their prisoners.'

George Ward had an extra large flask of instant coffee with him. He passed out mugs and Lewis and Charlie stood at the far end of the trailer, apart from the others. Charlie took a sip of his coffee and massaged his right temple with his forefinger. Lewis could see the strain across his eyes where the furrows cut deeper than usual.

'Are you worrying about the kids?' Lewis asked in a soft voice. Charlie looked down into the coffee and was silent for a little while.

'If we'd picked them up this wouldn't have happened. I decided we would go ahead with this . . .' – he gestured around the trailer – 'escapade. If those children are hurt, I will be responsible.'

'You didn't plan it that way, Charlie,' Lewis said in a flat voice.

'I don't see how that changes things,' Charlie said quietly. Lewis leaned against the wall while his boss continued. 'It's all part of the same war. Think of some poor, bloody general ordering an entire army into combat. He knows the kind of casualties they will take and most of them will be boys; they always are.'

He looked around the trailer and slapped the wall with the flat of his hand. 'Funny, they often sleep in a caravan like this before the battle. They always say in their memoirs what time they went to bed before the attack. Nobody says what time they got to sleep.'

Lewis put down his mug decisively and called to Sandy and Gordon.

'Right. Let's go and see the others. Gordon, bring the blueprint and the message from Colin.'

They left the trailer and Charlie Mars rejoined Prince Nazzan who was watching the street through the window. It was calm but they could all sense the tension. By now people had been posted to positions so there was little movement; just a feeling of expectancy.

'Lewis has gone to brief his team, Your Highness,' Charlie said and Prince Nazzan turned to him.

'I think it would be better if you called me Ali in less

108

formal moments. After all, Captain Horne does and you are his commanding officer, aren't you?'

Charlie reflected for a moment. 'I suppose I am,' he said then turned to Prince Nazzan. 'Do you know a poem called "The General"?' Nazzan continued to gaze out of the window, then he began to recite:

'Good morning, good morning!' the General said
When we met him last week on our way to the Line.
Now the soldiers he smiled at are most of 'em dead,
And we're cursing his staff for incompetent swine.
'He's a cheery old card,' grunted Harry to Jack
As they slogged up to Arras with a rifle and pack.

But he did for them both with his plan of attack.

*

Gordon Meredith slowly raised the skylight hatch and lifted himself on to the flat tarred area of the roof. One by one, Lewis, Sandy and the seven other members of their group surrounded him. They were all dressed the same, in blue-black coveralls, rubber-soled combat boots and with their heads covered in black ski masks. They carried a variety of equipment; Koch and Hechler sub-machine guns slung across their chests, Browning automatics in the holsters on their hips and webbing holding extra ammunition magazines and grenades. In addition, some carried coils of rope, harnesses and a variety of clamps and curiously-shaped pieces of metal equipment.

Lewis looked around the group. 'Everyone OK?' he asked in a low voice. When he was satisfied they were ready, he began to work his way across the roofs of the buildings towards the Embassy. The rest followed, crouched in single file. When they were on the correct rooftop Lewis looked around. There were low stone parapets at the front and back of the macadam-covered flat roof. Two low skylights were raised from the surface, one of them supporting a complex collection of radio aerials.

Lewis took the walkie-talkie radio that Sandy carried and switched it on.

'Charlie? Lewis here. We're in position.'

Charlie was in the communications trailer. He looked at the monitor screens that displayed the front of the Embassy.

'The listeners say nothing has changed and Colin Miller sent a similar message a few minutes ago,' Charlie said.

'OK,' Lewis replied. 'I'll call when we're ready to go.' He laid down the radio and watched as the dark figures set about securing clamps and running lines of cable between the two stone parapets. Eventually, they were finished. Meredith walked around and checked the tension of the cables, and everyone fitted themselves into the harnesses. Lewis took up the radio again.

'Charlie, we're ready to go.'

'OK,' Charlie replied. 'Still no change.'

All ten members of the assault team took the heavy metal clips that were attached by nylon ropes to their harnesses and snapped them to the steel cable that was held taut by the web of equipment stretched across the roof. Lewis made a hand signal and the men stepped onto the parapet at the front of the building and pulled goggles over their eyes.

Lewis placed a whistle between his teeth and very carefully took a grenade into his left hand. He pulled the pin and held down the lever.

For a split second he glanced up into a blue sky mixed with white fluffy clouds, then blew on the whistle and thrust off from the edge of the parapet. After a fifteen foot descent his feet came into contact with the white stone on the front of the building and he was aware of Sandy and Gordon close beside him. As they thrust away again he heard another blast of a whistle when the next group began their jump.

The one and a half seconds seemed interminable as the three of them swung back on the end of their lines, then simultaneously smashed through the tall Georgian windows of the Ambassador's office.

Once inside the three slapped the release buttons on their harnesses and Lewis threw the percussion grenade. Designed to stun and disorientate rather than destroy with fragments of shrapnel, the effect in the office was

110

devastating, despite the gaping hole already created by their arrival.

Lewis, on the right position, landed on his feet and instantly drew the Browning automatic from his holster. Meredith, to his immediate left, landed on top of the huge desk in front of the window. His body skidded across the surface scattering telephones, inkwell and paperwork to mix with the coating of broken glass that already lay across the room.

Sandy Patch had landed to the left of the desk and collided with an easy chair. At that moment they could hear the sound of other grenades exploding. As they had smashed through the window, each of them had concentrated on the left of the room where Colin Miller's messages had informed them they could expect to see two of the terrorists armed with sub-machine guns.

Lewis had his Browning levelled as he heard the sound of Sandy's Koch and Hechler firing. The terrorist in the corner who held a squat, little machine gun was thrown backwards on the highbacked chair so that his legs sprawled in a grotesque and graceless attitude. Next to him stood another empty chair where the other gunman should have been.

Lewis's eyes swept the room and took in the group of strangely-clad schoolboys who huddled together in various positions of defence. In the centre of the group, her back flattened against the wall, sat a youngish woman with short, brown hair, her blue angora sweater contrasting nicely with the Wedgwood colour of the office walls. Her eyes stared in shock.

The mahogany door of the office was swinging open and they could see the other man behind a wall of schoolboys. Colin Miller sprang to his feet from where he had been crouching and caught the Arab as he started to level the sub-machine gun.

With his right hand Miller pulled the gun towards him as he hit the Arab on the side of the head with the cupped palm of his hand. The sub-machine gun fired a short burst and the two stumbled away from each other. The Arab released the gun and scrabbled for the automatic pistol that was tucked in the waistband of his trousers as Sandy

111

fired. The man slumped against the door jamb and the pistol clattered from his hand as he fell sideways, half in and half out of the room.

Colin Miller folded his arms across his stomach and sank to his knees. Meredith got to him and he toppled sideways into his arms.

'He was going for a piss,' he said and he coughed and convulsed with the pain.

From somewhere else in the building the sound of gunfire came to them. Lewis crossed the room and hauled the Arab away from the door into the corridor outside and slammed the door shut. The boys seemed to have recovered quickly from their ordeal. They crowded around Lewis chattering with excitement. The young woman had got to her feet and looked around. She put out a restraining arm to one of the boys who was reaching for the Arab's handgun that lay next to the wainscoting.

'We told you, Miss Chambers, didn't we? . . . we said the SAS would come . . . you are the SAS, aren't you, sir? . . . course he is, look at his uniform . . . we said they would, Miss Chambers.'

Lewis pulled off his hood and goggles.

'Miss Chambers, could you get the boys to build a barrier behind the desk?' Lewis said. The woman gazed at him with a puzzled expression and Lewis gestured to the safe that they stood near. 'We may have to blow open the safe.'

She looked around blankly for a few moments, then the sound of two more shots in the distance seemed to bring her back to the present.

'Boys,' she said firmly. 'Turn the desk on its side.' The green-coated figures set about the work with gusto. Most of the time they were ordered to keep the world tidy. Now authority was encouraging them in disorder.

Lewis crossed the room to where Gordon had laid Colin Miller and knelt beside him.

'He's had it, Lew,' Gordon said softly. Lewis reached for Miller's jacket which was draped over the back of a chair and quickly covered his face. He said to Gordon 'Look after the kids.'

Sandy was at the safe against the wall methodically

working his way through the list of combinations he had been given. Lewis took up a position by the door.

'How's it going?' he called out to Sandy.

'Last one, boss,' he replied; then 'No go – I'll have to blow her.' Sandy unslung a small backpack and rapidly attached blobs of plastic explosive. He plugged in wires and took cover behind the desk. 'OK,' he called and Lewis joined them.

Sandy turned a handle to generate the current and the room shook again with the sound of the explosion. While the air was still full of dust, they moved forward.

'I'll check out the rest of the house. You two get to work,' Lewis said curtly. He stepped into the corridor outside the office and threw himself flat as automatic gunfire ploughed into the wall above him and stitched a line of holes in the wood panelling. He rolled back into the room, kicked the door shut and took Gordon's radio.

'Section Leader calling Stanhope.'

'Stanhope here, Section Leader.'

'What's going on?' Lewis asked.

'We got them all except for two positioned at the very top of the stairs above you.'

'OK,' Lewis said. 'Meredith and I will try to get down to them from the roof.'

'Understood,' Stanhope said.

Lewis looked around the room once again. Sandy knelt at the open safe methodically photographing the contents with a small, motor-driven camera he had carried in the same pack he had used for the explosives. Lewis crouched beside him.

'How long will you be?' Sandy shrugged as he sorted through the documents.

'Could be ten minutes.'

'Gordon and I are going to be busy for a while; two of them are still lodged at the top of the building. We're going to dig them out.'

'Right,' Sandy said in a preoccupied voice as he went on photographing the contents of the safe. Lewis slung his sub-machine gun across his chest and clipped the radio to his harness.

113

'Miss Chambers, please keep the boys away from Sergeant Patch and over here away from the door.'

She nodded and he noticed how composed she now looked but for the laddered shreds of her stockings. The boys gazed up at him with admiration.

'I want you all to do exactly what Miss Chambers says. Do you understand?' he said in a stern voice.

'Yes, sir,' they all chorused.

'Right, and stay here until we come back for you.'

With the last order given, Lewis pulled on his hood again and he and Gordon took the ropes that still dangled from the parapet and began to haul themselves back onto the roof. They made their way to the first skylight and tried to open it, but it resisted their joint efforts. The second one began to give but it made a tearing sound. Lewis got on the radio.

'Stanhope, make some noise five seconds from now.'

He and Meredith seized the edge of the skylight and on the count of five started to haul just as the crack of a percussion grenade sounded within the house. The skylight gave way with a ripping noise as the wood frame cracked and splintered. As they opened it wide, a bell started to clang.

'I think we've set off the burglar alarm,' Meredith said with amazement in his voice. They made their way down a narrow, wooden staircase into an attic room filled with trunks and packing cases. A door led out to a dark corridor. Their rubber-soled boots made a soft squeaking on the bare boards. Light flooded up the stairwell they could see before them.

When Lewis and Meredith reached the balcony, they crept forward until they could look down over the handrail. A window lighted their landing and the one below where they could see the two gunmen who commanded the stairwell. They wore pink and blue shirts and seemed to be relaxed as they looked down. The soft diffused light made the scene seem strangely peaceful despite the clanging that still emanated from the Embassy's alarm.

Lewis took another percussion grenade from his webbing and showed it to Meredith. Because the Arabs had been firing their guns in a confined space, Lewis knew

114

that the noise would have partially deafened them so they would be unlikely to hear anything as they edged towards them. When they were within a few feet of the men, Lewis threw the grenade over their heads so that the two Arabs started and turned to face the thump just before the grenade exploded in their faces.

Lewis and Gordon had crouched down to cover their ears. As the roar subsided they rose and clubbed the two stunned men who reeled before them. Gordon threw their weapons down the stairs away from the prone bodies and Lewis called the all clear. Slowly, they walked back to the Ambassador's office. The body of the Arab still lay outside. They stepped over him and banged on the door.

'OK Sandy, it's Gordon and me,' Lewis shouted and they entered the room again.

Sandy was still on his knees, but they could see the work was nearly done. Lewis called all the boys to the side of the room and had them line up in front of him. They stood to attention and waited for him to speak.

'You have all witnessed a secret operation,' he said, acutely aware of how pompous he must look and sound. He could see Meredith watching him as he ploughed on. 'I must ask you to keep everything you have seen here today completely to yourselves. Do I have your word that I can rely on you all never to speak of what you saw us do to another living person?'

'Yes, sir,' they all said in hushed voices.

'Good. Now I shall ask Miss Chambers to lead you all downstairs. Congratulations, you've all done well.'

Miss Chambers looked at him for a moment and Lewis wasn't sure what emotions she felt. Finally, she said: 'Thank you. I think those men would have killed us.'

Lewis nodded. He felt slightly embarrassed by her obvious gratitude.

'There's a man downstairs called Mr Mars. Will you please speak only to him?'

'Yes, if you say so. Come along, boys.'

As she was about to leave, Lewis called her back.

She turned and he said: 'Miss Chambers. Where were you going when you were captured?'

She smiled and took a moment to remember. 'Oh, to

the BBC to take part in a schools quiz programme on the radio. It was to be a treat for them.'

As soon as they left, Lewis picked up the walkie talkie and called Charlie Mars.

'Yes, everything all right?' he asked with a slight note of anxiety in his voice.

'There's a Miss Chambers and some boys on the way down. We'd better keep them in our custody for a while, otherwise the wrong people might get something out of them.'

'Right,' Charlie said. 'Can you get down here, we've got another problem.'

'Coming now.'

Lewis snapped off the radio and looked around at the room: it had taken years to weave the carpets and make the beautiful furniture that now lay smashed and blood-soaked after a few minutes of battle.

Lewis had a few moments conversation with Gordon and Sandy and then checked he had all his equipment with him before walking slowly down the staircase.

'Any wounded up there?' an ambulanceman asked and he shook his head. He could see into the room where the Embassy staff had been held. Five bodies were laid out. Sergeant Stanhope stood in the doorway smoking a cigarette, looking down at them.

'What's the damage, Bill?' Lewis said and the sergeant glanced up at him.

'Three wounded, two light, one nasty but not fatal . . . I heard Colin bought it.'

Lewis nodded. 'Yes.'

'You knew him pretty well, didn't you?'

'And his wife.' He passed on and down to the entrance and out on the pavement where a small Arab in a short-sleeved white shirt was shouting at Charlie Mars in Arabic. Charlie was playing the role of the silly ass and doing it rather well.

'Now here is the officer in charge of the operation. I'm sure he will verify everything I have told you, won't you, Captain?'

'What's that, sir?' Lewis said ponderously.

'This gentleman is the Comrade Secretary of the Quata-

116

ran Revolutionary Diplomatic Mission. I have got that right, have I not, sir?'

'Yes,' hissed the Arab in cold fury.

'Now, he wants to go to his office to check everything is in order and I've just been explaining to him that there could be explosives in the building and we are checking to make sure it's safe.'

'I demand to be allowed access. That is Quataran territory and you cannot keep me out. It is against all international laws.'

While the Comrade Secretary was still screeching, Lewis called Meredith on his walkie-talkie.

'Captain Horne here. Can you tell me if the building is secure, and, in your opinion, safe for inspection by the Comrade Secretary?' He turned and gave the little man a reassuring smile.

Gordon's voice crackled over the radio.

'Good,' Lewis said. 'You can go up now, sir.'

The tiny man stalked into the building and Lewis and Charlie followed. They had to move to keep up with him as he fairly raced up the stairs to his office. They were right behind him as he stood before the doorway. The body of the Arab had been moved. He thrust open the door and entered.

At first it was hard for Charlie to make out what had happened, so thoroughly had the room been devastated. But moments later it seemed to swim into focus and he could see the bodies of two Arabs by the blown safe.

One lay face down clutching a bundle of papers to his chest. They were stuck together in congealed blood. The other still held a sub-machine gun in his hand. On the other side of the room, wearing SAS combat clothes, lay the body of Captain Colin Miller. To the observer it appeared that he had shot the two Arabs as they were in the process of rifling the safe and had been killed himself in the exchange of fire.

Charlie walked over to Miller's body and looked down at him, then he turned to the Comrade Secretary who was also studying the scene.

'It would seem you owe this officer a great deal, sir,' he

said and he walked from the room as the Arab went down on his knees and began to peel the bloodsoaked papers from his countryman's body.

Far I hear the bugle blow
To call me where I would not go,
And the guns begin the song,
'Soldier, fly or stay for long.'

A Shropshire Lad
A. E. HOUSMAN

Chapter Six

Lewis looked in the mirror to check the knot in his tie and in doing so noticed that the collar of his shirt had started to fray slightly. He reached into the locker and examined the jacket of his grey flannel suit.

'Damn,' he muttered, as he detected the telltale signs of wear at the elbows and the pockets. The act of buying clothes bored him and he knew that a shopping expedition was now inevitable. He shut the locker door and heaved the dark blue canvas bag containing his uniform and weapons onto the bench seat.

'Take care of my kit, will you George?' he said to Ward who was still fiddling with radio equipment.

'Sure. Where do you want it?'

'In my room at Gower Street,' Lewis said as he made a final check that nothing had been left behind. Satisfied, he opened the door of the trailer and found Charlie Mars waiting for him in the roadway.

'Sandy Patch has taken the film to be processed. It'll be a couple of hours before we can look at anything,' Charlie said.

Lewis watched the crowd that was now surging along Great Titchfield Street. The noise had returned as the danger departed.

'What's going on?' he asked.

Charlie looked towards New Cavendish Street.

'Oh, Bellingford is back from Number 10. I gather he's giving television interviews and posing for Press photographs. Meredith had a look a moment ago and said he was denying he had played any part in the proceedings whilst somehow giving the impression he actually led the attack.' Lewis laughed.

'I thought that anorak of his wouldn't be wasted.'

'What are you going to do now?' Charlie asked.

'I'll go and see how Tony Cole is getting on.'

'He's at the Middlesex. The doctor told me he was hit

121

in the legs. They took Colin Miller's body there as well.'

Lewis looked towards the crowd again. 'Where's Ali?'

'I got Meredith to take him away before he was spotted by the Press.' Lewis nodded.

'I'll see you later at Gower Street,' he said and he set off away from the crowd towards the Middlesex Hospital.

When he got to the junction with Mortimer Street Lewis suddenly felt ravenously hungry as he realised that the last food he had eaten were the few spoonfuls of caviare in Sam's American Bar the night before.

He looked around for a few minutes and found a small café that seemed to fit into a crack between two large buildings, pushed open a door with a tinkling bell and stood at the counter next to a display case of sandwiches and rolls. The man in a well-cut blue suit who had been following him since Lewis had left Charlie Mars now hesitated on the other side of the road.

'Yes, luv, can I 'elp you?' a tiny, young woman with an olive complexion asked Lewis. He looked at her black hair and huge liquid brown eyes as she smiled up at him.

'Er, cup of tea and two cheese rolls, please,' he said casually, and instantly regretted his choice. She passed the cup of tea and he said 'Do you think you could make those rolls bacon?'

'Of course, luv.' Then he shook his head.

'No, one bacon and one cheese.'

'Blimey, luv,' the girl said in a distinctive accent that was a mixture of Cypriot and Cockney. 'It's a good job you're not in the SAS.'

'What did you say?' Lewis asked with surprise.

'The SAS, luv. They rescued them kids. It was just on the radio. If they 'ung about like you, them bleedin' Arabs would 'ave killed 'em all.'

'I see what you mean,' Lewis said as she passed him the rolls.

'One pound five pee, luv,' she said. Lewis paid and sat at a table by the window. Through a clear patch in the condensation he saw the dapper figure of Max Ernhart raise a hand in greeting as he entered the café.

He smiled at Lewis as he stood at the counter and waited for the girl to serve him.

'Yes, luv,' she said again and Ernhart spoke to her in fluent Greek. She beamed with pleasure and chattered for a few moments while she got him a coffee. He carried the cup to where Lewis sat and took the chair next to him.

'You seem to speak the language well,' Lewis said while Ernhart followed his gaze to the girl behind the counter.

'I spent a little time there during the war,' he said as he took a sip of his coffee and grimaced.

'Wehrmacht?' Lewis asked. Ernhart nodded.

'Paratrooper. Yes, lad, I were as slim as you in those days. And the girls. My God, if you were the airborne – *they* used to jump on *us*.'

'How did you find me?' Lewis said.

'Mr Bellingford is an acquaintance of mine. We're both on the same North-Eastern Development Committee.'

'Does he know you as Denis Slingsby or Max Ernhart?'

'Oh, I don't think he minds either. After all, we're all in favour of the Common Market these days.'

Lewis spoke through a mouthful of bacon roll: 'And there was me thinking you were a simple Yorkshireman.'

Ernhart grinned. 'Nationality's a funny thing. Take you, family in the same regiment, generation after generation. English to the core, most people would say. But your mother was Welsh. So who's to know you're not a secret nationalist, setting fire to English road signs on your weekends off?'

'I'm impressed by your research,' Lewis said. 'Now tell me what do you want?'

Ernhart reached inside the double-breasted jacket and took an aluminium tube containing a Havana cigar out of his inside pocket. He tapped twice on the Formica-topped table and looked at Lewis for a few moments.

'I'd like you to work for me.'

Lewis bit off another mouthful of roll and waited for him to continue.

'I'm knocking on a bit now,' he said 'and I've no son to follow me in the business. Oh, I could retire. I've made a pile, but I don't want to just sell up and see strangers take over a lifetime's work. You come in now and learn the business and in a couple of years I'll make you Chief Executive and pack it in.'

Lewis finished his roll and swallowed some tea.

'What kind of salary?' he said.

Ernhart unscrewed the cap and extracted the cigar from the tube before he spoke. 'Forty-five thousand a year to start with, plus a car and membership of BUPA, half a per cent of any business you close for me, two per cent of anything you bring in yourself. And all reasonable expenses incurred on behalf of the company.'

Lewis finished his roll and pushed the plate away.

'Thanks, I'll think it over. Where can I contact you?'

Ernhart produced a slim leather wallet and handed Lewis a card. All it had on it was his name and a telephone number.

'They'll take a message for me any time, day and night.' He took the large knife from his pocket, the same one he had used to cut up his lunch on the bank of the Seine, and sliced the end from his cigar.

'Why me, Max?' Lewis asked and Ernhart sat back in his chair and inhaled smoke appreciatively. Then he looked hard at Lewis.

'You can make me a fortune.'

'How do you know?'

Ernhart waved a cloud of cigar smoke away. 'That's what I'm good at. Knowing these things. Don't worry, I'll see you're all right – I'll have to, you couldn't make a penny for yourself. Think it over and give me a ring.' He got up and left Lewis at the table after shouting his farewell in Greek to the girl behind the counter.

*

As he walked towards the main forecourt of the Middlesex Hospital, Lewis thought how quickly circumstances altered. His father had been commissioned in time for the invasion of Europe in 1944 where he had taken part in savage fighting. His grandfather had been wounded twice in the trenches during the Great War. Now he had been offered a job by Max Ernhart, a charming man whom they would consider their mortal enemy. Then he put the thought – and its implicit irony – out of his mind as he approached the reception desk.

He waited for a few minutes before being directed to a

long corridor that was packed with people who moved like river traffic; some flowing gently with the current and others fighting against the stream. White-coated figures walked swiftly between people in dressing-gowns or street clothes.

Lewis looked above their heads for the directions to Tony Cole's ward. Finally, he found what he was looking for. He entered the large doorway, passed the staff nurses' office and saw two small glass-panelled rooms. One was empty, the other was screened off Lewis could not see the occupant, but he guessed it was Cole.

Standing over the figure was Hanna. She turned as he looked through the window, saw Lewis and came out to him.

They stood opposite each other in awkward silence for a few moments.

'You're looking better than the last time I saw you,' Hanna said.

'I was working then, Hanna.'

She nodded. 'Yes, I've just been examining one of your workmates.'

'How is he?'

'Fine.' Hanna spoke in her professional voice. 'Of course, the human body wasn't designed to be shot with high velocity bullets but, all things considered, Captain Cole is doing well. He's still under sedation.'

Hanna continued: 'It's funny how you're all captains in your outfit. My brother was in the Marine Corps and they used to have lots of ranks; lieutenants, majors, colonels. I heard they brought two captains in the Special Air Service in, one wounded, one dead.' Hanna opened the door to the empty room. 'Let's go in here.'

Lewis followed her in and watched as she folded her arms and looked up at the ceiling for a moment.

'I'm sorry, Lewis. I know you and Colin Miller were friends.' Lewis shrugged.

'He knew it could happen. We all do. You're right, we make lousy partners.'

There was a small washbasin in the corner of the room. Hanna leaned against it.

'It's not fair. If there was a war on, I could accept it.

125

Everyone would be in the same boat, but this is peace time.' Lewis shook his head.

'No, it's not. It just seems so to civilians.'

Hanna looked down at her shoes and Lewis had to ask her the question: 'Who were you with in Paris?'

She looked up at him. 'My cousin Adam. My family want him to marry me,' she said.

As he was about to reply, he saw Hanna look over his shoulder to do something that had gained her attention outside. Lewis turned to follow her gaze and saw Judy Miller. She recognised Lewis and Hanna and smiled in an anxious fashion as Lewis opened the door.

'Lew,' she said. 'I got a message that Colin had been wounded . . .' The words faded away as she looked into his face. He was about to speak but she held up a hand.

'He's dead, isn't he?' she said in a flat voice.

For a moment, Lewis looked around at the bustle of the crowded ward. There seemed to be so much vitality there.

'Yes, Judy,' he said finally.

Hanna put an arm around her and guided her to a chair.

'I'm all right,' she said almost lightly. 'I'm all right.' She looked up at Lewis. 'When did it happen?'

'This afternoon. It was very quick.'

She closed her eyes for a moment and the door to the room opened and a staff nurse stood in the doorway.

'Everything as it should be?' she said heartily.

'Yes, fine,' Hanna answered curtly and the nurse retreated.

There was a long silence, interrupted periodically by the muffled sounds from the ward.

'He grew up in a florist's you know,' Judy said eventually. 'That's what his dad did; still does. They've got a shop in Broadstairs,. they live in the flat above it. A florist's. When he was a child the other boys used to call him Pansy because of it . . . that wasn't why he joined the Army. He didn't mind people laughing at him, he always wanted to be a soldier though. He was so easygoing.' She took a cigarette from her handbag but fumbled for a light.

'Just a minute, I'll get you a match,' Lewis offered.

'No, don't bother,' Judy said. 'I know they don't like you

126

to smoke in here.' She looked at the cigarette and Lewis looked at her in turn. He had the sensation she was made of the finest glass, if he were to move towards her she would shatter into tiny pieces. As they watched, tears began to flow down her face although her features were calm. Then she said: 'Oh, Colin,' and all the grief that was in her sounded in the two words. She reached out and her body began to rack with sobs. Lewis stood helplessly by and Hanna gently indicated with her head for him to go.

*

He walked for a long way before the tightness in his chest subsided and he could breathe evenly again.

At Gower Street there was still no getting away from it; news of Colin Miller's death seemed to have seeped through the building. People stood in small groups talking quietly, and gave him sympathetic nods as he passed them.

When he got to Charlie Mars's room, he found him sitting on the leather chesterfield eating a toasted sausage sandwich from the canteen. Lewis could see smudges of blue beneath his eyes.

'These things are bloody awful,' Charlie said as he lifted the remnants of crust up to Lewis for inspection and let them fall back onto the heavy china plate. He sat looking at the plate for a while, his face cast into an expression of deep sadness. Lewis knew he was thinking of Colin Miller.

'You should have had a bacon roll with me,' Lewis said. 'Incidentally, I've just seen Max Ernhart again.'

Charlie raised his eyebrows.

'Again? I didn't know you were acquainted in the first place.'

Lewis described their meetings in Paris and the encounter in the Cypriot café while Charlie lay on the sofa with his hands clasped behind his head and listened intently. When Lewis got to the job offer he whistled.

'Now that *is* intriguing.'

'What do you know about him, Charlie?' Lewis said. 'All I have is what Claude Henderson told me in Paris and what Ernhart said to me today. What else should I know?'

Charlie stretched for a moment before he reclasped his hands behind his head.

'Max Ernhart was born in Berlin. His father had been an officer in the Prussian Guards during the Great War. He was a war hero and was decorated with the Knight's Cross by the Kaiser.

'In 1918, Max's father returned to run the family business in Berlin which was manufacturing radio equipment. When Max was still a boy there was a family scandal. He was found in bed with a maid. They tried to pack him off to boarding school but instead he joined the Merchant Navy and made for South America.

'He teamed up with a Yorkshireman called John Slingsby who taught him to be a gun-runner. Then they returned to Europe in '36, for the Spanish Civil War, where they made a lot of money as arms dealers. John Slingsby was killed in Madrid and Ernhart returned to Germany, where he continued his business in Hamburg, even though he was still a few months off his eighteenth birthday.

'In 1939 there was a killing and Ernhart was implicated. It looked as if he was going to jail, but the judge gave him an option. So Max found himself in the Wehrmacht, not as an officer in a distinguished regiment like his father but as a private in a penal battalion just in time for the invasion of Poland. He fought well and was awarded the Iron Cross, second class.

'After the campaign he was granted a request to transfer to one of the new paratroop battalions. In 1941 he fought against us in Crete and was wounded and decorated again. He was sent home to Germany for convalescence. While he was there he made discreet inquiries and discovered that his father had died in Ravensbruck and the rest of his family were all in concentration camps.'

'Why?' Lewis said.

Charlie folded his arms across his chest.

'Because Max Ernhart's real name was Adolph Wise. His family were Jews. German Jewish war heroes were not uncommon in the First World War. Subsequently Hitler had their names obliterated from the war memorials. When Max returned to his unit, he deserted to the Greek partisans and fought with them until he came to

128

the attention of British Intelligence in Cairo. He was brought out and trained as one of our agents and he operated as such for the rest of the war.

'Then he disappeared until early in 1946 when he turned up in West Berlin with a string of agents operating in East Germany and a thriving arms business. In those days he did most of his work for the Americans but we kept in touch. He was married at that time to a German woman, Eva Klemperer. They were a glamorous couple around post-war Berlin.

'Then, in the early Fifties, his network was cracked wide open. No one knew how it happened. The whole business was too complex. They were all executed; no attempt to turn any of them. Ernhart's wife was also killed though he got out, badly wounded, and seemed a broken man. For a time he retired to Whitby in Yorkshire. Oh, he had plenty of money so he could afford to do nothing. He acted as a sort of consultant for a while. And that's how Claude Henderson got to know him.

'Then, in the early Sixties, he moved to London and married again to Caroline Mendez. She was the young widow of a South American racing driver although she had been a model from Bradford called Carol Carter. They had one daughter in the late Sixties and seemed to enjoy one of those catastrophic relationships that never quite spill over into a divorce. Max has kept dealing in arms but no further espionage involvement that we can detect since his network was destroyed.'

'So what was he doing in Paris?'

Charlie shrugged.

'Everyone is being very close, dear boy. But I rather suspect he's putting together some joint arms deal with the Israelis and the Quataran Royal Family if they can get their country back.'

'Why does he want me?' Charlie shrugged again.

'Search me, maybe he thinks you'll make a good son-in-law. It's the sort of thing that dwells on the mind of men with daughters. Believe me, I know.'

Charlie yawned and pressed the buzzer on his telephone to summon Penny Rose.

'We don't see any of that photographic stuff for at least

a couple of hours.' He looked at his watch as Penny came into the room. 'Miss Rose, I am going to have a couple of hours' sleep. If anyone asks for me tell them I have been called away by the Prime Minister. If the Prime Minister calls, tell Number 10 I am with the Queen. Give me a call and a cup of tea at five forty-five precisely.'

As Lewis got to the door he could hear Charlie's breathing change to an even tone. When he reached his own quarters he found Meredith writing at the desk they shared.

'What are you doing?' Lewis asked, and Meredith paused for a moment.

'I thought you had rather a lot on your plate so I'm drafting your report of today's events.'

'This is an unparalleled act of generosity,' Lewis said. Then he remembered that he still had to prepare a report on the events in Paris or Claude Henderson would flay him with chains of paper clips. He decided he would work in Penny Rose's office where he could use the spare desk. He took some report forms from Meredith and made for her office.

*

He wrote in a fast even hand with only an occasional correction. After a while he became aware that Penny Rose was watching him. He looked up and she smiled brightly at him. He smiled back and tried to concentrate on the report, but she had successfully interrupted the flow of his thoughts. He glanced at her again and saw that she had lowered her head. Her shoulders gave a slight shudder and Lewis realised she was crying.

He cleared his throat and she looked up. Tears had fallen on the inside of her glasses and the tip of her nose was red. For a moment he thought of the pain he had seen earlier on Judy's face.

'What's the matter, Penny?' he said gently.

'Oh, I don't know what to do,' she said in a broken voice.

Lewis got up and took her by the shoulders.

'Come on, tell me what the problem is.'

She got up and walked to where her handbag was on top of a filing cabinet and took out a paper tissue to dab her face.

'Captain Horne,' she said suddenly. 'Have you heard any gossip about me?'

'What kind of gossip, Penny?'

She took a deep breath and then blurted out: 'Oh, of me being of easy virtue.'

Lewis fought to keep his expression under control. He knew how hurt she would be if he laughed.

'That's an old-fashioned turn of phrase. Where did you pick it up?'

Penny threw the paper tissue away.

'Sister Bernadette always used to say that at the convent school I went to.'

'Why should anyone be gossiping about your virtue?'

She paused and he could see it was difficult for her to begin.

'It started at Curzon Street. I wondered if anyone has talked about what happened there?'

Lewis leaned against the desk and indicated for Penny to sit in the chair he had just vacated.

'Begin at the beginning,' he said and she clasped her hands together.

'I started work at Curzon Street last Easter just a few weeks before Mr Crawshaw and Mr Herriot were retiring after thirty years in the department. There was a big party and, oh, lots of drink.

'During the evening, I went to get something from my desk. My office was not being used for the party and I thought it was empty but there was a man lying on his back. I thought he'd had a heart attack. His name is Jeffrey Curtis, he drinks and smokes a lot and he's overweight. Anyway he started to make a terrible sound so I decided to give him the kiss of life and that's when the conga line came into my office. He woke up then,' she said bitterly. 'He was just drunk. They all laughed and I was so embarrassed I laughed as well.'

Lewis was biting the inside of his mouth. He then turned away to regain his composure.

'So that's how the gossip started,' he said.

'No,' she said, 'not at first. It was the incident with Raymond Podmore.'

'Tell me about it.'

She let out a sigh.

'About two weeks later there was a warm spell. I'd stayed for the weekend at my grandparents' and I'd found some of my grandmother's dresses from the Thirties, lovely flimsy things. They're very fashionable now, they just float after you.'

'So what happened?'

'Mr Podmore kept making jokes about me and Jeffrey Curtis. I had to go and do some letters for him, Mr Podmore, that is. I came into his office and closed the door behind me.

'But I'd shut a lot of the dress in the door and when I walked towards him the whole frock ripped off and I was standing there in my undies. Well, Mr Podmore just went to pieces. He rushed out of the room and the girls in the typing pool stood up and they could see into his office and me with next to nothing on.'

Lewis began to snort with suppressed laughter. He turned it into a coughing fit and dropped his fountain pen. He and Penny both reached down for it and her hair became entangled with the buttons on the cuff of his jacket. Lewis encircled her head with his other arm and was standing in what appeared to be a close embrace when George Ward rapped sharply on the door and entered.

He stopped dead and started to back out.

'Get in here,' Lewis snarled. 'Help us to get untangled.'

Ward freed Lewis after a moment's effort.

'You've met Mr Ward, haven't you?' Lewis said. 'He's in charge of communications. He also briefs the rest of us on internal matters.' He turned to Penny and took her slim shoulders in his hands. 'Now Penny, I want you to tell the gallant Captain here exactly what you told me.' He picked up his papers from the desk. 'While I go downstairs to see Mary Brown.'

*

The machine clattered for a few minutes and Mary reached into the tray and handed the printout to Lewis. It was the text of the Washington conversation between the two KGB agents. Lewis glanced at it and thanked Mary who sat down at her desk once more.

132

'And nothing else has turned up?' Lewis said.

'No,' Mary replied, 'but it's not surprising. We only have the American stuff in the system.'

'I don't follow,' Lewis said.

Mary tapped his sheets of paper.

'That comes to us on disc straight from Langley in Virginia. This equipment is all manufactured in America, but half our girls aren't yet trained to operate it. We're weeks – months – behind in getting stuff into it. There's masses of material still waiting for processing. Orders are we do it alphabetically. Q for Quatara is a long way off.'

'Where is the unprocessed paper?' Lewis asked.

Mary nodded into the corner. 'In the old storeroom in box files.'

Half an hour later Meredith was seated on his chaise longue carefully touching up the varnish on a split cane fishing rod when Lewis backed into the room with four box files in his arms.

'Come on,' he said. 'Give me a hand with this.'

Meredith groaned. 'Oh, God. I'm supposed to be a man of action, not a box wallah.'

Lewis dumped two of the files in his lap.

'What are we looking for?' Meredith said as he laid the brush and fishing rod aside.

'Someone young. A left-handed shot connected with Quatara.'

'Is that all?' Gordon said plaintively.

'Get on with it.' Lewis sat down at the tiny desk and took a wad of paper from the first box file, while Meredith looked slightly piqued at the sharp tone of his colleague's command.

*

Two hours later they were staring at a pile of paper before them on the desk.

'Well that's it,' Lewis said.

At that moment Sandy Patch came in.

'How's it going?' Lewis asked as Sandy sat on the edge of the desk.

'OK, boss. The photographs I took are being printed. What's all this?' he said, gesturing to the paper work on

133

the desk. There were all sorts of documents before Lewis; newspaper cuttings, memos, witness statements, reports from field operators. Lewis pushed the paper towards Sandy.

'Take a look at this and tell me if there's a common denominator.'

After forty minutes' study Sandy laid the last sheet of paper aside and looked up at Lewis who put down the book he had been reading. Meredith glanced up from the fishing rod he had resumed varnishing.

'What do you think?' Lewis said.

Sandy ran a hand through his thinning hair. 'Billy the Kid is doing all the killing.'

'Why do you call him Billy the Kid?' Meredith asked.

Sandy turned to look at him. 'He was left-handed as well. Look, all the witnesses back it up. Gilligan gets the chop in New York as he's about to organise something at the United Nations. It appears to be a mugging, but witnesses say the mugger was white with the look of a rich kid. The strongest statement comes from an ex-cop who is a boxing fan. When he was asked if he was sure he held the knife in the left hand, he said he knew a south paw when he saw one.

'Sir Arthur Trialwood, one of the people who actually put the Quataran Royal Family on the throne after the war, goes to the Middle East to visit Arab leaders privately, but we know he's drumming up support against the revolution. He gets knifed in Beirut. Found dead in a lavatory at the airport. The cleaner says he was talking to a dark-haired boy. Once again, the wound indicates the killer was left-handed.

'Prince Fayeed in Vienna was killed and his driver wounded. The police say it was a Red Brigade's job. The driver is sure the assassin opened the right hand door of the car to shoot them. That would be very awkward for anyone but a left-hander.

'Lucien Cleward, multi-national industrialist and well-known poofter, is about to cancel a proposed desalination plant in Quatara because he doesn't like the rebels. He picks up a boy in an expensive gay club and takes him back to Mayfair. He prepares a light meal with his own hands and after supper gets strangled with a silk dressing-gown cord.'

'What indication does a strangulation give to him being left-handed?' Gordon asked.

Sandy smiled. 'There was a good copper on the job. Cleward didn't clear up after the midnight snack. The guest's wine glass was on the left and the knife and fork were the wrong way round on the plate. The common denominator is a one-man left-handed death squad. All he needs from London is the SP and he's away.'

'Then what does he need?' Lewis said.

'The SP,' Sandy repeated. 'The starting price – the off.'

Lewis shuffled through the papers rapidly checking something.

'Yes, it looks as if he's operating from London.' He watched Gordon for a moment who was still intently varnishing his fishing rod.

'We must assume our mole is in Government. The Civil Service or a branch of security. Taking communications between those departments into account, our friend waits until the maximum amount of suspects are in the know about a move being made by our side, then he unleashes his little playmate who flies off and checkmates our team members.'

Lewis got up and put the book he had been reading back on the shelf. He paused for a moment then turned to Meredith.

'Gordon, run a check on the airlines. He might just have used the same name for all the flights.'

With Gordon despatched on his errand, Lewis leaned against the bookshelves, his arms folded, deep in thought. Then he looked up at Sandy.

'I thought you were going to take an early night?'

'I'll stay if you like,' Sandy said easily

'It's the school concert, isn't it?'

'Yeah.'

Lewis grinned. 'Why should you get away with it? Go on, shove off. Take a bleeper with you just in case.'

'Are you sure?'

'Yes, and tell him if he plays any bum notes I'll burn his football boots.'

He watched Sandy go and then looked at the time. It was five minutes past five and he felt weary. It was going to be some time before Charlie needed him. He stretched out on Gordon's tatty chaise longue and instantly went to sleep.

*

'Captain Horne, Captain Horne,' a voice called anxiously.

Lewis came to and found Penny Rose bending over him. She had a mug of tea in her hand. He blinked and looked up at her.

'Mr Mars said the darkroom took longer than expected so he told me to let you sleep on.'

He took the tea and sipped it while she looked down at him as if he were a patient in a hospital bed.

'You're working late, Penny,' he said.

'Oh, I don't mind,' she said. 'I haven't got to go anywhere until seven-thirty.'

Lewis nodded and handed the mug back to her. When he got to Charlie's room he found him with Mary Brown. A screen was rigged up at one end of the room and a slide projector.

'The stuff is in French, Arabic and Russian,' Charlie said. 'We can all manage the French, Mary will do the Russian. I've asked Paul Renfrew to give you a hand with the Arabic, Lewis. I trust you won't be offended.'

Lewis smiled. 'Not in the least. My Arabic is a rough, army sort. Not in the same league as the graceful, purist phrasing of the Foreign Office.'

'You've a silver tongue in your head, Captain,' a soft voice said.

They all turned to welcome Renfrew.

'Will you pour me a glass of malt whisky, Charlie? I must have some compensation for the late hours we're keeping.' He glanced around the room and carefully flicked some ash from the cigarette he smoked in an ivory holder on to the carpet. 'This is a fascinating room, Charlie. What style of decor would you describe it as fitting? Oxford grotesque? Dear God, I know Polish land-ladies who would scorn the contents.'

Charlie gazed down at him through horn-rimmed glasses.

'I hardly think that anyone who wears a suit of that cut and texture is in a position to question me on a matter of taste,' he retorted dryly.

136

'I call it my traffic light look,' he said to Mary proudly as she passed him his drink. 'You see?' he said as he held a sleeve out to her. 'The tweed is a subtle mixture of red, green and amber. What do you think?'

Mary looked at him from head to toe.

'I think you were made for this room,' she said with a smile meant for them both.

'Right,' Charlie said as Meredith and Sandy entered each carrying a pile of photographic transparencies.

'Let's get started. If anyone else would care for a drink, help yourselves.'

'I'd like a glass of beer,' Gordon said. 'Anyone else?' He took orders as the others made themselves comfortable. Charlie turned out the lights and the first document was projected on to the screen. Renfrew started to translate a report from the Comrade Secretary on the state of political awareness amongst his staff. It was going to be a long night.

*

Eventually they had finished the final slide. Charlie turned the lights on and opened the two dormer windows so that a fresh breeze cut through the frowzy, smoke-laden atmosphere and stirred the loose papers that lay around the room.

Disappointment lay heavily on them all. Charlie leaned against the fireplace and gazed into the empty grate.

'So there we are. We know who they've had murdered and we know who does the dry cleaning for the Mission, how often they pay their grocery bill at Harrods and what the entire Russian Embassy staff like for lunch and dinner. We know those prominent people in British public life who sympathise with their glorious struggle, but we knew that already.'

Renfrew stretched and fitted another cigarette into his holder. His tenth of the night; Lewis had been counting.

'We've narrowed it down to someone in the Civil Service or in the Government,' he said. 'That stuff about the Peace Conference must eliminate anyone in security.'

'Yes, they seem rather keen to keep a tag on the intelligence agencies. How many names did we recognise apart from Lewis! Put the slide up again will you, Gordon?' said Charlie.

Meredith found the drum and pumped the button on the projector until the document Charlie had referred to came onto the screen.

'Names and job descriptions,' Charlie said. 'This list has been lifted from Curzon Street: Grogan and Willis, Thomson, Parker and Ranley, all our people. Jill Alcott, never heard of her.'

'That name was on an earlier list,' Lewis said. 'The one with addresses. Put it up again.'

Gordon found it and they studied the slide carefully. Lewis looked at the name again. Something disturbed him about it, then he read the address once more. He reached into his inside pocket and took out the piece of paper Jessica had given him in Paris.

It was the same number in Prince of Wales Drive.

*

Lewis crossed Chelsea Bridge into Queenstown Road and turned right into Prince of Wales Drive. It took longer than he had expected to find a parking space and it started to rain when he was still some distance from the flat. He buttoned up Rene Malle's trenchcoat and lowered his head into the driving wind.

The seemingly endless cliff of red brick and white stone rose up beside him on his right, parked motor cars on his left and the long, wet ribbon of empty pavement before him. Eventually, he came to the number she had given him. He climbed the flights of stairs to her flat and rang the bell. She opened the door and stood aside so that he could enter.

'I tried to telephone,' Lewis said.

'I've only been in for about ten minutes,' she replied.

He passed across a hallway and into a comfortable living room.

There were bookcases each side of the fireplace and prints of eighteenth-century London on the walls. The light came from table lamps about the room. The furniture was a mixture of good, solid, second-hand pieces chosen for comfort and the odd Victorian antique.

It was also the home of a childless couple. There were too many ornament in easy reach.

'Let me take your coat,' she said and he handed it to her. When she returned he studied her clothes. She was wearing a man's woollen dressing gown and a thick pair of slippers. The dressing gown was too large, so she had turned the sleeves back. She was hardly the picture of the seductive mistress; neither did she look like a spy.

'He's a lawyer, your . . .?' He waved around the room.

'Yes, how did you know?'

'The prints. They're all of the Inner Temple. '

She nodded.

'What shall I call you?' he said. 'I understand you could be Jill Alcott.'

'My name really is Jessica Crossley. Jeremy Bellingford gave me the name Alcott. How did you discover me?'

'You turned up on a list.' He ran his hand through his rain-soaked hair.

'We're all on a list somewhere, I suppose. I'll get you something.'

She turned with a towel and he rubbed vigorously for a few minutes.

'I'm sorry, Lewis,' she said when he had stopped.

'Why?' he asked.

'For deceiving you.'

'How did you deceive me?' She sat on the arm of the armchair and looked down at her hands.

'I didn't tell you why I was really in Paris. When we walked down to the Seine from the Louvre I took you to the fisherman deliberately. I knew he would be there. I met him with Jack Silver. He wanted to meet you.'

'That's all right,' he said as he put aside the towel. 'I didn't tell you the truth about myself either.'

'Yes, but I knew all along you were working for Gower Street.'

He smiled. 'There's a deep fault in your logic.'

'I suppose there is, but I still felt rotten about it. I don't think I'm cut out for a life of deception.' She held her arms out towards the walls of the flat. 'I know that sounds like hypocrisy – here of all places – but it's true. I thought you were coming here to accuse me of ... I don't know ... betrayal.'

Lewis shook his head.

'I didn't come to pass judgment on you, why should I? Anyway, in the essential things you told me the truth about yourself.' He stood up. 'I came to warn you. I imagine Bellingford set up whatever department you're in because he said he couldn't be sure of the established intelligence services.'

Jessica nodded. 'Yes, that's just about it.'

'How were you recruited?'

'I was working in the Foreign Office in translation. My Arabic is excellent and I have a good knowledge of the Middle East.'

'So Bellingford just trawled for you?'

'Yes and a couple of people recommended me.'

'The bloody fool – I suppose he boasted of his brilliant move to everyone he wanted to impress. Your cover's blown, you're in danger.'

She smiled.

'Who could want to harm me? I haven't done anything to anyone.'

Lewis realised that despite her intelligence, Jessica was completely guileless. The world of espionage to her was an abstraction that had no connection with life and death. Bellingford had recklessly pitched her into terrible danger because he was impressed by her academic brilliance. It was like encouraging a champion swimmer to practise in shark-infested waters.

The telephone rang suddenly on the table next to Jessica. She picked it up quickly.

'Hello. Yes. Thank you, I'm fine.' She hung up and Lewis looked at her face which had become thoughtful.

'Who was it?' he said.

'I don't know. Someone asked if I was Jill Alcott and said they were checking on behalf of Bellingford to see if I was all right.'

'Pack some clothes. You'd better come and stay at my flat.'

But even as he said it, he wondered if this small precaution would be enough.

'Wanderers eastward, wanderers west,
Know you why you cannot rest?
*   'Tis that every mother's son*
Travails with a skeleton.'

A Shropshire Lad
A. E. HOUSMAN

Chapter Seven

Jessica opened her eyes and saw close to her, in the half light, the outline of a hooded figure. Her head came off the pillow and she gasped in fear. The figure seized both her wrists as she began to struggle.

'It's me. Lewis,' he said urgently as he waited for her to be calm. Finally he let go and she sank back on the bed and pulled the cover over her again. He turned and opened the thin curtains so that the morning light illuminated his dark training suit with a hood that covered his head.

'I'm just going for a run, if you want to use the shower first,' he said as he sat on the end of the bed and tightened the laces of his training shoes.

Jessica raised herself on her elbows and looked around the bare room. There was a nondescript, dark-wood chest of drawers at the foot of the bed and a large, ugly, heavily-carved wardrobe with a mirror let into the door next to it. A wicker armchair that had been painted pale green at one time stood in the corner near the window. There was no carpet on the battered parquet floor and the cream-painted walls were without pictures. A plain whitewood table stood next to the bed with a black Anglepoise lamp on it and a pile of library books. She raised her knees beneath the duvet and looked at Lewis again.

'What time is it?' she said.

'Eight o'clock. I'll be back in about half an hour,' he replied.

Jessica nodded sleepily. She did not like to talk in the morning.

The sound of the front door closing came to her as she rolled out of bed and padded barefoot to the bathroom. In her hurry to leave Prince of Wales Drive the night before, she had forgotten her dressing gown and slippers. The bathroom was equally bleak. The black and white marble tiles on the floor were cracked and uneven and the walls were painted a drab pea green.

Instead of a bath there was an ancient reeded glass shower with chrome fittings that looked about the same vintage as the *Titanic*. She felt the towels on the rail. At least they were large and warm. Jessica opened the cabinet above the wash basin and gazed at the sparse contents. There were three disposable razors, a canister of shaving foam, a plastic bottle of shampoo, a toothbrush and a half-used tube of toothpaste: certain orders of monks lived in greater comfort.

While waiting for the shower to reach the right temperature, she examined a set of old-fashioned chemist's scales in the corner and then she stepped into the luke-warm water.

When she had finished, she wrapped herself in two of the towels and wandered into the living room, her wet feet leaving footprints on the unpolished parquet floor. Jessica could detect the same lack of concern for the decor. One wall was covered in books stacked on shelving made from grey strip metal. Under one of the two uncurtained sash windows was a table covered in a dark red cloth. Next to the other, a metal desk and a typist's chair. In one alcove beside the fireplace was a television set, and in the other a blackened and chipped military chest, bound at the edges with brass.

Two old faded armchairs stood in front of the two-bar electric fire; next to the door was a battered upright piano and resting on top of it the only ornament in the room – a carving, about twelve inches high, of an eighteenth-century rifleman presenting arms.

A rather elaborate art deco mirror with scalloped edges hung from a chain over the mantelpiece. Like the bedroom, there were no carpets on the wooden floor. Long playing records were stacked on the shelves in the alcove where the military chest stood, and to one side an old-fashioned record player.

Jessica crossed the room and sat at the desk. Lying on the top, weighed down by a glass paperweight, was a pile of foolscap pages covered in neat, bold handwriting. She glanced down at them and started to read. She was still there when Lewis returned from his run.

'What does this mean about the V-sign after Crécy?' she said.

Lewis walked over to her, unzipped his training top and looked over her shoulder at his notes.

'Legend has it the French chopped off the first and second fingers of the British archers when they caught them. After Crécy the archers are supposed to have held up their two fingers to the captured French aristocracy.'

'Do you believe that?' Jessica asked. Lewis shrugged.

'It sounds logical. The V-sign has always been a working class gesture and it does indicate the mood the bowmen were in after the battle.' She turned back to the notes.

'I didn't know the longbow affected history this much.'

Lewis peeled off the top as he made for the bathroom.

'If you think British soccer fans have a bad reputation in Europe, you should hear what they had to say about our archers,' he shouted as he turned on the shower.

By the time he had finished in the bathroom Jessica had dressed and made him a cup of instant coffee.

'The only food you have is some digestive biscuits and a bottle of stuffed olives,' she said as he quickly towelled himself dry and put on clothes.

'I don't eat here very often,' Lewis said as he noticed the clean shirt he had just put on was also showing the first signs of fraying at the cuffs.

'It doesn't surprise me,' Jessica called out as she glanced around the living room. 'The surroundings are hardly conducive to feasting.'

'I'm never here,' Lewis said as he brushed his shoes. 'But if I feel in need of home comforts, my sister Janet lives in the flat below and I can always drop in there for a few hours.'

The telephone rang and Lewis looked at his watch. 'Ten past nine,' he said. 'I have a feeling it's work.'

He was right. It was Charlie and his voice sounded tired.

'Have you seen the papers?' he asked.

'Not yet,' Lewis replied. 'Why?'

'Let me read you a selection of headlines. Mole Hunt in Whitehall. Hi-de-Spy. Minister Confirms Security Leak. That ass Bellingford told the reporters the siege was only a part of his duties. His major task was counter-espionage. The reporters flattered him a bit and then he told them about the mole. I suppose the bloody fool thought it was on lobby terms. Incidentally, do you know Jessica Crossley's whereabouts?'

'She's here with me,' Lewis said. There was a brief pause. Then Charlie said: 'Good. Bring her in to Gower Street, will you? I've already had a contrite Bellingford on the line. At least he was contrite when I chastised him for running a personal secret service. He's asked us to take her over.'

'You're to work with us,' Lewis said in an aside to her as Charlie spoke again: 'Tell her to ring Bellingford at Lord North Street. He's got something for you both to do. I'll see you later.'

Lewis hung up and then lifted the receiver again and handed it to Jessica.

'You're to ring Bellingford at his home number.'

Lewis went into the kitchen again and washed the coffee mugs while she made the call. Jessica joined him after a while.

'You're right. He just told me he thinks it would be best if I went to Gower Street. He gave me the impression it was his idea. Anyway, we have to call a man after ten thirty. His name is Brian Brewster, he's a friend of Jeremy Bellingford's who works in advertising.'

'Why?' Lewis asked.

'Something to do with Russia. He wants to talk to someone in British Intelligence.'

Lewis groaned as he dried the mugs and put them in a cupboard.

'Oh Christ. One of those.'

'One of what?' Jessica said in a curious voice as she traced a pattern of autumn leaves across the surface of the Formica-topped table.

'He's probably been to Moscow on a business trip and met a dissident in Red Square. It happens all the time,' Lewis said as he folded the teatowel neatly. 'A visit to

Russia can have a profound effect on some people. If they've got connections they invariably want to discuss their experience with someone in Intelligence. Most of them end up at Curzon Street but we get our fair share. Claude Henderson usually deals with them.'

'So you think it will be a waste of time?' Jessica said as Lewis held out her raincoat so she could put it on. He shrugged.

'Who knows? If I were a betting man I'd say there was as much chance of anything coming from it as there is of the secretary of the Supreme Soviet parachuting into Scotland and saying he wants to sign a peace pact.'

'But that's exactly what Rudolph Hess did in World War II,' Jessica said, and then she punched him when she saw his smile.

'Come on,' he said as he pushed her towards the door. 'You work for Charlie Mars now.'

Lewis looked out on to Lamb's Conduit Street. The part of the road in front of his flat was barred to traffic and had been turned into a walkway for pedestrians but no one strolled there now. Rain lashed down forming great puddles all the way to Guilford Place. To the left of the doorway they stood in was the entrance to the Old Times Antique Shop.

'In here,' Lewis said as he pushed open the door to the tinkling of a small bell on a spring.

Roland Perth looked up from the back of the shop where he was standing in a green baize apron polishing the pieces of a large, silver dinner service. He glanced towards them.

'Lewis, my dear, and the young lady who was once a mere acquaintance.'

'Have you got a brolly we can borrow, Roland?' Lewis asked as Jessica looked around the tiny shop.

Roland pointed with a tarnished fork to a corner.

'If you look between the desk and the commode, there's an elephant's foot with a golfing umbrella in it.'

Lewis carefully located the brolly and backed gingerly out of the shop.

'Thanks, Roland. I'll bring it back,' he said and Jessica smiled as she squeezed past the precious china.

'Remember,' Roland called out, '"Singin' In The Rain" has been done to death. If you're going to do a number, make it "Pennies From Heaven".'

Lewis opened the multi-coloured brolly and they walked beneath its cover towards Gower Street.

'It's just a house,' Jessica said in surprise as they stood at the Georgian front door and he rang the bell.

'And the two either side,' Lewis replied as he collapsed the brolly. 'It's bigger than you would think.'

The door opened and he led her into the hallway.

'This is Miss Crossley, Sergeant Major Watts,' Lewis said to the erect uniformed figure who had opened the door.

'Good morning, miss. I had word that you were joining us.'

'Is Mr Mars here yet?' Lewis asked as he led Jessica towards the staircase.

'Yes, sir,' Sergeant Major Watts said, 'but no sign of Captain Meredith yet.'

When they had got rid of their damp clothes, Lewis took her on a tour of the building ending at Charlie Mars's room. He rose to his feet as she entered and Jessica glanced around at the book-lined chaos.

'If you're looking for somewhere to sit,' he said, 'you can take the spare desk next door. I dare say Penny will be pleased to have some company.'

As they were about to leave, Charlie held out a restraining hand. 'How did Bellingford come to recruit you?' he asked.

Jessica stopped and looked puzzled.

'I thought you knew. Jeremy Bellingford asked Paul Renfrew if he knew of anyone who was a good analyst in the Foreign Office. In fact, he was helping me with an article on the Middle East when Jeremy recruited me.'

'I see,' Charlie said, 'and how many more were recruited for this department?'

Jessica shrugged. 'I really have no idea. I only did what Mr Bellingford asked me to do. I had no office, I worked from home and got most of my instructions on the telephone.'

Charlie stood with his back to the fireplace and jangled

the change and keys in his trouser pockets. His chin was buried in his chest and his eyes were on the tatty oriental carpet at his feet.

'How did you meet Lewis in Paris?' he asked without lifting his eyes. She thought for a moment.

'Jeremy Bellingford told me to stay close to Lord Silver because he wanted to know all I could find out about the arms deal that was being negotiated with Ahmed and Max Ernhart. Bellingford telephoned them to say Lewis was there so Ernhart had him followed. He asked me to bring him to where he was fishing so he could take a look at him.'

'He really does appear to be very interested in you,' Charlie said.

Lewis opened the door and gestured for Jessica to leave the room ahead of him. She was about to when Claude Henderson loomed in the doorway.

'Who's interested in you?' Claude asked.

'I'm being head-hunted, Claude,' Lewis said. 'I've been offered forty-five thousand a year and a company car to go into industry.'

Claude was visibly disturbed by Lewis's claim.

'By whom?' he demanded in a shocked voice.

'Max Ernhart,' Lewis said with a winning smile.

Claude was about to say something else when he noticed Jessica, but he found it impossible to acknowledge her until he was introduced. Charlie came to his aid.

'My deputy, Claude Henderson – Jessica Crossley. Miss Crossley has been seconded to us by Jeremy Bellingford, Claude.'

Henderson shook hands. 'How do you do, Miss Crossley,' he said with a formal smile. Then he turned to Lewis. 'I should take that offer; if Ernhart gets the deal he wants with the Israelis and the Quataran Royal Family his company will be in clover.'

'That good, is it?' Charlie said, and Claude nodded.

'Megabucks, as our American cousins say.'

Lewis looked at his watch and tapped Jessica on the arm. 'It's time we rang Mr Brewster.' They made for Lewis's room where they found Meredith on the chaise longue with all the morning newspapers spread around

149

him. He stood up and shook hands with Jessica. She sat at the tiny desk to use the telephone and Lewis glanced through the newspapers that Meredith had discarded. After a few minutes of switchboard and secretarial delays, Brewster was on the line. He spoke with a sharp, staccato delivery.

She replaced the receiver after they had exchanged a few sentences and studied Lewis and Meredith in their cramped study. Lewis looked up from his paper and saw the look of amusement on Jessica's face.

'This is the first time I've ever seen a stuffed owl in an office. I take it you didn't decorate the room?' she said to Lewis as she waved a hand around the cluttered quarters.

He smiled and shook his head.

'I thought not. It's much cosier than your flat.'

'What did Mr Brewster say?' Lewis asked.

'He's having lunch at the Savoy where he has invited us to meet him for a drink in the American Bar at one o'clock.'

Gordon rattled the newspaper he was reading and they looked at him expectantly. After a moment he spoke: 'Try the champagne cocktails. I can vouch for their excellence.'

*

'Keep in touch,' Charlie Mars said as Jessica and Lewis got out of the taxi in the Strand.

Lewis nodded a yes as Charlie gestured to the driver to take him on to the Reform Club.

'This is the only piece of road in Britain where they drive on the right,' Jessica said as they walked along the short cul-de-sac that led from the Strand to the entrance of The Savoy.

'I suppose it's to make Americans feel at home.' They passed through the revolving door and turned left at the florist's counter for the flight of stairs that led to the American Bar. Fittingly, as they entered they came upon a group of very old Americans shuffling to their seats for the serious ritual of drinks before lunch.

The three men were similarly dressed in muted tones of light grey that contrasted nicely with their pink complexions and white hair. Discreet touches of gold flashed at Lewis from spectacle frames and rings. The women were thin, like only the rich can be thin, and their clothes were made from silk, cotton and wool. It was clear they did not know the touch of man-made fibre.

A waiter looked at Lewis and Jessica.

'Yes, sir?'

'Is Mr Brewster here?' Jessica said as Lewis scanned the tables and decided a man lighting an enormous cigar was their host. He was right.

Brewster was tall and athletically built. His hair was thinning and what was left had been expensively barbered to create the illusion of fullness. The clothes were stockbroker style: a dark blue striped suit, heavy white cotton shirt, a red silk polka-dot tie and a tan which was as carefully cultivated as his hair.

He stood up and took the cigar from his mouth as they approached him, and Lewis noticed his long and slender hands. He handled the massive Havana with such confidence Lewis guessed he had started out on his career as a salesman.

'Drinks?' Brewster said.

They exchanged glances and Lewis asked for champagne cocktails although he noticed that Brewster was drinking Perrier water.

Across the room they could hear one of the ancient Americans questioning a white-coated waiter about the dryness of the martini he was ordering.

Brewster glanced at his wrist and Lewis saw that he wore a Swatch, the highly-fashionable Swiss watch that cost less than the cigar he smoked. The waiter brought their drinks and Lewis took a game chip from the bowl placed before them.

'How can we help you, Mr Brewster?' he asked politely.

Brewster selected a large, salted cashew nut and bit it in two. He studied the remaining half intently for a moment before popping it into his mouth and levelling his gaze at Lewis, who realised that the little tactic he had just witnessed was a sales technique to gain his total attention.

'Have either of you heard of Jack Lyte?' he said in his staccato voice.

151

'Yes,' they both replied.

Brewster looked a little surprised.

'He wrote *Soldier Without Fortune*,' Jessica said.

'That's right,' Brewster replied. 'Did you know he died last year?'

Lewis nodded. 'In Moscow, wasn't it?'

'Yes. He was my uncle. My mother was with him when he died.'

'But you weren't there?' Jessica said.

Brewster tapped cigar ash into the silver tray.

'I declined the trip this time. I'd never met my uncle so I had no feelings about him, but I have visited Russia before.' He paused for a moment. 'Tell me, have you ever been to Moscow?'

'No,' Jessica replied.

Brewster puffed on the cigar for a moment.

'It's like waiting in a long queue in a Post Office in Acton on a wet afternoon,' he said with feeling. 'And that's in their top hotels.'

Acton, Lewis thought, that's where he's from; there was still some West London tones left in the voice.

'I take it you don't subscribe to the Soviet system,' Lewis said lightly.

'Oh, I used to be left wing when I was younger,' Brewster said easily.

'What changed you?'

'Waiting for the lift in the Ukraina Hotel.'

'There's always the Bolshoi,' Lewis said.

'Bollocks to the Bolshoi,' Brewster said evenly. 'Art can't make you happy.'

Lewis was beginning to warm to Brewster whom he suspected might be one of those rare people who was capable of being completely honest about himself.

'What does make you happy?' Jessica asked.

'Sex, money and power,' he replied without thinking. 'At least, that's what makes *me* happy. I can't speak for the rest of the world. Anyway, let me come to the point.

'Jack Lyte, leading light of the British Communist Movement, was my mother's brother. He wrote *Soldier Without Fortune* after the Spanish Civil War and then went to live in the Soviet Union where he remained until his death.

'Last year my mother got a call from the Russian Embassy to say he was on his last legs and he wanted to see his sister before he died. The Russian official explained that as a hero of the Soviet Union his request would be granted and would Mother like to pop over to the nursing home he was in.' Brewster paused and worked on his cigar for a moment. He was aware that he had a deeply attentive audience and the salesman in him relished it.

'Let me explain. My mother is not a sophisticated woman. When my father died, I was eleven and an only child. There was enough money from what he left to send me to school but she had to work as a filing clerk for a building society. She is also a staunch supporter of the Conservative Party. I became the centre of her life. My wellbeing was everything to her.'

'But she still went to see her brother Jack,' Jessica prodded. Brewster nodded.

'Old-fashioned virtues can be rather impressive at times.' Brewster looked at his watch again. It was clear he was running late. 'To be brief, when she saw the headlines about a spy in Whitehall this morning, she rang me in a bit of a panic. She knows I'm a friend of Jeremy Bellingford. When she was in Moscow, Jack Lyte told her there was a big spy in Whitehall. It seems he also gave her some kind of manuscript. She was worried that any kind of publicity could hurt my career so she did nothing with it.'

'Evidently you don't share your mother's fears, Mr Brewster,' Lewis said politely. Brewster shook his head.

'I know people think I'm a self-seeking son-of-a-bitch, Mr Horne, but I'm a patriotic self-seeking son-of-a-bitch. I have a good life in this country.'

Brewster took a gold ballpoint pen and an elegant card container from his inside pocket and wrote down his mother's name and address. He handed it to Lewis as the waiter arrived with the bill. Brewster took a wad of money from his pocket and peeled off a twenty pound note which he put on the table without looking at the total or even

153

acknowledging the existence of the waiter. Now that they were moving towards the exit, Brewster gave the impression he had all the time in the world.

They stopped by the entrance to the Grill and Brewster shook hands again.

'Well, give my kindest regards to your boss,' he said.

'And to your mother,' Lewis said softly. Brewster registered a moment of uncertainty.

'How is old Jeremy? He went to Oxford, you know.'

'I remember him well,' Lewis said evenly.

'You were there too?' Brewster said casually. Lewis nodded.

Brewster pushed open the door to the restaurant then hesitated. 'You don't need a degree to get in here,' he said.

'What a ghastly man,' Jessica commented as they waited for the doorman to get them a taxi.

'I rather liked him,' Lewis said as he got into the cab after Jessica and remembered a tip for the doorman. Then he looked at his watch; still time to catch Charlie Mars before he went in for his lunch.

'Reform Club, please,' he said to the driver.

'Why do you like him?' she asked.

'I suppose because he didn't make any secret of his ambitions.'

'But he's obviously so ruthless.'

'Well, you always know where you are with ruthless people.'

The driver swerved to change to the left-hand lane and Jessica was thrown against Lewis.

'Where's that?' she said.

'Nowhere,' he replied cheerfully as they juddered to a halt at the lights in Trafalgar Square. 'As long as you never drop your guard with the ones who are fighting their way. It's ordinary people who are the ones to worry about. They can be unpredictable in the worst way, treacherous or noble at the oddest of times. It's the reason dictators hate the masses; the quirkiness of human nature terrifies them.'

The taxi lurched forward again and Jessica stayed pressed against him.

'Austen Mars taught you that.'

Lewis thought for a moment as Admiralty Arch passed to their left. 'Yes, I think he did.'

The taxi stopped outside the Reform Club and Lewis left Jessica in the cab and sprinted up the flight of stairs into the lobby. Another short flight of steps brought him into the great pillared saloon at the centre of the club. Natural light flooded through the glass roof and splashed onto the mosaic marble floor.

Groups of men sat on the leather sofas against the walls or stood around the heavy mahogany table to his right that served as a bar. Lewis spotted Charlie chatting to a couple of men who were laughing. He stood in Charlie's line of vision until he was noticed, then he moved to a wooden lectern near the entrance and read the news agency tapes that were displayed there.

After a few moments Charlie joined him.

'Wild goose chase?' Lewis shrugged.

'I'm not sure, it could be but it's worth checking out. We're off now. I've got a cab waiting outside.'

Charlie raised his eyebrows.

'Drinks at the Savoy and taxis. The department will be taking a very close look at your expenses.'

'Don't worry,' Lewis said with a sideways grin. 'We're only going as far as Green Park. We always get the tube from there.'

*

After a few minutes walk from Acton Town station, Lewis and Jessica turned into the street where Brian Brewster's mother lived. It consisted of long rows of late-Victorian terraced houses trimmed with white decorative stone. Somehow the street could not decide whether it was going up or coming down in the world. Some of the houses had fresh paint with elegant front doors and hanging baskets of flowers, while others stood grim and tatty behind over-grown privet hedges.

Mrs Brewster's house belonged to another category altogether and represented the original occupants of the street. Lower middle class respectability. The tiny lawn was neatly-manicured and two scrupulously washed milk bottles stood on the doorstep. All that the gleaming window panes revealed were net curtains like a sheet of frost masking the secrets of the parlour.

When Mrs Brewster answered the door, Lewis and Jessica smiled reassuringly at her as she peered anxiously out at them. She was a slight woman with a fluffy white hair, wearing a floral pinafore and comfortable slippers.

'Mrs Brewster, your son Brian asked us to come and see you,' Lewis said.

She seemed reluctant to let them enter and as they waited the sound of a heavy rock band came to them from the radio two youths played as they were repairing a car in the road several doors away.

'I do wish they wouldn't do that,' she said in a plaintive voice. 'I remember when this used to be such a quiet street.'

Lewis held out the sheet of paper so she could see her son's handwriting and she immediately opened the door wider to allow them to enter the narrow hallway.

'You can hang your coats there,' she said indicating a hat and umbrella stand that stood against the wall. Jessica closed the front door and the sound of the rock band receded into the distance.

'Come in here.' She led them into a small room that was so crowded with furniture and ornaments that Jessica was reminded of Roland Perth's shop.

'I'll just make a cup of tea,' Mrs Brewster said without waiting to see if her visitors wanted one or not. While she was gone, they looked around the room.

The furniture had all been made in the Thirties and showed the results of more than half a century of regular polishing. There was a piano , sideboard, table with four chairs, two reddish-brown armchairs with crisp white antimacassars and a collection of side tables. A photograph of a sailor in a petty officer's uniform hung on the wall above the piano.

For the rest, on every surface was a framed photograph of Brian Brewster shown throughout his life. He was there as a child cuddling a toy, at the zoo, in the Boy Scouts, in school uniform; then the progress of his marriage to a shy-looking girl and the birth of their two children.

156

Lewis was studying a holiday photograph of Brewster and his family in a sailing boat when his mother entered with a tray. When she had carefully poured the tea to their individual liking, they sat down.

'So you're friends of Brian,' she said and Lewis smiled at her.

'Not exactly, Mrs Brewster. We work for the Civil Service. Brian knows one of our superiors and they both asked us to come and see you.'

'Perhaps you can tell us about your brother Jack?' Jessica asked in a solicitous voice.

Mrs Brewster held her cup of tea with both hands as she drank.

'Jack – yes. Well, first I must tell you I hardly knew him. I was the baby of the family. Jack was the eldest, then there was my other brother, Ted. That's him,' she said, nodding to the picture above the piano. 'He was killed on the *Hood*.' She looked at them both for a moment. 'That was a ship that went down in the war.'

'Yes, Mrs Brewster, we've heard of it,' Lewis said gently.

'Not many young people know much about those days,' she said as if she did not quite believe him. 'Then there was my sister, Dolly. She went to Canada after the war, but she died in the Sixties. So there was only me. Of course I can remember Jack, but I was a little girl then. He used to have a motorbike. He gave me a lift on it once. Our dad was furious. We went right along Acton Vale.' She paused for a moment and a smile of remembrance lighted her face.

'He used to row something shocking with my dad. Always about politics. Dad was a real Tory. We had a hardware shop in the Vale then. Dad wanted the boys to go into the business with him. Ted would have, but Jack wanted to be a writer. He had a job in a garage in Shepherd's Bush, but all he was really interested in was going to meetings.

'Then he went to Spain when the Civil War started and he never came home again. Of course he was famous for a while when the book came out and I think Dad got a bit of a kick out of it although he always denied that. Anyway, it was more or less forgotten once the war started and that was it until last year when this man came to see me and invited me to Russia.'

She paused and drank some more of her tea. Faintly from the street came the sound of the radio playing rock and roll.

'What did you think of Moscow?' Jessica asked.

Mrs Brewster placed her cup carefully beside a photograph of her son on his wedding day.

'Well, it was quite nice, really. Brian hates it there. He's gone on business quite a few times. But I thought the hotel was ever so comfortable and the girl, Natasha, who took me around was lovely. The nursing home Jack was in wasn't like a hospital at all. It was in a wood full of silver birch trees, a big wooden house they called a funny name.'

'A *dacha*,' Jessica said.

'Yes, that's it. When we arrived he was sitting outside with a rug over him. He was just skin and bone. I didn't recognise him at all. He looked at me for a while and then he said: "Hello, Lily. Do you want to come for a spin on my bike?" and I knew it was him all right.

'We talked for a little while but he was ever so weak. He had to rest a lot. I stayed there a week with Natasha. She looked after him and gave him his medicine. It helped with the pain. In the mornings we used to walk to a little village that was quite close and get the shopping. They had most things there. I told Brian and he laughed. He said it was a special shop for the privileged. But it was only an ordinary place – not a patch on Sainsbury's.

'In the afternoons, Natasha would read to him for a couple of hours and it was early to bed after supper. When he had the strength he wanted to talk about England. Well, not England so much. More about what it was like around here when we were young. What was Shepherd's Bush and Acton Vale like now, and Ealing Broadway. Of course it's all changed. Except for the pubs; they're still there but the cinemas have all gone and they've pulled down Shepherd's Bush and most of Ealing Broadway and the shops are all different. Mind you, the parks are the same: the pubs and the parks.'

For a moment she slipped into the past again. The rock

music played on in the distance. Then she gave a little shiver and went on: 'The day before I was going to leave, he asked Natasha to bring the manuscript. He gave it to me while she was there and made me promise to show it to a publisher in this country.

'I asked if I could get into trouble with the authorities, in Russia I mean. And Natasha said she would personally give it to me at the airport, and she had an official letter to say everything was all right. That afternoon, Natasha went into the village after she'd read to Jack and I stayed with him, just the two of us. When he was sure she'd gone away, he acted funny. He made me promise that I'd take the book to the Foreign Office, explain who he was and tell them the code was in the gift edition.'

'The code was in the gift edition,' Lewis repeated.

'That's right,' Mrs Brewster said and she sat very still as a shaft of sunlight shone through the net curtains and motes of dust danced about her white hair.

'Where is the manuscript, Mrs Brewster?' Lewis asked and she got up and opened the lid of the piano stool. She took a pile of very old sheet music and dumped it on the table next to Lewis. The top sheet was *'Tiger Rag'*.

'No one's played the piano for years,' she said, 'since Ted, really. We used to have some fun in here when we were young.'

Outside, the rock music pounded on. They were a long way from *'Tiger Rag'*. She lifted out a bundle wrapped in heavy brown paper and tied together with coarse string. Lewis laid the package on the sideboard after carefully moving some of the collected pictures of Brian Brewster and untied the string.

The manuscript was at least four inches thick and written on an extraordinary variety of papers – lined exercise books, wrapping paper, flyleaves from books – anything that had come to hand over many years. All covered in a fine, highly legible copperplate script with occasional neat corrections and masses of footnotes. Lewis estimated that the whole bundle comprised about half a million words. The first sheet was much better quality than the rest: thick, heavy handmade paper, a light yellow colour. Stuck onto it was a page taken from an edition of the works of Shakespeare. It was the twenty-ninth sonnet. The words were set in archaic sixteenth-century style.

> When in disgrace with Fortune and mens eyes,
> I all alone beweepe my out-cast state,
> And trouble deafe heaven with my bootlesse cries,
> And looke upon my selfe and curse my fate.
> Wishing me like to one more rich in hope,
> Featur'd like him, like him with friends possest,
> Desiring this mans art, and that mans skope,
> With what I most enjoy contented least,
> Yet in these thoughts my selfe almost despising,
> Haplye I thinke on thee, and then my state,
> (Like to the Larke at breake of daye arising)
> From sullen earth sings himns at Heavens gate,
> For thy sweet love remembred such welth brings,
> That then I skorne to change my state with Kings.

Underneath, in larger handwriting than he had used for the rest of the manuscript, was the title *State of Kings: The Triumph of the Soviet System*, by Jack Lyte.

'Did he say anything else, Mrs Brewster?' Lewis asked casually. He had a feeling she was holding something back. She hesitated and glanced at them anxiously.

'He said there was a spy right at the top in Britain and that the authorities might be able to catch him with this book.'

Jessica placed her teacup onto the tray with great care.

'Why didn't you do anything until now?' she asked.

Mrs Brewster leaned against the sideboard and folded her arms across her chest defensively. She looked very fragile to Lewis. He tried to smile in a reassuring way but when she spoke she sounded guilty, as if trying to explain why she had been caught shoplifting.

'Jack was the black sheep of our family. I know that sounds funny these days but being respectable used to mean something to our sort of people. People had forgotten Jack. Brian was getting on so well in his career. His company does a lot of work for the Government. I just didn't want to bring it all up again and remind people, so I didn't tell anyone and Jack died, so I thought, best leave things as they are. Then there was all that in the papers and on the television about a spy so I told Brian and he said I had to talk to you.'

Her voice had changed as she spoke so that she ended on an almost defiant note. The rock music from the street was suddenly drowned by a shattering noise as the engine of the car was revved in a series of powerful crescendos. Mrs Brewster winced and the lines of her frown deepened. Lewis and Jessica stood near the door and Mrs Brewster realised they were ready to leave. As they turned to say goodbye on the door step, she seemed to have cheered up.

'You know,' she said as they shook hands, 'it was quite nice really, Russia that is. I often think of that nice little house near the village. Funny, isn't it?'

Lewis nodded as Mrs Brewster closed her front door on the present.

*

'So this is it,' Charlie Mars said as they looked down on the manuscript where it lay on the desk in Charlie's office. 'And you say the key is in the sonnet?'

Lewis nodded. 'Well, actually, the edition the sonnet is from.'

'Ah,' Charlie said, 'that could be difficult to track down.'

'Well, the boffins will be able to tell us if it's a British edition and after that we'll just have to rely on a great deal of boring searching until we do.'

'May I see that?' Claude Henderson said.

Jessica Crossley took the page and passed it to him where he sat at the end of the table. The light that came through the high windows was weak because of the heavily overcast sky. Henderson snapped on the large Anglepoise lamp and held the sheet of manuscript in the powerful light. He studied it for a few moments then cleared his throat.

'I think I might have this at home.'

'You, Claude?' Lewis said with a note of surprise in his voice.

Claude lowered his head and looked at him over his spectacles.

'Yes, Captain Horne,' he said dryly. 'Being able to

161

read was one of the necessary qualifications for entry to Cambridge University. Many of us went on to collect books and keep them in our houses.'

'But you think you may have this very copy?' Charlie said.

'I'm not a hundred per cent certain but it does look very familiar.'

'Can you lay your hands on it easily?' Charlie said and Claude shook his head.

'No, I'm afraid I'm going to need some help.'

*

As the duty car passed Hanger Lane, the leaden skies opened once more and torrents of rain slowed down the traffic that headed away from London on the Western Avenue.

As they came level with the regal façade of the Hoover factory, the image of Odeon-style splendour – slightly distorted by the heavy rain on the windows of the car – nudged Lewis's memory and he remembered a similar day when he had been an undergraduate and had hitched a lift back to Oxford.

'Turn right when we get to Greenford,' Claude said to Lewis who was driving the blue Ford Granada. Jessica sat in the back of the car and watched the suburban landscape as it rose towards Harrow-on-the-Hill.

As the road to the Hill became steeper, Claude Henderson directed Lewis to turn the car into a close that contained modern town houses. Green patches of lawn, shaved to geometric neatness, formed a quilt with the precise flower beds, wet areas of concrete and paving stones. Lewis stopped outside the house Henderson indicated. As he did so, the front door opened and a woman carrying an umbrella came out and made for the car parked on the forecourt.

Henderson got out of the car and turned the collar of his raincoat up against the rain.

'Edith,' he called out and the woman turned from the red Cortina and made for Claude.

'What are you doing here?' she said as she glanced into the car.

162

'You know Captain Horne, but you haven't met Miss Crossley.'

'How do you do,' Mrs Henderson said and Jessica looked up at a plump, pretty woman with a smiling expression and rather a lot of make-up.

'We've come to collect one of my books.'

'Well, you'll have to find it yourself. They're all still in the tea chests. I'm going to my committee meeting and I'm late. Delighted to meet you Miss Crossley. Nice to see you once again, Captain Horne. Now I must go, Claude,' she said as she made for the Cortina again.

Henderson waved as she drove away.

'My books are in here,' he said as he opened the door to the garage and revealed tea chests stacked like children's building blocks in the gloomy interior. 'We've only just moved,' Claude said in an apologetic voice. 'We've been meaning to since the children grew up. Since we've been here I've had to keep my books out here until I can get enough shelves built. You'd be astonished at how much it's going to cost.'

He switched on a rather weak naked electric light and looked at the piled chests.

'Well, shall we begin?' Henderson said and each of them began to dip into a different box. It was tiring work. Eventually the rain stopped and Mrs Henderson returned from her meeting and brought them out some tea. Finally Jessica held a slim book out to Henderson.

'Is this it?'

Claude took it into his hands and turned to the twenty-ninth sonnet. He took a photostat of the title page of Lyte's manuscript and compared them.

'I think we've got it,' he said in an excited voice.

'Oh, sick I am to see you, will you never let me be?
You may be good for something but you are not good for me.
Oh, go where you are wanted, for you are not wanted here.'
And that was all the farewell when I parted from my dear.'

A Shropshire Lad
A. E. HOUSMAN

Chapter 8

James Fitzgerald D'Arcy placed the manuscript of Lyte's book on the mantelpiece in Charlie Mars's office and opened Claude Henderson's book of sonnets. As he read he lifted his steel-rimmed glasses and massaged the red indentations on each side of his nose with his thumb and forefinger. D'Arcy was one of those men so thin his clothes always seemed baggy on his fleshless frame. Dark red hair that contrasted with his chalky white complexion grew in a shock from his head and poked around the edges of his clothes so that Jessica could see the coarse reddish fringes at the cuffs and collar of his checked shirt.

'Well?' Charlie said and D'Arcy glanced up in surprise.

'Oh, yes, well,' he said in a soft Trinity College accent. 'I can't see that it should take us long now we have the key. Without it, of course, it would have been an impossibility.'

Charlie got up from the sofa and switched on the swan-necked brass reading lamp behind his leather chester-field.

'OK, Fitz. Press on,' he said. 'Burn the midnight oil until the task is done.'

D'Arcy left the room and Charlie turned to Jessica and Lewis.

'So the solution lay in Claude's garage?'

Lewis nodded.

'I got the impression his wife would have liked us to take all the books with us.' Charlie looked to Jessica.

'And how are you, young lady?' She smiled.

'Fine, but I could do with a bath. It's strange how grubby one feels after rooting around among old books all afternoon.'

Charlie thrust his hands in his pockets and looked down at his brogues before clearing his throat.

'Are you, er . . . comfortable at Lewis's flat?'

Jessica could see the question embarrassed him and she felt rather touched.

'Yes,' she said, and to put Claude's mind at rest, 'Captain Horne has been the perfect gentleman.'

'Good, good,' Charlie said in a relieved voice. 'I think it would still be dangerous for you to go to your own flat just for the time being.'

'In that case, I'd better get her home and give her a wash,' Lewis said with a cheerful smile.

Charlie was about to retort stiffly when he saw that Jessica was smiling as well, so he just gestured with both hands for them to leave his office.

*

'What's your favourite food?' Jessica asked as she walked beside Lewis towards Lamb's Conduit Street.

'Bacon and eggs,' he replied firmly. It had been his experience that any other reply to a woman invariably led to gastronomic experiences of the forgettable kind. 'Why do you ask?' he said as they came out of Montague Street and into Russell Square.

But Jessica quickly changed tack.

'I thought you might want us to stay in tonight so you could cook me your favourite meal,' she said in an offhand way as they waited for a gap in the evening traffic.

'I used to care about food,' he said. 'But then something happened to me a few years ago.'

Jessica linked her arm through his and as they walked beneath the trees in the square he remembered the couple in the Boulevard St Germain-des-Près.

'Tell me about it,' she said. Lewis shrugged dismissively.

'I was captured by Bedouin tribesmen and they pulled out my tastebuds one by one because I wouldn't talk.'

'Why wouldn't you talk?'

'Because I didn't know the answers to their questions.'

'What were they asking you?' He shrugged once more.

'Big stuff – what's the meaning of life, does God exist, that sort of thing. I tried telling them the position and strength of our troops but they weren't interested.'

'How did you escape?'

'Some friends rode up in a pink Landrover and rescued me.'

'Are you sure it wasn't a pink elephant?'

'It might have been,' he said cheerfully. 'Frankly I was too tired to notice.'

After a few minutes' walk they reached Lamb's Conduit Street and Lewis unlocked his front door. They crossed the dim marble-floored hallway and climbed the stairs to his flat. Inside the doorway was a collection of cases: Jessica's clothes from her own apartment had arrived. Someone from Gower Street had packed them up and delivered them earlier in the day.

'I don't suppose they allow you an iron in the maximum security wing,' Jessica said as she looked around at her bleak surroundings.

'As a matter of fact, soldiers are pretty good at that sort of thing,' Lewis said as he pulled open a cupboard to reveal an ironing board.

'Excellent,' she said. 'When I'm clean again I shall press some of my frillies.'

Lewis was still laughing when there was a knock on his door. He raised his eyebrows to Jessica as he crossed the room to answer it. When he opened the door, Hanna was standing there.

'Lewis, I just wanted to . . .' Her voice trailed away when she saw Jessica. 'I'm so sorry,' she said quickly. 'I didn't realise you were with someone. I met Janet outside and she let me in. Forgive me for the intrusion.'

She started to leave and Lewis shut the door before she could back out.

'Hanna Pearce, can I introduce a colleague of mine, Jessica Crossley.'

The two women shook hands and exchanged glances that chilled the air around them.

'I won't interrupt you as you're working,' Hanna said in a sweetly frosty voice. 'What I had to say wasn't important.'

'Can I leave you alone for a while?' Jessica said with an edgy politeness that equalled Hanna's forced tone. Lewis decided to be assertive.

'Jessica, will you wait here for a while? I would like to talk to Hanna.'

'Of course,' she said. 'Do you mind if I take a shower?'

'Please do,' he replied as he avoided Hanna's eyes and opened the door to lead her out of the flat.

'There's no need for this,' she said as they reached the street. 'Don't let me keep you from your guest. What I had to say wasn't important.'

Lewis took her by the elbow without speaking and propelled her in the direction of The Lamb.

Once inside the bar, he glanced around and was glad to see it wasn't too crowded. He guided Hanna to a table and stood against one of the engraved glass partitions that divided the bars until he was served. Placing a glass of white wine in front of Hanna he took a swallow from the large whisky he had bought for himself.

Lewis looked at her. She was wearing a cheap raincoat tied at the waist with a belt and her hair was drawn back in a tight bun; she wore no make-up. Any other woman would have put a paper bag over her head rather than be seen to such effect. But Hanna looked marvellous. Lewis wanted to reach out and touch her.

'Where did you get the coat?' he asked instead.

Hanna glanced down at the sleeve in a distracted way as if she were seeing it for the first time.

'Oh, it belongs to one of the nurses. I borrowed it.'

He nodded and sipped some more whisky.

'I borrowed one the other day as well,' he said. 'I'm a better borrower than you. Mine is much more expensive.'

Hanna looked at the untouched wine before her then up into Lewis's eyes.

'Jessica Crossley – you say she's a colleague but I got the impression there's more to it than that. Am I right?'

Lewis looked at the engraved glass and mahogany surroundings of the pub. In a corner he could see Roland Perth drinking with a couple of youngish people Lewis took to be actors. Roland was scrupulously avoiding them.

'Well, is there more?'

Lewis looked at her as he drank some of his whisky.

'I have been faithful to you, Cynara, after my fashion,' he said.

'What does that mean?' Hanna said.

Lewis shrugged. 'I forgot you didn't read many romantic poets at Harvard Medical School.'

'You're right,' Hanna said. 'At the end of the day we could just about manage a cup of coffee and a Simon and Garfunkel record. Who was Cynara?'

'A girl that a poet called Ernest Dowson wrote about.'

'What about this other girl, Miss Crossley?' Hanna said in a gentler voice.

'That really depends on you, Hanna,' he said. 'I don't want anyone else, but if I can't have you . . . he shrugged. 'I'm a soldier not a monk.'

'You don't have to be either,' she said as she twirled the glass by its stem.

'Yes I do,' he said with conviction. 'I know that now. You caused me to give it the deepest consideration and it is what I have to do.'

'You've got to do what you've got to do?' Hanna said bitterly.

'Just like John Wayne.'

Lewis sighed. 'Look, I've tried to explain to you before, my work is as much a vocation to me as your being a doctor is to you. We have to hold the line. If we had the choice we would prefer to serve on a battlefield where we could wear uniforms, but the opposition have chosen the streets of our cities.'

Hanna pushed away the glass of wine and clasped her hands tightly together.

'We're not getting anywhere, are we?' He shook his head.

'Why did you want to see me?' he asked. She shrugged.

'I've got a couple of days off. I thought we might spend some time together.'

'What about your cousin?' Lewis said with an edge to his voice.

Hanna sat back with her hands in the pockets of the cheap raincoat so that her shoulders were hunched.

'I've known him all my life. I love him all right, the way I love the Chrysler Building. So how about it? A little time out of war?'

'I can't, Hanna,' he said sadly. 'I'm in the middle of a job.'

She got up and tightened the belt of her raincoat.

'And no one else can do it for you,' she said bitterly.

'You know better than that.'

'Yes,' she said in the same tone, 'I saw *High Noon*.'

'That was Gary Cooper, not John Wayne, and the girl came back to him.'

'Sometimes I wish life was like the movies,' Hanna muttered as they walked to the door. They stood in Lamb's Conduit Street avoiding each other's gaze. There was nothing more to say.

'Goodbye,' Hanna said finally, then she walked away with her head lowered, as if defeated.

*

Lewis crossed the street slowly and paused for a while before he let himself into the flats. As he passed his sister's door, he noticed it was ajar and she called out to him. He found Janet and Jessica in the kitchen seated at the scrubbed pine table drinking mugs of coffee. The tortoiseshell cat sat on top of the refrigerator and swished its tail at him as he entered. The cat was normally friendly, then he remembered it was female. The only thing with a friendly face in the room was a Donald Duck clock that grinned at him from the Welsh dresser.

'Would you like some coffee, Lulu?' his sister said in a voice that was notably lacking in warmth.

'No thanks,' he replied warily.

Janet sat with her elbows on the table and raised the mug of coffee to her mouth with both hands. Jessica did the same. Without looking at him Janet spoke.

'I've invited Jessica to stay here while she's away from her own flat. It's more convenient for a woman than your barrack-room upstairs.'

Lewis began to scent a conspiracy.

'If that's what you want. Fine,' he said in a non-committal voice.

'I think I'll go and get my things together now,' Jessica said as she swiftly put down her cup of coffee and edged past Lewis and out of the flat.

Lewis reached across the table and took her coffee mug.

172

The warm sweet drink washed the taste of whisky from his mouth.

'How did this piece of solidarity come about?' he asked as the cat swished her tail at him once more.

'You can be very hard on women, Lulu,' Janet said in a softer voice. He shrugged.

'I don't mean to, Jan. You know I don't like hurting people. But I expect them to know their own minds.'

'That's a bit insensitive, isn't it? That girl has had a deep shock recently, the equivalent of the death of a husband, she meets you and you show her affection. She returns that affection and then she discovers that you're simply consoling yourself with her because you're in love with someone unobtainable. How do you expect her to feel?'

He nodded bleakly, sipped his coffee and looked into the smiling face of Donald Duck. Janet got up and stood beside him. She slid her arm through his and rested her head on his shoulder.

'I'm sorry, Lulu. I don't mean to nag.'

'No, you're right,' he said with a light sigh. 'I think I'll push off for the rest of the evening. It'll give you both a chance to get settled.'

Janet squeezed his arm and he kissed the top of her head before letting himself out of the flat. Without thinking, he knew where he was going. Since he was a small child, Lewis had possessed a great gift. However painful life became, he could recover with books. Libraries to Lewis had become dressing stations where he knew his wounds would be healed. He headed for the British Museum Reading Room until he realised the time. Pausing for a moment he suddenly remembered a book in Charlie's office.

The door from the street was locked when he arrived as Sergeant Major Watts had long gone off duty.

He rang the bell and after a while George Ward came and opened the door. Lewis climbed the stairs through the half-deserted building and looked down to a line of light that shone beneath the door. He knocked and entered. Charlie glanced up from the desk where he was writing.

'Hello. I thought you were long gone?' Charlie knew Lewis as well as anyone. He could sense that all was not well.

'I saw a book earlier about the Battle of Naseby. Is it any good?'

Charlie leaned back in his chair and clasped his hands behind his head to ease the muscles in his back.

'Excellent,' he said.

'May I borrow it?'

Charlie waved to the pile of books on the mantelpiece.

'Of course, help yourself.' Lewis looked for a moment and found the book.

'I wouldn't mind a whisky,' Charlie said. 'Would you care to join me?'

Lewis reached down into the cupboard next to the fireplace and produced the bottle of malt and two cut-glass tumblers. He poured two measures, placed one on the desk in front of Charlie and took the other and the book to the chesterfield. Within moments both men were absorbed in their work. After a couple of hours, Charlie yawned as he dotted the last sentence he was going to write that night.

He screwed the top onto his old fountain pen, flipped shut the spiral-bound exercise book he had been writing in and laid his spectacles on top of it. Lewis glanced up from his book and Charlie looked at his gold pocket watch.

'Ten thirty-five. Do you fancy a bite of supper at Berto-relli's?'

'Suits me,' Lewis said as he shut the book on his lap.

'Are you going to take that with you?' Charlie asked, indicating the book Lewis held.

'Yes, if you don't mind.'

'Bring it here,' Charlie commanded and, unscrewing his fountain pen again, he took the book and wrote C. A. Mars in a legible hand in the fly leaf. Charlie let Lewis go first as he switched out the lights. Before he turned off the last, he picked up a telephone hand-set on the coffee table.

'George? Mars here. I'm going now,' he said to the duty officer. He locked the door behind him and both of them

174

walked the length of the corridor with the measured tread of those who have known a long day.

But when they reached the hallway, D'Arcy was waiting for them. 'We've cracked it,' he said in an excited voice. He held up a bundle of printout paper. 'It's all here. Fascinating stuff.'

Charlie took the wad of paper and strode purposefully into the Duty Room. Penny Rose and George Ward looked up startled as they entered.

'You're here late, Penny,' Charlie said in a preoccupied voice. 'Do you think you can get us some coffee?'

'Yes, of course, sir,' she said and Lewis watched her leave the room, her face glowing with embarrassment. George Ward tried a weak smile as Lewis sat down at the desk next to Charlie and took the first sheet of printout paper from Charlie's hand. Together they began to read.

'I am Jack Lyte, an Englishman and a socialist. Many would say the two terms are incompatible but I am the proof that this is not so. Those aspects of England that have moved poets, musicians and artists, have also made their mark on me. I bear the same stamp upon my soul. The kindness, courage and endurance of the people set the standards I measure my actions by and provide me with the source of my dignity and my pride. The history that formed the countryside, the towns and the character of the English formed me and other socialists like me. Ours is not a mystical belief; indeed, the very simplicity of our argument is such that it must be dealt with by the most devious type of sophistry. For who can face the relentless logic of an idea which states: in a world of material abundance where nature has provided men with a dazzling array of skills, from simple strength to minds that can calculate the distance between the stars, why should some have more than they could ever need if they were to live for a thousand years yet others suffer for lack of care?

'I gave my life to overcome those who would maintain such inequalities and I paid a terrible price. I chose exile from my country and the people whom

I loved and I would do so again even though I look back upon a life of bitter failure.

'I choose these words with care because I have seen and experienced the horror that good men and women are capable of when they follow the cold dictates of their minds. Socialists of my generation looked at the brutalities visited upon the lives of those least able to defend themselves and we decided to support a crucial decision which has almost ruined our cause. We agreed to fight fire with fire, and so the terrible philosophy was born: the end justifies the means.

'Now mankind has learned if human beings set about putting the world to rights by using terror, repression and cruelty, these tools will eventually pervert the user. In the beginning we convinced ourselves that we acted with the detachment of the surgeon where the swift cut of the scalpel will remove a malignant growth or ease a swollen abscess and a healthy life will quickly be restored to the patient.

'But instead, we practitioners found we were not in a hospital but an abattoir and the scalpel had become an axe to slaughter those who would not tread the ordained path of righteousness. Faith in one's fellow human beings is replaced by an implacable hatred for those who were seen to be tainted by thoughts that deviate from a narrow set of slogans.

'Those who dared to oppose were crushed lest they contaminated the innocents who were too unworldly to cope with the freedom of choice between ideas. Beset by such conditions the only reality becomes raw, naked power and the nightmare has reached full circle.

'Liberator becomes oppressor, freedom the chains of servitude. In a sense, this testament is to recall a journey, not the physical distances I endured but the long odyssey of my spirit.

'It began in the simplicity of my young manhood, through the agony of those dark, bitter years when I lost my faith and entered a wilderness of despair to the tranquillity I have found, at least, as I grow closer to death.

'The cause of my present peace of mind was not a Road to Damascus-like conversion, but the teaching of Professor Mikhail Andreyovich Chernovensky of the Academy of Soviet Sciences who died some time ago without leaving any close family and therefore can be named as a friend without fear of reprisal being visited upon those whom he loved. He taught me the meaning of evolution and in doing so pointed out that the world was in reality a time machine where those of us born in the advanced nations could visit any period of the past. So, if we wished to see life in the Stone Age we could go to the last of the aborigines in Australia.

'Places in Central Asia had not changed since medieval times and parts of China had not yet experienced the Industrial Revolution. In this way he demonstrated to me the brevity of mankind's struggle towards civilisation and the lapses into barbarity that accompany any seeming advancement. According to the Professor, we had so recently emerged from the dark, primitive forest it was folly to expect we were ready to embrace the philosophy of saints. He taught me that it would be centuries, maybe even thousands of years before the human race would be ready for the responsibility socialism demanded of everyone. Nonetheless, he had faith.

'His favourite quotation was from Chesterton: "If a black seed in the earth can grow into something as beautiful as a rose, what might not man's heart become on its long journey to the stars?" He believed wonderful things would be achieved, but not with the whip and the gun.

'With what he had taught me I thought again of England and I reached the conclusion that despite the inequalities that still existed there, democracy gave it a character that would vanish if that system was subverted by communism. Therefore I will tell my story and I hope with all my heart I will undo some of the harm I helped to engender.

'In the November of 1942 I was a war correspondent

attached to the First Guards Army before Stalingrad.
We were about to attack the Germans and the forces
we had amassed were awesome. Half a million men,
nine hundred of the new T34 tanks, one thousand
attack planes and a fantastic mass of artillery. I had
a great sense that I was about to see history made and
I felt a bitter disappointment when I received orders
from the political commissar of my division to
report to Moscow immediately.

'Most journeys are difficult in war time, and mine
was no exception, but eventually I reported to
Headquarters in Moscow as ordered and was
instructed by General Vladimirovich to go to an
address on Gorky Street and report to Oleg
Nikolayev. I made my way there and found that the
building was an enormous townhouse once owned by
a member of the Imperial family.

'A secretary took me to a magnificent hall that
had obviously once been a ballroom. The ceiling
was covered in a delicate eighteenth-century mural
and a tracery of gilding ran across the walls above
great rococo mirrors. The floor was sprung and highly
polished. In one corner, seated at a trestle table and
wearing a huge overcoat with a fur collar, was the
largest human being I have ever seen.

'He had a black beard that enveloped most of his
face and blue eyes that really did seem to twinkle
as he took my hand in his great pawlike grip. I am
above average height and in my greatcoat and the tall
fur hat I wore normally presented an imposing figure.
Oleg Nikolayev dwarfed me. He gestured to a chair
opposite his own and breathed heavily for a few
moments so that plumes of steam emitted from his
mouth into the icy air.

'Suddenly, he bellowed "Tania" in a voice that
sounded as loud as an artillery barrage, and a beautiful
woman came into the room. She wore tiny boots and
a silver fox fur coat and hat. Together they looked
like a pair who might perform some extraordinary
act at the Moscow State Theatre. "Take notes," he said
to her as he lit the long black cigar he held clamped

178

between his teeth. "Where are you from, Comrade?" he said in his booming voice.

"'England,' I said in what I suppose was a puzzled tone. He flicked ash onto the polished floor.

"'Be more specific, Comrade.'

"'I was born and brought up in Acton, a suburb in west London.'

"'Describe it to me,' he said in a pleasant enough voice. I thought for a while and then began.

"'There is no equivalent in Russia to the London suburbs. Throughout the last century the city grew with bewildering speed and it goes on to this day. Places I knew as countryside when I was a boy are now part of greater London. Once Acton was a village, so like other suburbs it has its own character.'

"'But there are similarities?' he said.

"'Oh, yes,' I replied. 'London grows in rough, concentric circles: each suburb usually contains a High Street of shops which are often part of the same monopolistic group, a recreation park and rows of houses inhabited by workers, petit bourgeoisie or professional people. The ruling classes do not live there.'

'Nikolayev looked up at the prancing nymphs on the ceiling and exhaled a mixture of frozen breath and Georgian tobacco. "Comrade, describe a collection of such shops and their function."

'I thought for a moment and then began as Tania wrote rapidly in a large notebook.

"'A public house, that is a premises licensed to sell beer, wine and spirits . . ." I continued for some time describing the flight of shops I had visited so often with my mother when I was a child. When Nikolayev stubbed out his third cigar, he held up his hand to stop me and reached into the pocket of his greatcoat and produced a bottle.

'He unscrewed the top and was about to swallow when instead he held it out to me. I took it as my body was numb with cold and swallowed a good mouthful. I had expected vodka, but the bottle contained a very good brandy. He took a long pull himself and passed it on to Tania.

'"You have an artist's eye for detail, my friend. I think our venture will be a success." He turned to Tania. "Bring the telephone and get me that clown in supplies."

'She left the ballroom and moments later returned with a military field telephone that snaked a cable behind it. After a few moments she made her connection and handed the instrument to Nikolayev. He spoke in a surprisingly gentle voice even though his words were full of dreadful menace.

'"My dear fellow. This is Nikolayev at Gorky Street. I must tell you my balls are a deep blue colour because of the freezing temperature here. At eight o'clock tomorrow morning Comrade General Beria is due to tour these premises. If my balls are still blue, I shall ask him for yours and I can guarantee he will give them to me. Do I make myself clear? Excellent."

'He replaced the receiver and smiled at me.

'"Any questions?" he said in the same pleasant voice.

'"What is this work going to be?" I asked.

'Nikolayev gestured across the polished expanse in front of him.

'"We are going to make sure you are not homesick, Comrade. We are going to build you a little Acton here in Gorky Street."

*

'He was as good as his word. While the greatest struggle in history took place a few hundred miles to the west we painstakingly constructed a beautiful scale model of a tiny piece of England. Researchers, artists and craftsmen worked with devotion for month after month until I finally, I could walk, Gulliver-like, once again down a street where the battlements of St Mary's Church now only reached to my chest.

'All the details were exquisite. The perfection of

the work was such that it fascinated everyone who came to see it, so that we had grown used to a stream of important visitors. Eventually, it was completed. Oleg Nikolayev and I remained behind that night and we stood looking down at my childhood memories. He passed the brandy to me once again.

'"Here's to the second stage," he said when he took the bottle and raised it to his lips.

'The following morning, Nikolayev and Tania took me to another part of the building on Gorky Street. I assumed it had once been a library because of the empty bookshelves that lined the walls, but the books had been removed along with the rest of the furniture.

'All that was left were some delicately carved chairs that were chipped and battered. Seated upon them was a collection of people who had clearly seen hard times. They coughed and shuffled as they looked around the room and at each other.

'I stood with Nikolayev and Tania for some time before the seated crowd and gradually I came to realise what they all had in common. At first some of them began tentative conversations with each other in Russian, and then gradually they all began to speak English and I could tell from the variety of accents that they came from all parts of the British Isles.

'"Ladies and gentlemen," Nikolayev began, "until now you have pursued a variety of careers and professions, but each of you has become a member of the party and each is consequently dedicated to world revolution. Now we call upon you to take up a new challenge." He turned to me with a gesture. "Your fellow countryman, Jack Lyte, is going to be in charge of turning you into a nation of shopkeepers."

'And so our new work began. While the Soviet forces smashed the Wehrmacht back into Germany we curious band laboured to make ourselves familiar with the lives and habits of the sort of people who inhabited the original buildings we had constructed so skilfully in miniature. At night, after supper, by way of recreation, we would watch the films that were on release in Britain at that time and listen to the radio and read the newspapers, so we remained familiar with life in the country we had once called home.

'Then in the spring of 1945 when we knew the Red Army was poised to cross the river Oder and fight the last battle, we were all suddenly transported. Nikolayev brought me back to the ballroom before we departed and I found Tania appropriately standing by the model of "The Six Bells" public house.

'"One last drink," Nikolayev said. "Tania must go on a long journey." Silently we raised our glasses and toasted the happy highways I had once known.

'For five disorientating days we were transported across huge distances in sealed railway compartments or covered trucks until we were finally unloaded at our destination.

'It was a massive tract of land cordoned off by a high, electrified barbed wire fence and guarded with dogs and watchtowers. We guessed that it was somewhere in Northern Europe and close to the sea by the plants and birds we observed. Within this giant compound was a town of pre-fabricated wooden cabins laid out with military precision and next to that township – the reason for all our training – a full-scale version of the model we had built in Moscow.

'Obviously additional information had been obtained, as it went far beyond my original descriptions to include alterations that had taken place in the war years. Our purpose was now quite clear. We were to train agents who were then to be infiltrated into Britain.

'The system from the beginning was extraordinarily effective. No amount of classroom theory can replace practical example and it was astonishing how oddly people will behave in a country if they have not learned her customs by example and observation.

'I will not attempt to describe those people that we trained. Most of them were mature adults and would, by now, be either dead or too old to be of any further harm, but believe me, for many years they were among you. As far as we know, no one was ever captured – such was the effectiveness of our enterprise. And it must be remembered the incredible lengths my masters went to in creating that playground. Even the weather was defied.

'Despite the severity of the winter, the High Street kept going as special underground heating equipment had been installed and a mass of Russian soldiers would arrive after any severe snowfall to excavate us from snowdrifts. Although the High Street was as accurate as could be created by all who worked there, one element was missing. No children ever visited; we lived in a world populated only by adults. Then, in the summer of 1946, this too was put right.

'Nikolayev called me to the hut he used as his quarters late one afternoon and invited me to sit down in one of the armchairs he had managed to obtain for himself.

'"I have a surprise for you," he said with a curious smile on his face. He called out: "Bring him in," and instantly a guard appeared at the door with a boy whom I judged to be about thirteen.

'"Jack Lyte, I would like to introduce John Smith."

'I gazed at him with deep surprise for a few moments, but not because of anything odd about his appearance; on the contrary it was the familiarity that caused my reaction. John Smith was wearing a uniform identical to the one I had worn at his age. It denoted him as a pupil of Acton Grammar School for Boys and the sight of those baggy, woollen flannel trousers and the blazer and cap touched my memory once again.

'The boy held out his hand to me and doffed his cap with the other.

'"How do you do, sir," he said with a slight bow and the trace of a German accent.

'"I want you to work with him as much as you can, Jack," Nikolayev said to me. "He has a natural ability for languages but I want his English accent to be perfect."

'I looked closely at the boy. He had hair the colour of flax and his fair complexion was as fresh as a girl's but there was something unchildlike about the features, a look around the eyes that gave the impression of a loss of innocence. And there was something else, a slight lopsidedness. I looked for the cause and I realised that the lobe of his left ear was missing.

'The boy came with me to the shop that I ran as my part of the project. It was a newsagent, tobacconist and confectioner's. When he saw the rows of sweet jars and boxes of chocolates his face took on a longing expression. I asked him if he would like something and he produced a ration book from his satchel and held it out to me without speaking.

'"What would you like, John?" I asked.

'"Chocolate, please."

'I waved away the ration book and handed him a bar of Cadbury's. He began to put it carefully into his satchel.

'"You can eat it now, John. We have plenty more."

'He looked at me with disbelief and then suspicion. When he realised I was serious he broke a piece off the bar and chewed it very slowly. Then he looked around the shop. He studied the magazines, comics and newspapers laid out on the counter, the display of greetings cards and the racks of paperbacks.

'Then he came back to the counter and, ignoring the comics, took a copy of the *News Chronicle* and began to read. He was behaving more like an adult of forty than a boy of thirteen.

'From then on, each day after he had finished his schooling in a part of the camp I was not permitted to visit, he would come to the shop and together we would read the papers and discuss their contents and what parts of them puzzled him.

'At first, his questions were about aspects of Britain

but gradually, as he became more familiar with the way of life through his prodigious reading, the questions became more abstract and even philosophical and I began to understand for the first time something of the rewards of teaching.

'The days passed pleasantly enough, and the months quickly, but after a few years I found the routine boring and I applied to the head of my section, the man who had replaced Nikolayev in the early fifties, for permission to return to Moscow and take up my work as a writer once more.

'The man, who was as drab and boring as Nikolayev had been flamboyant and extrovert, said he would forward my request and a few days later he coldly informed me that my present work was considered to be the utmost importance by Moscow Centre and I was to put out of my mind any thought of leaving the camp until I was ordered to do so. With this decision passed on me like a sentence, I began to settle into an undemanding way of life so that I hardly noticed that I had passed from young manhood into early middle age.

'John Smith also altered. He lost some of his boyhood shyness and became quite outgoing. He developed an easy, bantering style of conversation but when he was about sixteen, he had started to go away for long periods – sometimes months on end – and I soon realised how much I missed his company.

'The days passed each like any other, and the years just seemed to melt away as they do when your life enters a prolonged period of undemanding routine. John Smith and I had developed the kind of relationship that could be described as uncle and nephew. I say this with care because in those years I realised that a part of me was missing. I did not possess the capability to love as other people did, therefore the relationship I had with the boy, or youth as he now was, did not develop into a father and son bond.

'Sometimes I felt he may have wished for that dimension in our attitudes towards each other, but I was unable to supply the necessary affection. Which was as well, because in the summer of 1953 John Smith disappeared from the camp and I did not see him again for thirty years.

'My own life only had one more chapter of interest. In 1956 I was still in exile at the camp when I was suddenly summoned to Moscow. Despite the incredible imperialist posturing of Britain and France over the seizure of the Suez Canal by Colonel Nasser, the Russian invasion of Hungary had been a serious setback for Soviet world relations.

'I was called back and told by Moscow Centre that I was to go to Budapest immediately and begin a series of articles extolling the virtues of the Red Army. I was to stress that it had come to assist the gallant government and people of freedom-loving Hungary in their struggle against the fascist counter-revolutionaries and their plutocratic accomplices from the so-called democracies. It was a nightmare.

'Ordinary men and women were actually on the streets of Budapest fighting with their bare hands against a modern army. My dream had come full circle. From my years of reading the English newspapers I could see that although there were massive faults in the country of my birth, it did not need tanks to keep order. I decided that I would escape to Austria and was about to do so when I was wounded in the street fighting.

'With perfect irony I came to in a hospital bed in Moscow where I was fêted as a hero! My wounds were quite bad and I was some years recovering from them, and in that period I met my dear friend, Professor Chernovensky, who began my period of true education. At last, this friendship brought me the tranquillity I had hoped for. Then I began to write this memoir and there seemed to be a small purpose to my life.

'I had at first intended it to be a polemical work but it must serve another purpose.

'In the September of 1984, I attended a performance

of the ballet "Icarus" at the Hall of the Praesidium
inside the walls of The Kremlin. As usual the theatre
was packed and before the ballet began I was
suddenly surprised to hear "God Save The Queen"
being played. Like the rest of the audience I looked
up to the VIP boxes to see who warranted the honour
and saw the British Foreign Secretary standing to
attention with several members of his entourage.

'You may be able to guess how I felt when I saw a
familiar figure standing beside him and looking every
inch an English gentleman. It was, of course, John
Smith.'

The mortal sickness of mind
Too unhappy to be kind.
Undone with misery, all they can
Is to hate their fellow man;
And till they drop they needs must still
Look at you and wish you ill.

A Shropshire Lad
A. E. HOUSMAN

Chapter Nine

The squat, stubby shape of a barge ploughing its way down river towards Gravesend caught Lewis's attention for a moment. He turned from Charlie Mars who sat with him in the back of the duty car as they cruised along Chelsea Embankment and watched as it cut a swathe through the dark waters. The harsh light from the sodium street lamps seemed to emphasise the bleakness of the empty road ahead and gave the foliage of the trees they passed beneath an artificial greenness.

There were no pedestrians to be seen. It was as if a curfew had cleared the streets of life. Lewis looked ahead where he could just see the glow in the sky from the Albert Bridge where it blazed like a giant fairground ride with the thousands of lights that studded its superstructure.

Usually he enjoyed the dazzling vulgarity it brought to this part of London. Somehow it was right that down-to-earth Battersea should be linked by this extraordinary umbilical cord to the smart raciness of Chelsea, but tonight it did nothing to cheer him. Instead it served only to contrast sadly with the melancholy purpose of their journey.

Charlie Mars shifted slightly in his seat and Lewis glanced at his profile. Charlie's head was sunk into his chest and his eyes were hooded in meditation.

George Ward was driving and as he swung out to overtake a cruising taxi, Charlie's head lifted with the sideways movement of the car.

'Were you and Renfrew close friends?' Lewis asked in a casual voice.

Charlie thought carefully about the question, then he raised his right hand palm upwards and let it fall into his lap again.

'Not what you would call close when I come to think

191

about it. I suppose we confuse the length of time we know somebody with the depth of feeling we have for them. Rather like unhappy marriages. But we saw quite a lot of one another when we were young. Sybil and Claire were school friends. They were also the two prettiest girls at Lady Margaret Hall.' Charlie smiled for a moment. 'But I must add in all honesty that the competition was not very fierce.'

'I don't suppose there can be any doubt that it's Renfrew, can there?' Lewis asked.

Charlie wiped his face with his hand before he replied with a shake of his head.

'He came up to Oxford on a good scholarship to read modern languages in 1953. We were both freshers. He'd gone to a grammar school in west London but his parents had been dead for some years. He always tended to be vague about his childhood and could be rather sardonic with us public schoolboys. I remember his saying we were all retarded by boarding school. He seemed rather sophisticated to all of us. No one had his self-assurance. Sybil and I took Claire to a party and she seemed to fall in love with him instantly.'

Lewis shrugged.

'There doesn't seem an enormous amount of evidence. And all of it is circumstantial. Surely there must be others with the same approximate dates? It doesn't sound all that conclusive.'

Charlie nodded.

'There *are* others with the same dates, but the clincher is the ears. I remember Sybil and Claire talking about him and Claire told her that he'd had plastic surgery on them. They were laughing because Sybil thought she meant he'd lost one of the lobes in an army accident and they had trimmed them both to match. She also said something rather shocking about another part of his anatomy and how she was glad that hadn't been trimmed.' Charlie smiled again. 'In those days I didn't quite appreciate how basic women can be about life.'

They passed the Albert Bridge and Charlie leaned forward. 'Over here on the right, George,' he said and Ward turned across the empty street and double parked at the top end of Cheyne Walk. They were in front of a narrow Georgian house with age-blackened brickwork, a bright red door and a lacework of iron railings. Lights were on downstairs. Charlie stopped for a moment and seemed to brace himself before he rang the bell. They heard a voice call: 'I'll get it, Edna.'

After a brief wait the door was opened by a thin, drably-dressed woman who seemed to be in late middle age. Lewis could see from her bone structure that she had once been beautiful but now her face was harsh and angular. Her eyes were sad and the deep creases each side of her mouth emphasised the air of melancholy she had about her.

'Hello, Claire,' Charlie said in a quiet voice.

She peered at him for a moment and then her face softened into an open smile.

'Charlie,' she said and Lewis could hear the warmth in her greeting. 'How lovely to see you. How are Sybil and the girls?' She gestured for them to come into the hallway.

'They're fine, Claire. I don't think you know Mr Horne.'

'No I don't. How do you do, Mr Horne.' She turned and shook hands and Lewis was suddenly aware of her cold, delicate hand. It was as if he could feel the bones through the thin flesh.

She led them along the narrow hallway past a pair of carved and gilded eighteenth-century mirrors and into a living room that was furnished and decorated with exquisite taste. Yet there was an air of neglect and dowdiness about the room as if the people who lived there had given up caring a long time ago.

'I see you still have all your father's furniture,' Charlie said. She looked around the room.

'Yes, I suppose it must be worth a lot of money these days,' she said in a disinterested voice.

Charlie looked at a secretaire that was delicately inlaid with fruit woods and contemplated that it had been worth a lot of money in any day.

'It's some time since you were last here, Charlie,' Claire said and he made a mental calculation.

'Before the girls were born.'

'Good heavens,' she said sadly. 'And I understand

they're both up at Oxford now. Sybil wrote to me some time ago.' Charlie nodded.

'Yes. At my old college; they take girls now. Oxford has certainly changed.'

She looked around the room for a moment. 'Like everything else.'

'Claire, we've come about Paul,' Charlie said gently, and she smiled a little bitterly.

'I didn't think I was the purpose of your visit, Charlie.' She rang a bell next to the fireplace and an ancient maid, in a black and white uniform that must have been made in the Thirties, came into the room. Charlie could see that she had not changed at all in the twenty years that had passed since last he saw her. 'Is Mr Renfrew at home, Edna?'

'Yes, Miss Claire.'

'Thank you. I won't need anything else tonight.'

Edna opened the door. 'I'll go up when you've gone to bed.'

During this exchange Charlie and Lewis stood on the rug before the fireplace, and looked round rather awkwardly at their surroundings.

'Won't you sit down?' Claire still spoke warmly, despite the purpose of their visit, and they sat side by side on a faded silk-covered sofa.

'Do you mind if we ask you a few questions about Paul?' Charlie said and Claire sat upright in an armchair that matched the sofa, as if steeling herself for an interrogation.

'I'm afraid I won't be much help. Paul and I are virtual strangers these days.' She fluttered her hands for a moment. 'What am I saying, these days? We haven't lived together as man and wife for many, many years.'

She turned her face from them and Lewis could feel an almost tangible sadness.

'Do you know much about his movements?' Charlie asked and Claire shook her head.

'We lead completely separate lives. He comes and goes as he pleases.'

'Does he go out a lot in the evenings, Mrs Renfrew?' Lewis asked and she studied him before she replied.

'According to Edna, he's out most evenings.'

Charlie folded his arms across his chest and cocked his head to one side.

'How long has this state of affairs existed, Claire?' She shrugged.

'I can't really remember. He's so charming to people, they have no idea how cold he can be. Indifference from someone you love is a cruel thing to bear.' She paused for a moment and then went on. 'It has made an old woman of me, Charlie.'

'Why didn't you get a divorce?' Charlie asked gently.

Claire looked at him with a sudden stiffening of pride.

'Three of my ancestors went to the stake for the sake of our faith, Charlie. I cannot deny my whole existence for the sake of expediency. Besides, I have had the love of my life. It took place in the summer of 1953.'

'Why do you think he didn't leave you if he was so indifferent?' Lewis asked.

'I can only imagine it's my money. He has acquired expensive tastes, you know. Not of the self-indulgent kind but his stamp collection is apparently exceptional. It seems such a silly thing to do for a grown man, sticking enormously expensive little pieces of paper in a book.'

But a good way of easily transporting a large sum of money around the world, Lewis thought as he looked into a far corner of the room where he noticed a patch of damp on the ceiling and wall. It had been years since the room had been decorated. It wasn't dirty, but the neglect showed in the touches of shabbiness marring the genteel grandeur; the worn edge of a carpet and the fabric faded by sunshine.

Charlie cleared his throat and looked down at his hands which he had clasped between his knees.

'Did he ever have any visitors here?'

She shook her head.

'No one has come for a long time, Charlie. The atmosphere is hardly conducive to encouraging a full social life, is it, Mr Horne?'

Lewis was surprised she had clearly been observing him so acutely as he had studied the room and its owner.

'I couldn't say, Mrs Renfrew,' he replied.

The atmosphere was oppressive. It was strange how a house absorbed the personalities of the people who lived in it. As if the very walls could reflect the emotions that the occupants had spent within them. He had known of the effect since childhood and had passed miserable nights in houses where there was a wrongness about the rooms. He often wondered whether people who saw ghosts had a similar but greater sensitivity to their surroundings. Lewis was beginning to hate this house and he looked forward to their departure.

Claire interrupted his reverie. 'Why are you asking all these questions, Charlie? What do you want with him? Is he in some kind of trouble?'

'We think so, yes.'

'What has he done?'

'It's to do with security. That's what I do now,' Charlie said.

She nodded again.

'I'd heard that it was something to do with that, your job, I mean. Are you saying Paul is a traitor?'

Charlie shook his head.

'No, we couldn't say he is a traitor, but he is in trouble.'

She sighed and looked distractedly around the room for a moment.

'I can't say that I feel anything about it. This thing he's done, it has something to do with betrayal?'

Charlie paused. 'It could have.'

Claire looked around the room again.

'Yes,' she said, her voice suddenly full of bitterness. 'He's an expert on betrayal.'

Lewis and Charlie rose to their feet, signalling an end to the interview.

'Can you tell us where he is?' Charlie said.

She sat stiff-backed in the chair and looked at them.

'His rooms are on the second floor, on the right at the top of the stairs. Forgive me if I don't come up and show you the way. I haven't been welcome there for some years.'

As they were about to leave, Charlie stopped.

'Was Paul a Catholic when you met him?'

'Oh, yes,' she said without hesitation. 'From the cradle.

It meant little to him though and he stopped all pretension of following the faith after a few years, but he often told me how pious his mother had been.'

Charlie nodded. 'Odd he never mentioned it before he met you.'

'I don't suppose it meant anything to him. Catholics tend to be undemonstrative about their faith when they are with Protestants. Passionate convictions are considered rather un-English. Strange, isn't it? My family fought against the Norman invasion yet by practising the religion of my ancestors I can be made to feel foreign.' She stood up and showed them to the door.

Awkwardly, they made their way out of the room and climbed the flights of stairs to the second floor. This part of the house had clearly been remodelled to suit quite another taste. The Georgian characteristics of the lower floors had been completely eliminated and replaced with an almost featureless modernity: pale beige carpeting, unadorned doors with plain chrome fittings and lamps that could have come from a motorway hotel.

Lewis could hear music coming from the first room. It was a Mahler symphony. The Ninth. He knocked and after a few moments Paul Renfrew opened the door. Although he was wearing pyjamas and a large, old-fashioned dressing gown, there was something more familiar about him than Lewis would have expected from their previous brief meeting.

At first, Renfrew's expression was blank and humourless. Then when he saw Lewis and Charlie he smiled and the transformation was astonishing. It was like lights being turned on in a shop window.

Instantly, Lewis wanted to smile back in response but then he remembered the sad woman below made desperate by this man's cruelty. When Renfrew saw their grim expressions, he stepped back into the room and let them enter his antiseptic domain.

The corridor outside had set the tone for the rooms exactly. It was just as if Charlie and Lewis had walked into a hotel room anywhere in Europe. There was an inexpensive featureless comfort about the rooms. Bright rayon carpet, plain beige walls, white furniture adorned with brass ornamental handles, a television set and a rather good quality music centre.

Renfrew seemed to consider the symphony unsuitable. He turned off the stereo and stood facing them impassively with his hands in the pockets of his dressing-gown. This time he did not attempt to charm with his smile and Lewis could see that he seemed much tougher-looking without the grin. The face was more roughly cut and the mouth harder.

'Would you care for some coffee?' he said almost lightly and he gestured towards a complicated machine that was filtering the dark liquid into a glass container.

'No thank you,' Charlie said politely and Lewis shook his head.

'Well?' Renfrew said.

'We know everything, Paul,' Charlie said. 'We've come to take you with us.'

He raised his eyebrows at the lack of emotion in Charlie's words.

'No remonstrations about betraying my country?'

Charlie shook his head. 'It would be hard to put a name to your country, Paul. The Third Reich? The Soviet Union?' He held up his hands. 'Here? Somehow I think not.'

Renfrew nodded. Lewis noticed he was smiling again but there seemed little humour in the face now.

'Oh, I had a country once,' he said in a voice so quiet Lewis only just heard him. He did not speak again until he was dressed. 'Where are you taking me?' he said.

'Somewhere special, Paul. A place we haven't used in a long time.'

*

Big Ben chimed the half-hour past midnight as George Ward drew the car to a halt on the Embankment. Paul Renfrew got out last as Lewis looked across the river to County Hall. When they were all together, they waited for a newspaper lorry to pass them and then crossed the road and walked down the stone steps to Westminster Pier. On the landing stood the burly figure of Commander Lear.

As they approached, he flipped the small cigar he was smoking into the black lapping waters and put his hands into his jacket pockets.

'All ready, sir,' he said to Charlie and they boarded the police boat that was moored for them. The engine coughed into life and the barge nosed its way into the stream. The coxswain opened up the power and they moved swiftly down river. Lewis looked towards the Embankment and imagined how the view would have looked in times past: anything to stop him dwelling on the bloody present.

When Romans had brought their galleys through its malarial swamps and kept a guard against the savage tribesmen who watched them from the banks; the water-borne traffic jams of medieval times and the might of Victorian England when the stinking, polluted waters served the greatest port in the world.

The water was cleaner now. Fish were living once again in the protected depths and the great ships were gone.

Lewis looked towards the south east and saw the familiar shape of Tower Bridge, then the floodlit walls of the Tower. From his expression Lewis guessed that Renfrew realised where he was going. The oldest prison for enemies of the Crown. For a thousand years its cells and dungeons had been used to jail those judged to be a danger to the state. Noble and base, heroes, villains; all had known the grim embrace of those grey walls.

When the police barge passed through Traitor's Gate, the warden stood on the landing flanked by guardsmen with fixed bayonets. Their gaudy uniforms did not look picturesque in these small hours. Suddenly their purpose was clear and went with the weapons the men carried. The ceremony of the day became the reality of the night. They flanked Renfrew and escorted him to his rooms.

Lewis and Charlie were taken through the Tower by a Beefeater. They had arranged to be picked up by George Ward outside the main gate. Lewis could feel the fortress about him. He had only been here once before on a summer bank holiday years before but he could still remember the crawling sense of apprehension as he had walked through certain parts of the Keep.

The great slabs of stone wall loomed alternately harsh in the floodlight or in deep, black shadows.

'Do you think it was worth bringing him by river?' Charlie asked. Lewis shrugged.

'It scared *me* – God knows what Renfrew thought.'

They walked on in silence for a few minutes and as they approached the main gate, Charlie spoke again.

'Do you think he'll crack?'

Lewis shook his head.

'No, I don't.'

'I'm inclined to agree with you,' Charlie said.

The Beefeater let them through a side gate and directed them so that a few minutes later they found themselves walking beside the empty moat in search of the duty car.

'Over here,' Lewis said as he saw George Ward holding his hand up to gain their attention.

As they strolled across the wide cobbled road, Lewis thought once again of the house in Chelsea and the sadness he had felt there. Charlie had obviously turned his mind to the same subject.

'We must ask Claire to Oxford for a visit,' he said.

'Did you have no idea that they were living that kind of life?' Lewis asked curiously.

'No idea,' he replied. 'It's rather startling to realise how many years have passed. We saw them from time to time at various social occasions but when you have a family you tend to lose touch with the friends of your youth. I now feel ashamed of neglecting Claire.'

Lewis shrugged. 'You and Sybil weren't to know. Obviously she concealed the situation from you both. Keeping up appearances, I suppose.'

They reached the car and Charlie paused before he got in.

'Yes. Well, I don't really have any excuses. In future I think I shall check up a bit closer on those people I care about.'

They did not speak again until Lewis said goodnight when the car stopped at the end of Lamb's Conduit Street. As he walked the few yards to his front door, the rain of the last few days began again. He stood in the doorway for a while and watched as gutters overflowed and torrents flooded the road before him. The smell and damp of the rain filled the stuffy little hallway, and the patter of rainfall began to mesmerise him.

Lewis thought over the events of the last few hours. He wondered if Renfrew had ever really loved Claire; he wondered how she could manage to stay with someone so cruel and his thoughts, as ever, led to Hanna.

His was not the usual career of an army officer. He knew the sacrifices his mother and grandmother had made in their lives, the long separations, sometimes for years, and the deep, aching fear that came to women when their men were on active service. And then he saw what it was like for Hanna.

His work was all active service. Any day could bring a bomb, a hijacking, an assassin's bullet. All the horrors of modern urban violence affected him and his work was to seek out the danger. There was no home posting; no safe commission in which to pass the time in training and ceremony. Just permanent standby, the never-ending tension of time before battle. He thought of the fear he felt whenever he was taking off in an aircraft and realised what she was trying to escape from.

The rain hissed down in the warm air and he remembered being in a car with his parents when he was a small boy. Janet was just a baby and it was late at night. His father sat in the front with the driver. He could recall how safe he had felt in the car. That's what Hanna wants; what he had in that car. A feeling of love, the protection she needed from the rain outside. All he had to offer was the eye of the storm.

Lewis shivered involuntarily, closed the door on the rain and slowly climbed the stairs to his own rooms. Only now did he let exhaustion overwhelm him.

*

The sound of the doorbell woke him. He pulled on his training shoes and made for the front door, grabbing Rene Malle's raincoat on his way out. As he passed his sister's flat he could hear the sound of someone moving but did not pause to say good morning. The bell was still ringing in his flat; whoever waited outside was clearly determined to see him.

When he opened the door Max Ernhart stood there, protected from the rain by a huge black umbrella held for him by the same sinister figure who had driven his car in Paris. The minder had a square body that would run to fat in later life but now, in his early forties, it had the appearance of a concrete block house. The sports jacket he wore hung on the powerful frame like drapes on an unveiled statue.

Despite the dark glasses, Lewis could see most of the face. It was fair and pink, the kind of skin that would never take a tan. The hands were short and stubby and seemed almost childlike beneath the Harris tweed sleeves.

'Have you ever been a soldier, m'sieur?' he asked the man. The minder smiled without humour.

'*Oui, m'sieur,*' he replied.

'Paras?' Lewis said on a hunch.

The bodyguard nodded.

Ernhart took the cigar from his mouth and smiled. Everything about him was fresh and crisp. Lewis caught the scent of his after-shave lotion and he felt frowsty as he rubbed his own whiskered cheek.

Ernhart held out a red leather pilot's case.

'If you allow me to come in, I will pour you a very good cup of coffee. I understand you live in rather primitive conditions.'

Lewis shrugged and held open the door for him.

'Wait for me,' Ernhart commanded his driver then followed Lewis up the staircase.

'I see the description of your apartment was not exaggerated,' he said, placing the pilot's case on the table near the window. 'If you could provide me with two cups and some small plates.'

Lewis fetched the crockery and Ernhart examined the mugs with a slight sigh. From the large leather bag he took a vacuum flask, a container of cream and a paper bag containing fresh croissants.

Lewis brought some sugar and stirred his coffee. Ernhart looked with disapproval at the spoonfuls of sugar Lewis had put in his cup.

'I wonder if you would use so much of that substance if it were called white death?' he said in a conversational tone.

'I thought that was salt,' Lewis said as he took a sip and looked out onto wet rooftops. Ernhart shrugged.

'Take your pick. They're both a slow form of suicide.' He swallowed a mouthful of croissant and coffee. 'You picked up Paul Renfrew last night.'

'I suppose Bellingford gave you that information,' Lewis said in a cheerful voice.

Ernhart nodded. 'Do you think he'll talk?'

Lewis swallowed more coffee and ran his fingers through his tousled hair.

'I doubt it. Drugs will be of no use in these circumstances. He feels no sense of shame. Sometimes when people are caught they need a release and you can't stop them talking. But Renfrew cares nothing for his wife. It's my guess that he'll sit tight and wait for Moscow to make an exchange or spring him.'

Ernhart took another swallow of coffee.

'Will they spring him? He *is* rather a special case.'

Lewis nodded.

'They know how good it is for morale. The whole world knows they bring their own home and they never give up the search for anyone who harms them or theirs. He knows it's only a question of time. It all makes for a very resolute prisoner.'

'No, we are really going to need some luck to turn Paul Renfrew. We'll just have to cut our losses and settle for the fact that we've captured him. At least we'll be able to operate for the first time without Moscow knowing every time someone wipes their nose in Whitehall.'

'Could anything make him talk?'

Lewis sat back in his chair and placed the coffee mug before him.

'Some kind of shock, possibly.'

Ernhart took a piece of paper from his jacket pocket.

'Lyte says that Renfrew's name was originally Peter Holtz and he came from the Spandau district of Berlin. Correct?'

Lewis nodded. Ernhart relit his cigar and examined the

203

end for a moment. Then he stood up and walked across the room to where the model of the rifleman stood on the piano.

'There may be someone who could deliver such a shock,' he said while examining the figure intently.

'You know a great deal about this business, don't you?'

Ernhart puffed on his cigar again and then turned to study Lewis. It was some moments before he spoke again.

'After the war, I ran a network in East Germany. I started it with the help of my wife. Early in 1953 we heard that the Russians were going to pull off something big. I put the whole network on to it. That was when they hit us – everyone was killed except me. I now think Renfrew was the reason they took us out. They wanted to bring him over to the West and they couldn't risk us finding out about the operation.'

He handed the piece of paper to Lewis. It was a cutting from a German paper. He could not understand the text but the photographs showed an old lady with well-defined features and a young boy in the uniform of the Hitler Youth. The caption gave the woman's name as Frau Holtz.

'The copy says that Frau Holtz is still seeking her son whom she does not believe was killed in the War,' Ernhart explained. 'Life is a jigsaw puzzle. The pity is, you generally get the relevant pieces at the wrong times. Still, it might be the right time for you.'

They both remained silent for a while and then Lewis spoke.

'When did you get this?'

Ernhart shrugged. 'I still have people in Germany to look after my interests. I received this two months ago.'

'Why should it have been of any interest? You didn't know then that Renfrew was really Peter Holtz.' Ernhart nodded.

'No, but my contact knew it had been planted by the KGB.'

'Why should they do that?' Lewis asked.

'Because this is not Peter Holtz's long-lost mother.'

'Then who is it?' Lewis asked.

'My wife, Captain,' Ernhart said without emotion. 'Also known as Tania Chenkolia of the KGB.'

'And all these years you thought she was dead?'

'Yes.'

'Why weren't you killed?'

'I got a tip off, a telephone call, that the two men I was with in a café in the Kaiserhof were going to kill me when they dropped me off that night at the Brandenburg Gate.'

'Who made the call?'

'I never found out.'

Lewis looked at Ernhart with fascination. What an incredible journey had brought him to this room in London. He had crossed the world living out his life against the history of the century. Somehow, Lewis thought, the final act in Max Ernhart's drama was still a long way off.

'I hope what I've told you is some use. If you want me you can get me on the number I gave you.'

Lewis walked to the door with him. Ernhart looked around and smiled sardonically.

'If you worked for me I could promise you something better than this, you know.'

'But would I be happy, Max?'

Ernhart patted him on the shoulder.

'You don't want to be happy. If you did, you would marry Hanna Pearce.' With that final shot he turned and ran down the stairs while Lewis waited until he heard the front door close before he shut his own. How light on his feet Ernhart had sounded for such a big man.

Lewis walked back to the table and drank a final mouthful of coffee. He looked at the time and decided to shower before ringing Charlie Mars. Eventually, he dialled the number but as he waited for a reply there was a knock. He replaced the receiver and opened the front door to Jessica Crossley.

'We've got him,' he said as he picked up the telephone once more.

'Who?' Jessica said.

'The mole . . . the one we've been hunting,' Lewis said as he redialled.

'He has talked?' Jessica asked.

Lewis shook his head.

'. . . Hello, Sergeant Major Watts? Captain Horne here, has Mr Mars arrived? Good. No, don't bother. I'll be there with Miss Crossley in a few minutes.' He turned and took Jessica by the elbow. 'Come on, I'll give you the details on the way.'

During their walk, Lewis told her of the arrest but before he could tell her of Ernhart's visit they had arrived at Gower Street.

'Will you question him?' Jessica asked as they entered the house.

'No. I don't do that kind of work,' he said. 'It's a specialist trade.'

As they crossed the hall Sergeant Major Watts called out: 'Miss Crossley I got a message for you from Mr Bellingford; he says will you go right away to Curzon Street. There are some documents they want you to translate.'

'Right away?'

'Yes, Miss. There's a driver waiting to take you there.'

'See you later,' Lewis said as he started to climb the stairs.

He made his way to Charlie's office where he found him installed with Claude Henderson. The two men listened as Lewis repeated the story Ernhart had just told him. Charlie thought for a moment.

'I think they had better go and see if they can find Mrs Holtz, don't you?'

Claude nodded.

'I'll contact Arthur Chapman in Berlin. If we want to bring her back we had better make sure she has a passport.' Claude started to leave. 'I'll get the duty office to book you on the first available flight and get Chapman to meet you at the airport.'

*

The airbus levelled off for its approach into Tegel Airport and landed in brilliant sunshine. Lewis released his grip on the seat arms and watched the other passengers as they scrambled for the exits. The only people who seemed relaxed about their arrival were two privates who had celebrated the return to their unit with just enough drink to keep them off a charge.

Lewis came out of the main door to be greeted by

Chapman, a stocky young man with light brown hair and a chubby, boyish face.

'We think we've located her,' he said with the sort of excitement ill-fitted to a young man engaged in security work. He led Lewis to a BMW with a crumpled offside wing and opened the door. The inside of the car was a chaos of toys, comics and empty sweet packets.

'Sorry,' Chapman said. 'I borrowed it from Edwards and he's a family man.' Chapman deftly manoeuvred the car through the Berlin traffic and Lewis looked through the windows at the city. Despite the modern buildings and the impressive display of Germany's economic miracle, there were enough remains of the past, where parts of the old city poked through like the bones of dinosaurs, to remind visitors that some cataclysmic event had taken place. Lewis had not visited Berlin often but each time he felt he was in a haunted city.

Finally, Chapman stopped the car before a block of modern flats in the Spandau district. They went to a flat on the ground floor and rang the bell. There was no reply. Lewis looked at Chapman in frustration for some time as he leaned on the bell. As they waited, an old man came shuffling along the corridor. He was wearing an alpaca jacket and grey slacks with sandals; one claw-like hand clasped a polished walking stick. The old man's head was hairless and marked on the dome with large liver spots. He looked as fragile as an eggshell. Only his eyes seemed alive.

Chapman, questioned him in German and he answered in a high quivering voice.

'She has gone to her allotment,' Chapman said.

'Allotment?' Lewis repeated.

'You'll understand when you see it,' he said and returned with Lewis to the car. They drove for some time until they came upon a huge area of allotments similar to the ones around English cities but there was a difference. Where the huts on the British counterparts are shack-like affairs knocked together from corrugated iron, odds and ends of packing cases and waste lengths of wood, the Berliners had constructed quite elaborate chalets with flower pots, window boxes and trellis works covered with roses.

Chapman parked in an access road and they asked directions from a pair of middle-aged sunbathers who sat in front of their chalet as if on the Riviera, studiously ignoring the section of motorway flyover that passed a few metres from them. Following their instructions, Chapman and Lewis picked their way through the plots until they came upon the one pointed out to them.

A small woman with iron-grey hair was trimming a rose bush with methodical snips of her secateurs. Lewis judged her to be in her seventies but her figure was erect. She stopped still and watched as Lewis and Chapman approached; it was as if she had been waiting for them a long time.

'Frau Holtz?' Lewis asked in a friendly voice.

She nodded and Chapman launched into a flow of German that Lewis could not follow. After a few minutes he recognised the name Peter and watched as the elderly woman let the secateurs fall as she raised both of her hands to her face. Half an hour later they got back to her flat in Spandau.

*

The rooms were modern and sparsely decorated, the floors were polished wood and the colours pastel. On a long low sideboard was a collection of photographs. The elderly woman took a silver-framed picture and handed it to Lewis. It was of a boy in field grey. Clearly Renfrew.

Lewis took the photograph and spoke quietly to Chapman, 'Tell her that I talked to her son in London last night.'

Chapman translated the message and they could see the effect it had on the woman.

'Tell her we have a ticket for her and we can be with him this evening,' Lewis said as gently as he could. She took the photograph again and held it so tightly that her hand became white and the blue of her veins showed darkly on the pale skin.

It was easy to bring her out of Berlin. As Lewis had said, within a few hours they had cleared customs at Heathrow and were getting into George Ward's car to make for the reunion she had been promised. As they crossed the concourse to get to the car, a heavy figure watched them from the balcony. He didn't alter his gaze until the car had melted into the general traffic.

*

Lewis and Charlie stood at the end of the garden at Charlie's house in Oxfordshire. They leaned against the five-bar gate and looked towards the lights that shone onto the lawn. The rain had eased leaving the night sky bright from the moon so they could see the trees around them and the tennis court to their right.

'So we're sure it's her?' Charlie said and Lewis turned and looked over the paddock.

'Quite sure. Did he say anything during interrogation?' Charlie slapped the top of the gate.

'He talked a lot. We got the whole story of how he was exchanged. The real Renfrew had no family so the Russians just killed him. Holtz took his place and went straight up to Oxford.'

'Will it work now?' Lewis asked.

Charlie nodded. 'I think so – it should all go as we intended. They've had long enough together. Let's get back to them.'

They walked slowly to the house, through the conservatory and into the stone-flagged kitchen.

Once through the hallway they entered the large living room where Renfrew and his mother sat on a chintz-covered sofa under a portrait of Sybil and her daughters.

Charlie's dogs followed them into the room until they were ordered back into the kitchen where Sybil had remained. Peter Holtz stood up.

'Anything you want, Charlie. I'll co-operate totally.'

Charlie and Lewis exchanged glances of relief and Charlie crossed the room in a few long-legged strides and clasped Holtz's hand.

'My dear fellow, I'm delighted. You'll see, we will give you a new identity and you and your mother will be able to live together without any danger. I give you my complete assurance.'

'What about my department?' Holtz asked.

'You telephoned yesterday and said you had a slight migraine,' Lewis said with a smile.

'You seem to have thought of everything,' Holtz said as he sat down on the sofa again and linked arms with his mother, looking happy at last.

Look not in my eyes, for fear
They mirror true the sight I see,
And there you find your face too clear
And love it and be lost like me.
One the long nights through must lie
Spent in star-defeated sighs,
But why should you as well as I
Perish? gaze not in my eyes.

A Shropshire Lad
A. E. HOUSMAN

Chapter Ten

At ten thirty in the morning, along with other small groups of men who were muttering to each other, Charlie Mars and Lewis stood together in a large conference room in the Foreign Office. Charlie leaned against the mahogany-panelled wall to watch Paul Renfrew as he stood with two other civil servants and began to relate some anecdote with vigorous charm.

'One has to admit, he is a remarkable man,' Charlie said as they watched Renfrew's group burst into laughter at the end of the story.

'I wonder what language he dreams in?' Lewis said softly as he looked down at the worn cuff of his shirt.

'Probably six or seven different ones,' Charlie replied. 'It must be like the United Nations up there in his head. A French king said something about languages, I seem to recall.'

'Charles the Fifth,' Lewis answered. '"To God I speak Spanish, to women Italian, to men French, and to my horse – German."'

Charlie yawned.

'I can never remember that anecdote. I suppose it's because the man who told it to me at school was so detestable.'

Lewis smiled.

'I thought you loved your schooldays, Charlie.'

'I love liquorice allsorts, but I cannot bear the white cog-shaped ones. And that was what that dreadful man was – distinctly cog-shaped. We used to call him The Flogger. His father had been a missionary in Matabeleland. No wonder we lost the Empire.'

At ten thirty-two precisely, Jeremy Bellingford entered. He was accompanied by Prince Nazzan who stood next to him as the meeting came to order and the others

213

took their places at the long table. The portraits of long-dead dignitaries gazed upon the proceedings.

'Gentlemen,' Bellingford said. 'Before I say anything more I would like you to give your attention to His Royal Highness General Prince Nazzan who has something to say to us of the utmost importance in our deliberations about events in Quatara.'

Bellingford sat down and assumed an expression of grave concern as Prince Nazzan smiled at the assembly. It was clear from his demeanour that he was perfectly at ease.

'Gentlemen, thank you for your attention,' Nazzan said. 'It is with the heaviest of hearts that I must tell you of the decision that I and the exiled members of my country's legitimate government have reached after the bitterest of heart-searching.' Nazzan paused and watched the ripple of concern his words brought to the men seated before him. Their previously impassive features had taken on new expressions of interest.

'As you all know, for some time my father, the King of Quatara, has been held hostage along with most of the other members of my family in the Royal Residence. The people responsible for this act of terrorism are the so-called People's Revolutionary Government – a group of criminals who are supported by other international gangsters wishing to destabilise the balance of power in the Middle East.

'So the army of my country, the Loyal Legion, has been unable to destroy the traitors who perpetrated this monstrous deed for fear of endangering the lives of the Royal Family. This state of affairs can no longer continue. I am sure you are all aware that His Majesty, my father, has always made it clear that Quatara stands shoulder to shoulder with all the other civilised nations in our joint endeavours to fight the dark forces who would bring a new age of anarchy to us all. So it is with great sorrow that I say we can no longer yield to blackmail.'

Nazzan paused again and Lewis heard one of the Permanent Secretaries close to him mutter: 'Christ, he's going to invade and let his father get the chop.' When the murmuring voices around the table stopped, Nazzan continued.

214

'We know the gravity of the course we are set upon, but we also know it is the responsibility of Quatara to set an example in fighting for freedom. Therefore, with the co-operation of our ally in the north and with the assistance of Her Britannic Majesty's special forces we shall launch an attack upon the rebels who have usurped the power of the throne of Quatara and restore our great country to the brotherhood of the Free World.'

His speech over, Prince Nazzan sat down to the muted sound of those around the table discussing the implication of his words in low voices.

As they spoke, a thickset man with carefully brushed, greying hair rose slowly to his feet and removed his glasses which he placed neatly on the writing pad before him, regarded them for a moment and then reached out and made a slight adjustment. Once he had positioned them to his satisfaction he put his hands into the pockets of his double-breasted jacket, turned his body in the direction of Prince Nazzan and Jeremy Bellingford and squared his wide shoulders.

'Your Royal Highness, Minister, you may or may not be aware that I was part of the commission that was proud to serve your father when he declared the Kingdom of Quatara in 1947. Since that time I have always been honoured to consider myself one of His Majesty's devoted friends. Therefore, I must state, without equivocation, my attitude to this dubious escapade.'

The speaker paused and thrust his hands deeper into the pockets of his jacket.

'Sir Patrick Congrave,' Charlie whispered to Lewis.

'A very tough old nut.'

Congrave cleared his throat and continued:

'I consider the action you are contemplating rash and dangerous. Far from proving to the rest of the free world our resolution in standing up to terrorism, we shall be seen as cynical adventurers if we perpetrate a bloodbath such as that last demonstrated to the world by the Bolsheviks at Ekaterinburg when they slaughtered the Czar and his family.

'While the King and your Highness's other relatives are safe we must use every other method to ensure their

215

release. May I remind you, we are not in a situation where the Revolutionary Government is demanding anything from us and we are therefore hardly under any immediate pressure. So strongly do I feel on this matter, I must withdraw from these proceedings. I expect that my words have been minuted?'

He nodded to the secretary, took up his glasses and walked with calm deliberation from the room.

Bellingford stood up again and rapped on the table for attention. All eyes turned to him and he looked down at Prince Nazzan who now sat with his eyes fixed upon a crystal ashtray on the table before him. All heads in the room then swung to the top of the table to watch the expressions on the faces there.

'I am sure we all know that Sir Patrick feels very deeply about the course of action we intend to embark upon, but laudable though his emotions may be, we all must know that he was somewhat overstating the case.

'The plan we are contemplating is the only way we can be sure of stabilising the situation in the Middle East, and one that we have agreed upon with our allies after a great deal of heart-searching.

'Your Royal Highness, may I express the sincere gratitude of Her Majesty's Government for your courageous stand on this vital matter and add our sympathies to you and your family at this trying time.'

Bellingford cast his eye around the table and came to rest on the tall, plain-looking man who sat to the right of Lewis.

'I should now like to call upon Colonel David Ferguson of the Special Air Service who will instruct us in the strategy that will be employed by the forces of Quatara in the forthcoming campaign. Gentlemen, Colonel Ferguson.'

The tall figure buttoned the jacket of his two-piece grey flannel suit and walked to a display stand at the head of the table. As he passed Lewis he gave a curt little nod which Lewis acknowledged in kind.

Ferguson pulled a toggle and a small curtain arrangement swung back to reveal a large-scale map. He coughed to clear his throat and stood with one hand in his jacket pocket.

'Your Royal Highness, Minister, gentlemen. This is a crude map of the Kingdom of Quatara. I am sure you are all familiar with the geography of the terrain but to refresh you: Quatara is predominantly a desert country shaped like a pear with the tip pointing south into the Gulf of Aden. The blunt end is defined by the Mountains of Rage and the interior is desert occupied by nomadic tribesmen who owe traditional loyalty to the Royal Family. The port of Quatara, which is at the tip of the pear and which gives its name to the Kingdom, is the only city of any size and it contains the bulk of the population, the Royal Palace and the government. To the west, here, are the oilfields.

'The only practical invasion route from the north through the mountains is the Atzar Pass which is defended at the moment by a battalion of the Revolutionary Army. The plan, which has the gracious approval of General Prince Nazzan, is as follows:

'At 0400 hours on the 17th, two days from now, units of the Special Air Service will have infiltrated south of the Atzar Pass. They will begin a diversionary attack on the defending Revolutionary force and when they are fully engaged, the Loyal Legion will attack in strength through the pass and sweep into the interior.

'There they will advance on a fairly broad front with the purpose of reaching those tribesmen who can be relied upon to rally to the Royal Family. To this purpose it is essential that His Highness be with the Legion to show himself to the loyal tribesmen and thus rally their support. It is to be expected that this action will cause the Revolutionaries in the capital to threaten the blanket execution of the Royal Family unless the invading Legion withdraws.

'We expect them to fulfil this act and announce their actions on Quatara Radio. Our agents have persuaded the loyal tribesmen who have infiltrated the capital to use this announcement as a signal for a general uprising so that the Revolutionaries will be forced to keep a significant section of other forces in the capital. Thus the Loyal Legion will be able to fight two major engagements and by so doing destroy the Revolutionary forces piecemeal

217

rather than fight one set-piece battle, the outcome of which could not be guaranteed.

'So gentlemen, as you see, it is essential to the plan that the Loyal Legion first destroys the Revolutionary Government forces at the Atzar Pass, then goes on to destroy the rest of their forces in another engagement. We hope to achieve this by leaking information to the Revolutionary Government that it is imperative that they keep their main force in the capital.'

There was a stunned silence in the room until a slim gentleman in a well cut, three-piece suit stood up. He brushed aside a shock of white hair that flopped over his forehead and spoke in a rather actorish voice: 'So what you are saying, Colonel, is that the success of this plan relies upon the Revolutionaries murdering the Royal Family so that it will create the proper diversion. If that is so, I begin to think that I should have left with Sir Patrick Congrave.'

Before Colonel Ferguson could answer, Prince Nazzan stood up and banged the table for attention. When he spoke his voice cut through the babbling exchanges. It was the voice of a ruler, stripped of charm and manner. The words were driven like nails and the audience fell silent as he spoke.

'This plan is not the responsibility of Colonel Ferguson. It could only have been contemplated with my acquiescence. Let me remind you, gentlemen, it is my family who are to die and they will do so in the full understanding that such a sacrifice is no more than any loyal patriot of our country would make if he were called upon to do so.'

At that point Bellingford joined Prince Nazzan to signify the end of the meeting. The crowd began to chatter again but gradually the buzz around the table died down and Lewis watched as the white-haired man leaned towards Paul Renfrew and said, 'And we wonder how we earned the sobriquet "Perfidious Albion"?'

Paul Renfrew smiled towards the man.

'Come on, Noel, the British Empire has paddled in muddy waters before now. Just look on it as another opium war, or another Saigon, come to that.'

The civil servant stood up, his anger barely contained.

'That was quite another war and we were fully justified in our actions.'

'Were you, Noel? Aren't you just a teeny bit doubtful? Couldn't it be that the Vietnamese were little oriental people who jolly well ought to be told what to do by Europeans, whereas the Arabs are proud, independent sons of the burning sands?'

The older man produced a scarlet silk handkerchief from the sleeve of his jacket and rubbed it across his brow. Then he threw his head back.

'Really, Renfrew, with your attitude towards the Arabs I often wonder why you never became our resident Zionist.'

And then he turned in a curiously feline way and walked quickly from the room. Renfrew grinned up at Lewis who had kept an embarrassed silence throughout that exchange.

'There is nothing more petulant than a Foreign Office queen. I know Noel of old. He'll be doing his needlepoint all afternoon after that exchange and his secretary will be in tears by tea time.'

'What did the reference to Saigon mean?' Lewis asked, as Renfrew snapped shut his briefcase and turned the combination wheels with his thumbs.

'Oh, he was in the Far East at the end of the war after the Japs surrendered. The British got to Saigon first and found it being run by the guerrillas who, along with American special forces, had been fighting the Japanese. The British re-armed the Japanese who had surrendered and booted out the natives. You see Britain, France and Holland had done a deal to safeguard each other's colonies. The disgruntled natives took to the jungle and that's how the Vietcong first came into being.'

As Lewis nodded a goodbye to Colonel Ferguson he muttered in response, 'It's a complicated world.' Renfrew grinned again.

'Young man, as our American friends would put it: "You can say that again."'

Lewis grinned back as Renfrew and he fell in step behind Bellingford and Prince Nazzan. Charlie joined them at the doorway and as they walked from the room Renfrew lit a cigarette and inhaled deeply.

'Sorry,' he said and offered the packet to Charlie.

'No thanks,' he said with a shake of his head. 'I've finally given them up.'

They made for the Whitehall exit where Charlie had a car waiting, and when they were out of earshot of the others he turned to Renfrew who seemed preoccupied.

'So when will you make the first contact?' Charlie asked as they stopped beside the car.

'I already have,' he said quietly.

'How?' Charlie said with a certain surprise in his voice. Renfrew inhaled again from the cigarette and dropped it to the ground.

'Somebody saw me come out of the meeting smoking without a cigarette holder. At this moment a telephone call is being made to set up the chain.' He turned to Lewis. 'Would you care for a game of squash, Captain? I'll meet you at the RAC Club at 1 pm.'

*

Renfrew was good at squash, too. Despite their age difference he held Lewis to a draw for most of the game but age told in the end. They were both soaked in sweat as they came off the court and made for the showers. Although he was watching carefully, Lewis almost missed the changeover. It happened as Renfrew laid his racquet down for a moment next to a dark-haired young man who was tying his shoe.

As Lewis made for the bar with Renfrew, he glanced in the direction of a loud, braying laugh and caught a snatch of conversation between two young men about a party attended the night before.

'Lovely chaps,' Renfrew said as he waved to catch the barman's attention. Lewis looked at him, puzzled. 'Those clowns in the changing room – you don't approve?'

Lewis nodded a little ruefully. He did not like to let his thoughts show so obviously.

'Strange,' Renfrew said. 'You remind me quite a lot of my old commanding officer.'

Lewis glanced around to check they were out of earshot.

'Your Russian commanding officer?'

Renfrew laughed. 'No, Frederick Kahz was not a Russian. He was a Prussian guardsman.'

Lewis calculated for a moment.

'But you couldn't have been more than . . .'

'Yes, I was very young,' Renfrew said.

'Hitler Youth?' Lewis asked.

Renfrew ordered their beers before he answered. He took the first mouthful and then placed the glass carefully on the bar.

'Until our first engagement, the young man who was leading us had ambitions. He was killed along with the rest of my unit. I was picked up by the regular Wehrmacht and stayed with them till the end. As I say, the officer of my company was a lot like you. Funny, I ended up with the Iron Cross, not that ignorant fool who got the rest killed.'

Lewis looked at Renfrew. His face had become like a mask. It was impossible to find any flicker of emotion; suddenly his companion had become a closed book again.

Lewis finished his lager, bade farewell to Renfrew and then walked the few yards along Pall Mall to the Reform Club. As he did so, he looked up at the buildings that flanked Pall Mall and felt reassured by the dignified façades that spoke of wealth, security and privilege. He tried to imagine scuttling among their ruins, fighting an invading army. To his dismay, he could imagine it all too easily.

He found Charlie Mars sitting in the balcony that overlooked the grand salon.

There was a whisky and soda in front of the empty chair that faced him. Lewis sat down and took an appreciative sip.

'Well?' Charlie said. 'Did he tell you what he was going to pass on?'

Lewis reached inside his jacket.

'Better than that, he gave me a Xerox copy.'

Charlie took the sheet of paper and put on his glasses. He read the message aloud softly.

'"Expect attack timed 0400 hours 17th. Reinforce Atzar Pass but hold small force to put down insurrection in capital city. Loyal Legion troops have been subjected to heavy propaganda campaign to convince them that Revolutionary Government will not dare to execute Royal Family. Suggest major psychological blow to fighting spirit of Legion if Royal Family is seen to be liquidated in public. Would suggest Press invited to witness act so attacking troops are convinced of their deaths."'

Charlie folded the paper carefully and put it in his inside pocket before taking another pull at his drink.

'You know, Sybil's family got me into this business. They were doing it for years. In the last century, when they used to play the Russians in Afghanistan and along the Silk Road to Samarkand, they called it "The Great Game".'

Lewis stretched out. He felt relaxed after the violent exercise and the alcohol he had taken.

'If it's a game, it's a lot more complicated than squash,' he said quietly.

'Come on,' Charlie said suddenly. 'Let's see what's left to eat in the cold room.'

They helped themselves to plates of food and sat down at the last empty table. After a few mouthfuls a figure loomed over them. It was the civil servant Renfrew had called the Foreign Office queen earlier that morning.

'Charles,' he said in a light, waspish voice. 'How nice. We didn't have a chance to speak earlier.'

'Hello, Noel,' Charlie said without warmth. 'Do you know Lewis Horne?'

The man pursed his lips in a sort of smile and slightly nodded his head.

'Noel Landis,' he said. 'I've seen your name on the conference lists, Captain Horne.'

Lewis nodded and concentrated on a forkful of ham and coleslaw.

'What is that you're eating, Charles?' Landis said in the sort of penetrating voice that caused heads at a nearby table to turn.

Lewis thought instantly of the two men at the RAC Club. He felt like directing Landis there so he could harmonise his petulant falsetto tones with their self-satisfied bellowing.

Charlie poked at the pie-crust with his fork.

'Chicken and ham – I think. Anyway, it's very good.'

Landis ate some tomato and lettuce. 'Pie,' he said with great depth of feeling. 'I always think pie is such a brave decision.'

Charlie paused with his fork halfway to his mouth.

'Noel, we're in Pall Mall, not Rawalpindi.'

Landis looked surprised.

'Well of course we are, old boy. You wouldn't catch me eating salad there.'

They munched on in silence for a few minutes until Landis put down his knife and fork.

'What did you think of this morning's proceedings?' he said in a slightly quieter voice.

Charlie shrugged non-committally but Landis prodded further.

'It does seem as if some awful risks are about to be taken, wouldn't you say, Charles?'

Charlie laid down his knife and fork and took up his glass of wine.

'I don't follow, Noel,' he said with great caution in his voice.

Landis leaned forward across the table and spoke very quietly.

'Well, everyone was at this morning's meeting as usual, which rather points to the fact that the mole is still at large, or he has been caught and turned. The action we embark upon is decisive, terminal even. I'm sure the Russians will make an effort to understand what we are up to and one must always remember that they are a chess-playing nation. Complicated manoeuvres are their forte.'

Charlie and Lewis exchanged glances as Landis's eyes flickered between them.

'Well, I must be off,' Landis said as he drummed all his fingers on the edge of the table as if playing a small piano. 'There is still a minor amount of influence we can exercise around the globe, gentlemen.'

He pushed back his chair and made for the pay desk, leaving Lewis and Charlie to think about his words in silence as they finished their wine.

*

Gordon Meredith was lying on his chaise longue with a squash racquet in one hand and an Arabic phrase book in the other when Lewis entered their room at Gower Street. He dropped the large blue plastic carrier bag that he held on top of the desk and flipped through the papers there to check for anything important.

'What did you think of my performance, old boy?' Gordon asked as he gazed steadily at the page of Arabic before him.

'It sounded like a Harrod's mating cry,' Lewis said. 'You must have had maidens pawing the ground and sniffing the air as far away as Sloane Square.'

Meredith grinned.

'It's a bloody sight harder than you may think, keeping up that kind of half-witted conversation, but Claude Henderson was right. You can be inconspicuous by making a lot of noise. The fellow Renfrew made the exchange with didn't give us a second glance.'

As he spoke, Gordon got up and walked over to the desk where he poked inside Lewis's shopping bag.

'You've bought a lot of new clothes that look like your old clothes, dear boy,' Meredith said in a surprised voice, and just then Jessica Crossley looked round the door.

'Charlie Mars says can you come up?' she said and they both followed her to his office.

'I understand you put up a very fine performance as a flannelled fool at the RAC Club,' Charlie said to Gordon Meredith as they filed into his room.

'Thank you, sir,' Gordon said. 'But I hope I won't be typecast in the future.'

Charlie gestured to them to sit down and Jessica squeezed onto the chesterfield with Claude Henderson and George Ward. Gordon took a chair and Lewis remained standing against the bookshelves while Charlie spread his arms along the fireplace.

'Claude, will you tell us all how the operation went? Please don't spare any detail, it is imperative that we all know how things are proceeding.'

Henderson sat forward with a hand on each knee and cleared his throat in a rather self-conscious manner.

'As you all know, Renfrew told us he was going to pass

224

on the information we wanted our Soviet friends to know by his usual methods. As is customary in these cases, the chain would be organised by the receiver and altered at regular intervals. All Renfrew knew was that if he had significant information to pass on from Foreign Office briefings, he was to leave the meeting smoking a cigarette without using his holder and then play squash that day. The contact who saw him was a civil service messenger called Alfred Reese who we know to be perfectly harmless.

'Reese always thought that Renfrew was a secret gambler whose signal meant that he wanted to place a bet that day at a bookie's in Soho. Reese would call at Renfrew's office and take the money for which he was paid a small commission and place the bet at a bookmaker's in Dean Street.

'The bookmaker who took the bet understood that this transaction in fact meant that the services of a certain young lady who works in a massage parlour were required for the gentleman who placed the bet and she was alerted. But I get ahead of myself in the sequence of events. Meredith can take over here.'

Gordon brushed a hand through his short hair.

'I was informed Renfrew would exchange his racquet when he came off the court with Lewis. It was very expertly done. Had I not been warned I doubt if I would ever have noticed. The fellow who made the exchange was just going on to play. He finished his game, had a light lunch and left the club to walk to Soho.'

Charlie held up his hand at this point.

'Do we know who he is?'

'Yes, Charles,' Henderson said. 'He works for Aeroflot in Piccadilly. No other form; it seems he's just used for this function.'

'Go on,' Charlie said. Meredith continued.

'I left the club with him and gave the nod to George here, who was disguised as a potential taxi driver on the knowledge.'

Everyone glanced over to Ward who blushed slightly.

'The fellow set out on foot along Pall Mall and up the Haymarket towards Soho. He went into the Swedish

Girls' Massage Parlour in Dean Street which is above the bookmakers Claude mentioned earlier.

'I had kept Claude on RT all the time so he was there in one of our cars as the courier entered the building.'

Claude leaned back and crossed his arms on his chest. He looked very embarrassed.

'I had adopted the guise of a northern businessman who was well oiled and looking for gratification.'

'A northern businessman, Claude?' Charlie said with a certain levity in his voice.

'Certainly,' Henderson replied. 'I was born and bred in Leeds and can still manage the accent.'

Charlie bowed his head in acknowledgment.

'Please continue.'

'The place was quite small and run by a statuesque woman with platinum-blonde hair. By acting the blundering innocent I managed to persuade them I was prepared to pay a great deal of money but unable to perform any feat of sexual prowess. Their greed overcame them and I was allowed to watch the other customers through the bouncer's peepholes.' He glanced around the room. 'They have them in case any customers cause difficulties, you know.'

'You continue to enlighten us, Claude,' Charlie said.

'Yes, well. I found our Aeroflot friend having his two penn'orth all right. When she was finished he unscrewed the end of his squash racquet and handed her a piece of paper.

'I made out to my guide that I was in danger of passing out or worse and was unceremoniously dumped on the pavement outside, where I was able to identify our lady courier to George Ward.'

Ward leaned forward again. 'She got a taxi in Shaftesbury Avenue and went directly to the White Lodge Hotel in Lancaster Gate. Within minutes Claude had arrived on the scene with an ops van and staked out the place.'

Claude produced a brown manila envelope from the side of the chesterfield and held it aloft in triumph.

'Precisely twenty-five minutes later this gentleman was seen to enter the premises.'

Claude held out the envelope and Charlie took it from his hand. He pulled out six, grainy ten by twelve inch photographs. Lewis leaned forward to look at them over Charlie's shoulder. They showed a large, smartly-dressed man in his fifties with a forehead made even more pronounced by receding black hair, walking up the short flight of steps to a pillared entranceway. Charlie looked at the top picture for a moment and held it so Lewis could see it more clearly.

'Klashkov,' Lewis said and Charlie nodded.

'The bait appears to be inside the bear. If our friend the Cultural Attaché is as efficient as usual, we can be sure the information is already with Moscow Centre.'

He carefully placed the photographs on top of the pile of books on the mantelpiece before turning to the assembled company.

'Thank you all. Claude, Lewis, will you hang on?'

The others left the room and Charlie crossed his arms and spoke with obvious sincerity. 'Thank you, Claude, for a fine piece of work. I'm very impressed by your expertise.'

Henderson smiled sheepishly.

'Thank you, Charlie, your words are appreciated.'

'Tell me,' Charlie went on with a smile, 'what was the Swedish Girls' Massage Parlour like?'

Claude shrugged.

'I must confess I found it rather dreary. I imagined that it would be erotic but the actual experience saddens rather than arouses.'

Charlie nodded.

'I think it best to keep some of our fantasies firmly in place; reality can be the greatest of disappointments.'

He moved from the fireplace and sat down on the vacated chesterfield.

'I asked you to stay on for a moment because I wanted to let you know that Lord Silver and Max Ernhart are on their way here. All the arrangements are made. I dare say there are personal things you want to do, Lewis?'

Lewis nodded.

'Yes. I think I'll pop along to Boots and buy myself a bottle of suntan lotion. Oh, by the way, what will you do with Renfrew and the old lady?'

Charlie looked up from a piece of paper he was studying.

'I'm putting them in a safe house tomorrow with Jessica Crossley and George Ward to look after them.'

Lewis nodded.

'OK. See you later.'

As he passed Penny Rose's office the door was ajar. She was standing at her desk speaking on the telephone. George Ward stood next to her and they were holding hands. Lewis smiled as he walked on. They managed to look silly and rather touching at the same time, he thought. And then his mind turned to Hanna. He collected Rene's raincoat from his room and his bag full of new clothes and set off for home.

The sky was a sullen grey and shed a shadowless light over the city. Once inside his flat he rang the Middlesex Hospital and asked for Hanna's department. He got through to a secretary and asked what time she was off duty. The girl told him seven o'clock.

He thanked her and hung up, went to the bathroom, shaved and then laid his new clothes out on the bed. The creases in the blue Oxford-weave shirts annoyed him. He set up the ironing board and pressed all six of them. Then he dressed quickly in the new dark grey flannel suit and gave his shoes an extra shine. Before he left the flat he rubbed the wooden soldier for luck.

Half an hour later he stood in the forecourt of the Middlesex Hospital and waited for Hanna. She came out walking quite slowly, and when she saw him kept the same grave expression on her face as she stopped and waited for him to speak.

'What's a nice girl like you doing in a joint like this?' he said. She closed her eyes and smiled at him, and taking advantage of the opportunity, he leaned forward and quickly kissed her. Even though the contact was brief he felt the same familiar current pass between them. A sensation he had never felt with any other woman.

She opened her eyes and said, 'Of all the gin joints in the world, why did you have to walk into mine?'

Lewis thrust his hands into the pockets of Rene's raincoat.

'I'm supposed to say that. You're supposed to say "Just hold me, Ric. I don't want to think anymore."'

They looked at each other for a few moments as other people passed them by, and Lewis felt that he had never loved her as much as he did at that moment.

'I'm a hungry, lonely man looking for a rich woman to buy him a meal – any chance?'

She cocked her head to one side, then said 'OK – providing you don't talk politics.'

'We never discuss that subject in the mess, that or sex.'

He took her arm and they walked at an easy pace towards Charlotte Street.

'I ought to go home and change, but what the hell. Do you mind eating with a dirty doctor?'

'Say what you like about me, but I'm no snob when it comes to hygiene.'

'Where are we going?' she said.

He pointed ahead.

'The White Tower has a reservation in your name. I told them to cook us a crispy duck and not spare the apple sauce.'

'It sounds good. I'm in no mood to choose from a long menu.'

Lewis kept the conversation light. They drank their aperitifs and ate a selection of delicious pâtés with thick, freshly-made toast. Neither of them was in the mood for a difficult confrontation so the time passed in easy affection.

When Lewis had swallowed the last of his brandy he looked at his watch.

'You're not going to believe this, but I've got to have an early night.'

She smiled. 'Suits me, soldier,' she said.

He paid the bill and they strolled back towards the Middlesex where Hanna's little black Scirocco was parked. She opened the door and turned.

'Can I drop you off?' He shook his head.

'No thanks, I think I'd like to walk.'

She looked into his face and her hand tightened its grip on the top of the car door. Lewis reached inside his jacket and took out an envelope which he handed to her.

She took it and he said, 'Goodnight, Hanna,' and quickly walked away.

Slowly she got into the car and held the envelope for a moment. There was something hard and lumpy inside. She opened it and took out a sheet of paper and a shiny metal emblem. The letter read:

Dear Hanna,

I do not possess anything of value but I treasure this badge more than anything else. It belonged to my great-grandfather. I am going away tomorrow and the plain fact is that I might not get back. What I must tell you is that I love you. And my life changed and was better for knowing you. I wish I could be something else, but I am what I am.

Yours ever, Lewis.

She sat for some time without moving, then she spoke in a soft voice:

'Damn you, Lewis . . . damn you . . . you'll break my heart if I let you.'

And as she looked down again, tears fell onto the page and caused the ink to run.

230

Clay lies still, but blood's a rover;
Breath's a ware that will not keep.
Up, lad: when the journey's over
There'll be time enough to sleep.

A Shropshire Lad
A. E. HOUSMAN

Chapter Eleven

Lewis raised his binoculars towards the south-west and looked at a landscape that dissolved into shimmering bands from the heat of the sun. The only colours he saw were the white-grey of the dusty concrete runway which merged into sand and the pale blue of the sky.

As he watched he could feel the perspiration soaking into his khaki service shirt where it stretched tight across his back. He lowered the binoculars and wiped his eyes, then raised them again.

A dot that altered in shape and size seemed to swim into the scope of his vision. After a time it gradually grew into the outline of a fat, insect-like object and finally, the recognisable shape of a Hercules C-130 transport.

Lewis lowered the glasses again and wiped the perspiration from his forehead, then turned and walked towards a low concrete building that barely showed above the level of the runway.

As he descended the steep, narrow stairway the metal railing was hot to his touch. He entered the underground complex and Charlie Mars looked up from a copy of that morning's Nicosia paper.

Charlie was dressed for the tropics. He wore a straw panama hat, a blue-and-white striped seersucker suit and a pair of old, white canvas shoes.

'They're coming in,' he said. 'I just heard on the radio.' He nodded towards two men in white short-sleeved shirts who maintained contact with the aircraft. They were seated at a brightly-lit control centre at the far end of the room. Charlie sat further back in the cool, air-conditioned gloom. 'How is it out there?' he asked, and Lewis smiled back at him.

'Like the desert always is. Hotter than chilli peppers and drier than grave dust.'

Charlie folded his paper and laid it aside on the metal-framed table.

'Curious language, modern Greek,' he said as he tapped the newspaper. 'I don't think I shall ever learn to enjoy it. By the way, where are Meredith and Sandy Patch?'

Lewis sat down next to him on one of the tubular metal chairs, took off his beret and laid it on the table with his binoculars.

'They're strolling around the perimeter. It takes a little time to adjust to these weather conditions after the temperate climes of England. I don't want them sweating too heavily on the streets of Quatara.'

'How about you?' Charlie said and he reached for the glass of iced tea that rested at his elbow and took a few appreciative sips.

'You forget I was here recently. My tan's hardly faded or hadn't you noticed?'

Charlie tipped his hat forward over his eyes and sat back in his chair with his long legs stretched out before him. He seemed curiously relaxed.

'Do you know my grandmother never had a holiday in the sunshine. She couldn't believe it when my mother and father took to going to the South of France during the summer. My grandparents had a house near Cannes which they kept closed from March to November. In their time, only peasants had suntans, and certain foreigners of course.'

As he finished speaking, Sandy Patch and Gordon came into the bunker and flopped down on to the other chairs around Charlie. Their uniform shirts were soaked in sweat, but Charlie could see that despite the hostile conditions all three men were very fit.

They listened to the crackling radio conversation between aircraft and control centre until it was clear that the Hercules had come to a standstill. Lewis left the bunker and made his way to the aircraft that was standing on the edge of the airfield casting dark shadows on the heat-soaked runway. Some of the passengers had already disembarked and were standing under the wing to take advantage of the shade.

234

'Hello, Lew,' Colonel David Ferguson said as he approached. 'What's the state of play?'

'Sod all here, David, I'm afraid. They only open up this strip when they decide to have a war. There's a little shade and air-conditioning but it won't take more than half-a-dozen at a time. But at least they've got a large supply of a fizzy drink that tastes of ice-cold chemicals. I suggest the aircrew refuel and we get the lads to put up some kind of canvas shelters they've got stored. At least it will keep the sun off them and it won't be for too long.'

'Right,' the colonel said. 'Take Wally and Andrew and show them where that stuff is you mentioned. Incidentally, how are our hosts?'

Lewis was distracted for a moment as he watched the troopers bringing the first of their Land Rovers off the back of the Hercules. Then he turned back to the colonel with a grin.

'Oh, you know, same as ever. Arrogant bastards but good at the job.'

Colonel Ferguson nodded.

'Sure. Well, I'd much sooner have that than charming inefficiency.'

Major Andrew McQueen joined them and heard the colonel's last words.

'Any information on when our allies are due to arrive, Lewis?'

After consulting his watch, Lewis said that they could expect the others within the hour, then he led them to the storage area before he rejoined Charlie.

'We'd better try and get a few hours' sleep,' he said to Sandy and Gordon. 'There's a little room at the back there that should do the job.'

'Height of luxury, boss,' Sandy Patch said. 'They've even got bunks.'

'Tell the others we're going to get our heads down, will you, Charlie?'

'Certainly,' Charlie Mars replied as he picked up the newspaper again and turned to the crossword puzzle.

Once inside the tiny room Lewis looked around at the dusty racks of bunks with their hard, straw-filled mattresses, and clambered into the one nearest the door. As he lay down he looked up at the wooden slats of the bunk above him and thought of the pilots who had rested in the same bed. Then he closed his eyes and slipped into sleep.

He came to with a trooper shaking his shoulder and holding out a mug.

'Tea up, guv,' he said in a Geordie accent.

Lewis sat up and took the steaming drink. It was British Army brew all right – dark, hot and sweet, with a slight disinfectant tang. Lewis drank some and shivered. The air-conditioning was blasting away but he knew that outside the heat of the day would soon leave the parched landscape and a coldness would come to the rocks and sand. The three of them left the small room and entered the control area once again.

The fluorescent lights caused them to blink as they gazed around the concrete bunker. Charlie was sitting at the same metal table playing chess on a tiny, travelling set with one of the flight controllers.

'We're on our way to a briefing, Charlie,' Lewis said and Charlie raised his hand in acknowledgment, but kept his eyes on the board.

The three collected heavy canvas bags full of equipment and left the bunker. The recently deserted airstrip had undergone a transformation. Now, in the crystal-clear night air, lines of Hercules transport planes stood on the runway behind them, rows of tents were pitched in a mathematical precision so they created a neat canvas township of narrow alleys and broader streets. Lights powered by humming generators were strung from poles, and as the three walked towards their own headquarters, they looked back into perfect illumination and watched the troops of the Quataran Loyal Legion going about the business of camp life exactly as soldiers had done for thousands of years.

When they reached the command tent they dumped their gear just inside the entrance and joined the other officers and NCOs who had been eating a picnic meal of cold meat and fruit. There were even a few bottles of wine.

Lewis made himself a chicken and ham sandwich which

he ate quickly and then he took his time to munch his way through a large, green apple as he looked around the tent at his companions. Each man wore the same distinctive sand-coloured beret but that was the single common feature of the group.

There was a sense of calmness about them: a relaxed atmosphere that professionals give, like an orchestra before a performance. Eventually, Ferguson stood up and the conversations died away.

'Gentlemen,' he began. 'If you will come closer; Wally, the map if you please.'

The officers and NCOs left their camp stools and folding chairs and gathered around a map which revealed the familiar contours of Quatara.

There was a good-natured groan from the assembled crowd and the colonel held up his hands in mock protest.

'All right, all right, you've seen a lot of this corner of the world recently, but just one more time, OK?'

Lewis glanced at the group. Despite their earlier protestations they faced the colonel with grim attention.

'Quatara,' the colonel said as he slapped the map with the palm of his hand. 'A pear-shaped country with the capital at the tip which juts out into the Gulf. One flat plain of desert and an outer perimeter of mountains as rough and nasty as shark's teeth. One pass to and from a friendly country to the north and held by one battalion of the Revolutionary Army. The other two battalions are in the capital, impressing the populace and holding the Royal Family hostage. What we and our friends are about is quite simple. We are going to help the Loyal Legion to take back the country. Our specific tasks are not difficult.

'Captain Horne and Captain Meredith will take a small force into the city of Quatara. They leave in a few minutes. The rest of us embark soon and we will be landed here.'

He pointed with his forefinger to a place on the map before the Atzar Pass.

'Now this part of the desert is flat and clear enough to land a Hercules. The local tribesmen who are loyal to the Royal Family have made sure that it's free of obstructions and they will guide us in. We have to move forward and hold the Revolutionary Army in the pass by giving the

237

impression we are a much larger force – radio signals, dashing about in desert vehicles, that sort of thing. But we must hold until we are either relieved or they overrun us. If the latter should happen, don't try to make it through the interior. Circle around and try for here, here and here.'

He pointed to three spots on the map to either side of the major pass.

'You won't make it in the Land Rovers but the mountains can be climbed and when you get over, make for this spot.'

He pointed once again to a place on the map beyond the mountains.

'In four days' time at 1300 hours there will be a pick-up. Major McQueen will give you the exact co-ordinates for your map references. But let's hope all that will be unnecessary.

'Remember, a handful of Spartans held a pass much wider than this one against an entire army of Persians. They all got killed in the end, but that was because they were a load of dozy Greeks and we are not, gentlemen. So get to your positions and see that your men are ready for the events that the day will bring.'

Lewis walked back to the food table and took another apple. Curious, he thought, it was a fruit he never ate in England but here, in the desert, it took on an exotic quality that the grapes and peaches somehow lacked. He found himself standing next to Andrew McQueen.

'How about your co-ordinates, Lew! Where do you make for if things get a bit ropey in the city?'

'We just melt into the crowd, Andy.'

McQueen grinned. 'And then you all swim back several hundred miles to Cyprus?'

Lewis took another apple and put it in his trouser pocket.

'You know the old saying, Andy. You shouldn't have joined if you can't take a joke.'

He made for the exit and bumped into Meredith.

'We're all ready, Lewis. Our gear is aboard. Take-off in seven minutes.'

Lewis nodded.

Outside, Charlie Mars was standing with the Colonel in the cold, clear night. Above them the sky glowed with starlight. Lewis shook hands and walked swiftly to the waiting aircraft. Inside, Sandy and the ten troopers had strapped in for take-off. Meredith appeared in the dim interior lighting with the pilot. Lewis took one of the apples from his pocket and tossed it in his hand like a cricket ball.

'OK. Just one more time. We come in parallel with the beach at three hundred feet and jump four miles to the east of Quatara. The sea shelves sharply there so we will be close to the shore. On the beach, we regroup and make for the capital. A Bedouin tribe who we rendezvous with will take us in. Clear?'

'All clear, boss,' they answered.

'Who jumps first?' Lewis asked.

'Me, sir,' said a trooper with a Scots accent.

'Right, MacDonald, you win the prize.' He tossed him the apple, sat down in his seat and strapped in.

'No standing in the aisle,' the pilot said. 'Good luck, lads.'

After a few minutes the engines' roar reached a thunderous pitch and the aircraft swung out onto the runway. The lights in the interior went out and Lewis was suddenly glad of the darkness.

As the engines revved to even greater thunder, he could feel the familiar tightening in his chest and the sweat run in his palms. He wanted to leap to his feet and throw himself from the monstrous machine that held him in its bowels. Then the pilot released the brakes and the aircraft lurched forward and began to accelerate down the runway. Finally, it lifted into the sky.

Eventually, they levelled off and the engine note settled down to a steady drone as they headed south. The lights came on again and Lewis could look into the unconcerned faces of his fellow passengers. They made themselves as comfortable as they could for the long boredom of the flight, and time passed with the usual aching slowness. Finally, the co-pilot came back and indicated that they were within half-an-hour of their dropping zone. The men began to check their equipment and then the aircraft came down low and they began their run for the jump. They were in the sea within seconds and quickly into the self-inflating black rubber boats that had hit the surface moments before their own descent.

As they rowed for the shore they could see flickering lights and black robed figures came across the beach and helped them drag the boats ashore. They followed their guides across a wide expanse of flat, firm sand and then on to a camp that was alive with yapping dogs and moving people. Beyond the camp, camels were tethered in lines.

Flames from cooking fires flickered up into the dark night as Lewis was taken aside and led to a tent. Inside was a figure dressed in the same dark clothes as the other Arabs.

'Hello, Lewis, nice of you to drop in,' Prince Nazzan said with a grin. 'Forgive me for the cliché, but I'm afraid I really couldn't resist the temptation.'

Lewis shook hands.

'Everything seems to be going according to plan,' he said, 'but it's early yet. The Loyal Legion must be under way. It's imperative that my men and I start for the city immediately.'

'That has been arranged,' Nazzan said. 'Your equipment has been loaded onto camels; your men and some of my Bedouins are to go in to the market.'

Nazzan had spread a map on the large table that stood in the centre of the tent.

'You recognise the map of the city. The Palace here against the sea, then the outer circle of the old walls, and finally, the new suburbs of the city.' He tapped the map. 'The market is here next to the old wall. Inside is the barracks of the Revolutionary troops. You have to get inside the old wall, past the troops and then inside the Palace itself.' Lewis nodded.

'I'd better get dressed.'

Nazzan gestured to the corner of the tent.

'Your clothes are ready.'

Lewis quickly put on the black robes and made his way to where his men were waiting. Nazzan came with him and held out his hand.

240

'God be with you,' he said and stood impassively to watch Lewis and the rest of his group lead their camels on the road to the city. They passed across rocky scrubland for a while until they came to a macadam-surfaced road and their guide indicated they should keep to the side.

'Soldiers in lorries drive along very fast,' he informed Lewis in English who passed word to the others. And a few minutes later as if to confirm the guide's advice a lorry came swaying along the centre of the roadway and blew its horn continuously as it passed the plodding camel train.

Lewis caught a glimpse of troops watching them without curiosity as the lorry swayed past. They looked like arrogant boys, each clutching shining new Kalashnikov rifles as if they were birthday presents.

Eventually, the train reached the first buildings on the outskirts of the city and occasional patches of vegetation where irrigation had brought palm trees and flowers to the once rough countryside. Most of the buildings were new, including the Hilton Hotel which had been seized by the Revolutionary Government and now housed emissaries from those countries friendly to the new regime.

Lewis noticed that the ubiquitous Mercedes stood in their usual ranks, and he imagined the sleeping dignitaries from Iron Curtain countries tossing in their air-conditioned rooms, dreaming of postings to the capital cities of the West where their wives could find happiness in the shops of the decadent.

As they got closer to the old city walls they could sense the tension: scout cars buzzed angrily through the streets and they were ordered to the side of the road on two occasions as staff cars drove past with darkened windows and flying insignia. When they reached the city wall and turned for the market place, the huge gates of the ancient town were open and bright lights showed the activity inside. Motor vehicles began to stream from the gates and Lewis could see that the Revolutionary Army was on the move. They stopped their caravan and watched as armoured cars, troop carriers and artillery began to form in convoy.

Ignored by the modern army that passed them, Lewis

and his group stood and watched and counted the strength of the enemy. Two battalions, Lewis calculated and one battalion at the Atzar Pass. That was it. There could only be a light garrison left inside the walls.

Lewis nodded and Meredith, along with two troopers and two of the camels, detached himself from the group to move slowly ahead.

The first stallholders were setting up their wares as Lewis and his remaining men settled down beside the walls. Very soon the first streaks of light began to illuminate the sky and, as the shape of the city became clearer in the dawn light, a distant rumbling caused the early workers to pause for a moment while, from the west, the dark forms of massive transport planes came in low and parallel with the coastline.

'OK,' Lewis said, and his men began to strip the loads from the camels and assemble their equipment to the fascination of those market workers who stayed to watch. The ten men quickly set up mortars which they loaded with charges and grappling hooks. On an order from Lewis, they fired simultaneously so that ten ropes snaked into the air and curved into the battlements of the old wall.

Together Lewis and Sandy Patch ran forward to the gate and thrust satchels against the steel-reinforced wooden staves. Moments later a shattering explosion reverberated through the city and a gaping hole was blown in the ancient wooden doors. Lewis and Sandy tossed canisters into the breach which exploded into a dense, white smokescreen.

Meredith and his men had reached the section of the city wall where it became part of the Palace. They had also prepared their equipment so that when the sound of the explosion came to them, they fired off their grappling hooks and began to climb the walls. By the time they were on to the battlements, four guards who were nearest to them had recovered from the shock of the explosion and were looking around in alarm.

They were too late to bring their rifles to bear on the intruders. Meredith and his men fired simultaneously so that the camouflage-suited figures fell into untidy heaps on the white stone battlements of the Palace.

242

Across the roofs Meredith could see the crouching figures of other guards firing as they advanced.

'Take care of them,' he said almost casually as he looked intently across the white-painted rooftops of the Palace for a certain architectural feature. He had been told that an air-cooling vent gave near access to the quarters of the Royal Family.

He scanned the shapes before him until he located the one he sought. Only then did he take notice of the fire they were drawing from the rooftop guards.

'Cover me,' he said and he edged forward and wedged himself against the object that resembled a Chinese pagoda. He attached two satchel charges and twisted the time detonators. Then he ran back again with bullets kicking chunks of stone and plaster from the surrounding surfaces.

'Down,' he shouted and all three men flattened themselves simultaneously as the charges blew the pagoda in the air. It tumbled back to crash on to the roof a few feet away. Firing as they edged forward to the hole they had blown, they looked down into the interior of the building.

'Christ, it must be a thirty-five foot drop,' one of the troopers gasped as they looked at a mosaic floor covered in debris beneath them.

'Keep holding them,' Meredith said and he worked his way back to the battlement walls and recovered one of the grappling hooks and rope. Snaking his way back, he paused for a moment and through an ancient archer's slit in the walls, looked beyond the city to where he could see the fleet of aircraft landing on the firm sand near the sea shore.

As the transports touched down, the bellies of the planes opened and men and machinery began to pour out. Prince Nazzan stood on the head of the beach with an Israeli general and watched as the Loyal Legion disembarked from the planes and formed into a convoy.

As the last units took their places and began to move out, the Prince turned and shook hands with the sun-burned figure beside him.

'General Kahn,' the Prince said with grave courtesy,

'the people of Quatara will never forget the debt to Israel that we have incurred today. Please convey my deepest gratitude to your Prime Minister, and my sincere thanks.'

The General turned and smiled.

'I shall be delighted, Your Highness, but this occasion gives me even greater pleasure as I am performing the service for a fellow school friend.'

Prince Nazzan raised his eyebrows in astonishment and the General nodded.

'Oh yes, a few Jews get in as well, you know.' He started to walk back to his aircraft and as he did so called over a salutation *'Floreat Etonia'* as Prince Nazzan continued to gaze after him.

A staff officer hurried over to the Prince. 'We are ready to move, sir.'

'Very well, Captain. You know what to do.' And as he spoke, the sound of gunfire rolled back to them from the city.

*

After Lewis and Sandy had exploded the smoke canisters, armed figures began to emerge from the nearby buildings and stormed the gaping hole in the gate. They were the Bedouin tribesmen whom Prince Nazzan had ordered to infiltrate the city, and they pressed into the breach with fanatical courage as the remains of the garrison inside began to defend their position. Lewis and Sandy rejoined their troopers and scaled the walls to where the others were waiting.

'Action at Captain Meredith's position, boss,' one of the men said, and Lewis peered through the smoke that had drifted up from below towards the rattle of fire.

'Come on,' Lewis said, as they followed him. 'We can't have them winning all the medals.'

The irony of his words was not lost on them; no matter how desperate the engagement, no medals would be awarded for their part in the events of the day. As they moved forward, Lewis glanced over the battlements to the point where the walls joined the Palace. The garrison appeared to have their hands full with attacking Bedouins. He prayed that the defenders wouldn't realise the existence of the Fifth Column.

After a few yards they came under fire from the same guards who had engaged Meredith. One of Meredith's troopers had been left to cover while he and the other man descended into the Palace.

When Lewis and his force had worked their way forward to the hole, he left two others to give supporting fire and the rest of them shinned down the rope into the shadowy interior of the Palace.

*

The officer commanding the second and third battalions of the Revolutionary Army was riding at the head of his force in a staff car when he was overtaken by a Jeep with a lieutenant waving frantically for him to pull out of the convoy. With some irritation he ordered his driver to take advantage of a widened section of the road used for overtaking and the officer saluted.

'Well, comrade lieutenant?' he demanded coldly.

'A message, comrade colonel. The city is under heavy attack. The garrison is calling for assistance.'

The colonel looked non-plussed by the information. He had been told that there was no threat to the city.

'Are you sure this is accurate, lieutenant?' he asked suspiciously.

'Look, sir,' the junior officer said and the colonel followed his pointing finger towards the capital. They could see plumes of smoke rising from the city.

'Take me to the rear of the column,' he ordered his driver, and they swung the car around and drove on the rough surface beside the convoy-jammed road.

At the rear, the colonel found a group of his senior officers gazing towards the clouds of billowing smoke that had risen into the sky.

'Comrades,' he shouted. 'Turn your vehicles and follow me back to the city.'

The order was obeyed with some difficulty, but eventually the column turned and set off in the direction of Quatara. About three kilometres from the outskirts of the city, the ground fell away on each side of the road to leave a raised surface. The area was about thirty metres wide where the road covered it. When the returning convoy was stretched along the section, the armoured vehicles of the Loyal Legion rose from the concealed slope that was nearest to the sea and concentrated fire on the exposed flank of the Revolutionary battalions.

Those that tried to escape the initial onslaught drove into the Loyal Legion artillery waiting at the base of the slope on the other side of the road. After fifteen minutes the Revolutionary force was destroyed.

Prince Nazzan slowly rode past the rows of blazing vehicles and the piles of dead that lay in their huddled masses. When he had reached the end of the column, he called to an officer who was reassembling his men by the roadside, 'Colonel, take your detachment and relieve Captain Horne in the city. We go on to the Atzar Pass.'

The colonel saluted and immediately began to shout orders to his subordinates. Prince Nazzan turned once again and drove through his triumphant forces who now began to cheer him as the staff car drew through their ranks.

*

Lewis lowered himself into the hole and slid down the rope. After the blinding light on the roof, the gloomy coolness of the interior seemed safe and quiet as the sound of gunfire receded, but the illusion was not to last. As he dropped the last few feet, two of his men opened up with their sub-machine guns as guards came at them. Lewis saw they were standing at the exact corner of two corridors where they met at right-angles. To the left they could see a large area of light against the high, decorated walls cast by the wide expanse of a great stairwell.

'This way,' Lewis said as he made for the illuminated section. As he came to the banister that protected the balcony, Lewis could see that a massive double staircase led up to the corridor they now moved along.

The banisters, which curved away gracefully from the head of the stairway, were a masterpiece of carving. On each complex pattern was a delicate geometric lacework of marble. Hanging from the ceiling was a brass chandelier that swirled and gleamed with inlaid silver.

As Lewis came to the edge of the stairwell, he could see

guards running up the far staircase. With Sandy beside him, he raised his sub-machine gun and fired. The heavy-calibre ammunition tore into the delicate tracery of the staircase carvings and pieces of white marble shattered, flying in all direction like exploding clay pipes on a fairground rifle range.

Behind Lewis three troopers shouted a grenade warning and Lewis and Sandy flattened themselves against the wall as three grenades curved past them. The explosions that followed sent bomb fragments and pieces of marble singing through the air and ricocheting off the walls.

'Those are the Royal apartments,' Lewis said, pointing across the killing ground to where the corridor continued. 'Sandy, you come with me. Gordon, you hold this stairwell with the others.' He looked around at Sandy who was bleeding from a slight cut on his left cheek. 'Ready?'

Sandy nodded.

'OK,' Lewis said. 'Let's go.'

They sprinted across the exposed area of corridor, past walls being raked with automatic gun fire. Lewis could feel his robes being plucked and pulled as if by invisible fingers and at any moment he expected to feel the numbing blow of a round hitting his body. They threw themselves the last few yards to the welcome safety of the corridor walls.

'OK?' he gasped.

'OK, boss,' Sandy replied and they grinned at each other with the relief of having lived through the shooting gallery.

At the end of the corridor stood the massive brass doors that Lewis knew led to their ultimate goal – the Quataran Royal Family. He and Sandy turned the huge levered handles and it took both their strengths to haul open one of the great double doors. The room they revealed was massive and the sight that greeted them so astonishing, they stood momentarily frozen with surprise.

Inside the great throne room was a Bedouin encampment almost identical to the one they had been in a few hours before. The room was misted with smoke as fires burned in braziers about the hall and the smell of roasting meat came to them.

Three goats gently butted against Lewis and Sandy's legs. Ranged before them were the men of the Royal Family gathered around the King. But they were not dressed in the elegant white clothes of the aristocracy; these were resolute tribesmen in the dark robes of their ancestors.

The women and children were grouped behind their menfolk chattering noisily above the sound of bleating goats. Lewis stepped forward and bowed to the King who looked at him impassively.

'I am Captain Lewis Horne of the British Army, Your Majesty, at present acting under orders from your son, General Prince Nazzan. We are an advance party, but we expect to be relieved by your Loyal Legion at any time.'

From behind him Lewis was aware of the continuing gunfire as Gordon and the others continued their battle at the staircase. The King stepped forward and spoke in a quiet voice, despite the relentless noise a few metres away.

'Do you have any other weapons, Captain Horne?'

Lewis reached down and took his Browning automatic from its holster and handed it to the King, butt first. The King took the pistol, checked the magazine, cocked the weapon and began to walk purposefully past Lewis towards the sound of the gunfire.

'Sir,' Lewis shouted, and in desperation seized the King's arm and stopped him walking further. The men of the Royal Family surged forward at this insult until the King held up his hand to subdue them.

'Yes, Captain?' he said in the same courteous voice.

'I beg you to stay here with the Royal Family,' Lewis said. 'I understand your reasons for wishing to join the fighting but my men are pledged to save your life and they might have to take unnecessary risks if you are beside them.'

The King paused for a moment, then nodded.

'Very well, Captain. We place ourselves under your protection.'

Lewis sighed with relief.

'Thank you, sir. If you could please ask the Royal Family to gather themselves against that far wall and not to move about, we should be grateful.'

The King shouted the orders in Arabic and his tribe moved to the position Lewis had indicated. Sandy and Lewis ran back along the corridor to where they could see their men pinned down by the richochets from a light machine gun that was pouring fire from the stairwell below.

They stood out of range a moment as they checked the magazines on their sub-machine guns.

'OK, boss,' Sandy shouted above the echoing gunfire.

'Together,' Lewis shouted. 'Now.'

And they leapt into the open and poured concentrated fire for three seconds onto the machine-gun crew before jumping back into cover.

The machine gun stopped and Lewis looked across the landing.

'Anyone hit?' he shouted to his men and the call came back: 'Two light wounds, boss, nothing serious but ammo is getting low.'

Lewis and Sandy each took two magazines from their webbing and threw them across the open corridor. That movement set off another burst of fire from those below. They lay on the floor and took stock of their situation. Between them they had four grenades and eight magazines for their sub-machine guns.

'Pull back,' Lewis shouted. 'Let them try a charge.'

Meredith raised his hand in acknowledgment and Sandy and Lewis withdrew to the end of their section of the corridor. The others retreated to the hole in the roof from where they had entered the Palace interior.

Lewis and Sandy sank down and sat with their backs to the great doors to load the last of their ammunition. Each took a grenade and waited. The attackers below sent a storm of fire on to the balcony and when it was not returned, Lewis distinctly heard the order in Arabic for the charge. A few moments later the corridor in front of them was filled with camouflaged figures.

Lewis and Sandy threw their grenades into the packed mass and began to fire. The doors at their backs juddered from the weight of ammunition that was pumped into them and Lewis snapped his last magazine into the breech. As he did so, he heard the distinctive coughing bark of heavier calibre machine gunfire and shouting from below. Gradually the firing ceased from the mass before them and after a few moments a tall figure wearing the immaculate uniform and Arab head-dress of the Loyal Legion picked his way over the heaped bodies at the head of the stairs.

He walked along the corridor to where Sandy and Lewis were sprawled.

'Captain Horne? I am Colonel Al-Akmed.'

The elegant figure turned and looked along the ruined corridor to the huddled mass of the dead lying amid the debris of battle.

'The nearest run thing you've ever seen in your life.'

Lewis nodded as he listened to the clipped English tone. He looked at Sandy who sat with his back to the brass door and his empty sub-machine gun across his lap.

'He's quoting the Duke of Wellington,' Lewis said in a hoarse voice. Sandy smiled wearily as he looked along the smoke-filled corridor and the chaos before them. 'Jesus, Boss, it's an education working with you.'

*

The Russian ambassador banged the air-conditioning unit with the flat of his hand but it continued to make a loud, rattling noise. He turned once again to look with distaste at the slouching figure in camouflage combat fatigues that sat in front of his desk, nursing a chrome-plated Colt .45 automatic in his right hand.

'You were saying, comrade?' the ambassador prompted in a curt voice.

The President of the Quataran Revolutionary Government waved the pistol in the direction of the elderly Russian and spoke loudly, his hysteria barely concealed: 'You have betrayed us. All the information you gave us is wrong. The Legion has wiped out most of our army and is now on the way to the Atzar Pass to finish the job. You should be shot as traitor.'

The ambassador intensified his state to one of loathing. He walked around the desk and quietly snatched the flashy gun from the President's grasp.

'Comrade, I suggest you end this fantasy of shooting people and think about your own life. As for our information, clearly our man in London has been tricked, or turned into one of their own agents. These things happen. All you can hope is that the King continues to respect our diplomatic immunity or there will be a public execution for the loyal citizens of Quatara to attend very soon.'

The Arab's face seemed to crumple, but the ambassador offered no comfort. As he heard the sound of cheering from the streets, his thoughts turned with pleasure to the prospect of returning home to Moscow.

*

Prince Nazzan stood next to the armoured car that he had used in the recent battle. The field dressing on his left arm was looser than he would have preferred. He called an aide over to tighten it and as the young Captain nervously adjusted the bandage he felt the wound begin to throb with pain.

Around them the desert was littered with the broken and burning shells of wrecked vehicles and the untidily sprawled bodies of the dead. Nazzan watched the medics moving through the landscape looking for survivors for a moment then he waved over a signals officer who came to attention before him.

'Major, prepare a message to the King.'

The officer took out a notebook and Prince Nazzan began to dictate.

Your Majesty. It is my honour to report an overwhelming victory against those traitors who sought to overthrow your reign. The Loyal Legion has annihilated the Revolutionary Army in two engagements that took place today and the remains of that army are held prisoner for your judgment.

It is also my sad duty to inform you of the gallant allies of Her Britannic Majesty Queen Elizabeth's special forces who are missing after this glorious struggle. Before the Atzar Pass, Colonel David Ferguson and his detachment of officers and men were overrun by numerically superior forces. The bravery with which they fought and the losses they inflicted upon the enemy will inspire those who learn

of their deeds in the future. Signed, General Prince Naz-
zan. Get that off to the capital immediately.'

The signals officer saluted and Nazzan turned away
from the battlefield and looked towards the distant mountains that stood jagged along the skyline like broken glass
on a wall. He massaged his wounded arm for a moment
and spoke softly.

'You're up there, aren't you, David? With your bunch
of bloody cut-throats, eating lizards and staying alive.'

Oh soon, and better so than later
After long disgrace and scorn,
You shot dead the household traitor,
The soul that should not have been born.

A Shropshire Lad
A. E. HOUSMAN

Chapter Twelve

''Ere you are, son. You deserve it,' Lord Silver said as he handed Lewis the champagne. 'And you, Charlie.'

Charlie carefully placed the drink in the indentation on the plastic table before him. The three of them sat in the otherwise empty first-class compartment of a British Airways Tristar, half an hour out from Tel Aviv bound for Heathrow.

Lewis wore a pair of slacks and a lightweight jacket he had bought on the way to the airport. Charlie was dressed in the same seersucker suit which was beginning to show its age. The old canvas shoes had given out completely, and the seams were beginning to split. Lord Silver looked as if he had been on a long holiday. He wore a short-sleeved shirt, and a few hours' sunshine had left him with a deep suntan that would take most people several weeks to acquire.

'Obviously the deal has come to a successful conclusion,' Charlie said and Silver nodded vigorously.

'When the peace treaty is signed next week,' he said, 'Max's company will supply electronic equipment to the Israeli Army and the Loyal Legion, and Israel will train Quataran pilots. In exchange they'll have a base there.'

'Where did the Israelis get all those transport planes from?' Lewis asked suddenly.

'The Yanks,' Silver said as he sipped his champagne. 'But the pilots were their own.' He looked either side of him at the profiles of Charlie and Lewis, then he nudged Lewis in the ribs. 'Come on, tell me 'ow you did it.'

'Ask him, he worked it all out.' Lewis smiled, looked across at Charlie and then beckoned to the ever-attentive air hostess for some orange juice.

Lord Silver turned to the older man.

'Come on, Charlie. You know I've been vetted by security. Blimey, even the Prime Minister 'as to trust me.'

Charlie stretched as best he could and sipped his champagne. At that moment the air hostess returned with a jug of orange juice. Lewis drank half his champagne and held out the glass.

'That's Premier Cru, you know, son,' Lord Silver said in a slightly wounded voice.

'Sorry,' Lewis said, 'it's all the same to me.'

Silver shrugged with good humour once again.

'Ah, what do I care, you can pour it over yer bleedin' 'ead if you like.' He turned once again to Charlie. 'Come on, tell us 'ow you pulled it off.'

Charlie put down his glass again.

'It's a long story, Jack. Are you sure you won't be bored?'

'Try me,' Silver said.

Charlie nodded.

'It goes back to the war. Nikolayev was one of Moscow Centre's most brilliant planners. Of course, it didn't save him in the end. Beria had him executed in one of Stalin's purges. Before the war he had known Max Ernhart in Hamburg. He had the foresight to know that Max would be in a position of power one day and he wanted a way of infiltrating his organisation.

'Nikolayev originally met Tania Chenkolia at a party given by the Director of the Moscow State Theatre. She was a brilliant actress and everyone expected her to become a great star. Instead she went to work for Nikolayev. Together they thought of the idea of training a captured child but Nikolayev had other plans for Tania as well.'

Lord Silver nodded and Charlie continued: 'When Zukov's army entered Berlin in 1945 Tania went in with the front line troops with orders to find the right kid. She found Renfrew, or Peter Holtz as he then was, and brought him back to Russia. He was indoctrinated until he was ready to serve his new masters and then he was transferred to the model village at Riga where he spent the next seven years.

'The real Paul Renfrew was a National serviceman in the British zone of Berlin in 1957. After the army he was due to take up a scholarship at Oxford. His family had been killed in the Blitz so no one cared too much about him. The day after he was discharged the Russians killed him and substitued Peter Holtz who took up his place at Oxford.'

Lewis could see that Lord Silver was intrigued by Charlie's narrative. His champagne remained untouched before him.

'So what about Max and Tania?' he asked.

'After Tania brought out Peter Holtz she was sent back to Berlin when Nikolayev discovered Ernhart was starting up his network there.

'She got a job in one of the drinking clubs that were springing up in the ruins. They were fantastic places, full of high-ranking officers trading cigarettes for anything they wanted.'

Lord Silver smiled. 'You forget I was there, Charlie. I remember it well. But go on.'

'Max was introduced to Tania by Nikolayev and he fell for her immediately. She was a brilliant linguist and highly intelligent. They got married on Christmas Eve 1945 and she helped him to set up his network in the east, so of course when the Russians wanted to close it down they just killed them all. But they missed Max. He was tipped off.'

Lord Silver thought for a while:

'There's still something missing, isn't there?'

Charlie and Lewis exchanged smiles.

'Quite right, Jack. There was Nikolayev's master stroke. When they wiped out Max's network, Tania went on to play her final role. She became Peter Holtz's long-lost mother.'

'Good God,' Silver exclaimed. 'You mean the woman in London is Max's wife?'

Charlie nodded.

'But surely Max would have recognised her?'

'That's why he wanted to hire Lewis. The Russians made three recent attempts on his life and Max didn't know why. You see,' said Charlie, 'if Renfrew's cover was blown, they were going to leak to us that his mother was still alive so we could find her and Renfrew would pretend he had been turned to our side. The last thing they wanted was Max Ernhart finding his wife again. So they made a concentrated effort to knock him off. But that dreadful ex-Para of his always managed to thwart them.

'Look,' Charlie said, and he reached inside his jacket and produced a wad of cuttings. 'These are stories planted in the West German papers about Frau Holtz's long-lost son, Peter. They put these in to act as a lure to us as well.'

Silver took the cuttings and looked at the picture of Renfrew as a boy in his Wehrmacht uniform.

'Bloody incredible,' he said. 'Bloody incredible.' He handed them back to Charlie. 'So it's all over now except the sweeping up.'

'We hope so, Jack. The deal we've done with Max is that we hand Tania back to Moscow and in exchange we ask them to stop trying to knock Ernhart off.'

'So that puts your offer of a big job with him out of court, lad,' Silver said. 'Could you have kept him alive?'

Lewis shook his head.

'No, the assassin always gets through. So far, Max Ernhart has been incredibly lucky, but Moscow Centre will get him in the end if they really want him; unless returning Tania buys them off.'

'So it would have been a short-term contract anyway,' Lord Silver said sympathetically.

Lewis nodded as he raised his glass once again.

*

Eventually, the hostess returned and asked them to fasten their seat belts for the landing. The aircraft taxied to a halt and they looked out onto a weeping sky and the greyness of Heathrow.

After the usual trudge, they cleared Customs and stood on the concourse with their hand baggage. Lewis could see two figures making for them. Claude Henderson, his face creased with anxiety, weaved through the crowd and Raoul, Ernhart's bodyguard, pushed past people until they both stood before them.

'Bad news, I'm afraid,' Claude said first. 'They've flown the coop.'

'Who?' Charlie asked.

'Renfrew, his mother, and they've taken Jessica

Crossley with them. George Ward is badly wounded. Almost dead.'

'What happened to him?' Lewis asked.

'He was stabbed by somebody left-handed, according to Commander Lear,' Claude said.

'Herr Ernhart wants you to come with me,' Raoul said to Lewis. 'He says he can be of some help.'

'You had better go with him,' Charlie said. 'It sounds as if we can use all the help we can get.'

When they got to Ernhart's Rolls Royce, Lewis was surprised to see there was another passenger sitting in the back seat. It was Ernhart's daughter.

Raoul opened the door and Lewis slid in beside her.

'I hope you don't mind,' she said rather distantly. 'I just came along for the ride.'

'Not at all,' Lewis said, but he could see she wasn't really interested in his reply.

'Where are we going?' he asked Raoul.

'Not far,' he replied and deftly pulled out in front of a battered red Capri with a rebuilt wing the colour of putty.

Lewis caught a glimpse of pure hatred from the young black driver then looked into the rearview mirror to see a brief smirk of satisfaction on Raoul's face.

'Don't think he's only prejudiced against black people,' Sharon said coldly. 'He hates everyone with equal passion. It could just as easily have been a Swede in the car.'

Lewis nodded.

'I've met his type before. He's probably very fond of animals.'

'I once killed two Alsatians with my bare hands,' Raoul countered, his voice full of self-satisfaction.

Lewis smiled up at the face in the driver's mirror.

'Yes, it's a sad business, drowning puppies,' he said with deliberate misunderstanding.

Sharon squeezed his arm in warning and Lewis took the hint. He tried some small talk with his fellow passenger but she merely glanced at him and then lowered her eyes.

'What's up?' he said quietly and then, as will often happen with strangers, she told him how unhappy she was.

259

Lewis listened in silence until she had finished.

'So you've left him and come home to Mum and Dad?' he said, and she nodded.

'And you say he's a psychiatrist?'

She nodded again. 'But he could be much more than that. He's absolutely brilliant, but all he wants to do is work in that grotesque little place in Hammersmith.'

She held up her hands. 'I don't understand. He could have everything.'

Lewis looked across at the beautiful, sulking girl beside him.

'Maybe you were driving him crazy.'

She looked at him quickly and laughed for the first time. 'That's what he said. "You're driving me crazy."'

Lewis folded his arms.

'Did he say anything else?'

She thought for a moment.

'He used to say that Lennon and McCartney got it right: "All You Need Is Love!"'

Lewis thought about the statement for a while. Hanna would certainly agree. And that, of course, was the root of their problem. One love, but two incompatible jobs. With no solution to his problem, he turned his thoughts to Renfrew.

What did he love? Certainly not his wife. A country? But which one? Somewhere there had to be a clue, Lewis thought.

So immersed had he become in the Renfrew conundrum that Lewis, at first, didn't notice the changing landscape. They had come to a road on the edge of a Thirties estate with a long, high-security fence on one side. Behind the fence there was a long mass of shrubs and bushes. It was the sort of growth one saw on the embankments of railways or patches of waste ground, a tangle of hawthorn, elderberry and crabapple.

They drove alongside the fence for a time until Raoul reached forward and took a small box with buttons on it like a calculator, punched a series of numbers and pointed it at a set of gates that immediately swung open.

As they drove on, the tangled wood gradually gave way to trees that had obviously been chosen by a landscape gardener rather than the random hand of nature. The rutted gravel road they drove along finally stopped before a magnificent Tudor house that was surrounded by lawns and orchards. The car purred to a halt before the entrance and Lewis could see a row of hothouses filled with flowers and fruit, and beyond, a box hedge that had been trimmed into a series of geometric shapes beside an oval-shaped swimming pool.

Sharon and Lewis got out of the car and Raoul drove it away to park in a stable courtyard to the right of the house. The door was opened by a heavy-set, square-faced woman with sturdy limbs and braided corn-coloured hair.

'This way,' she ordered Lewis in a thick accent.

'See you later,' Sharon said as she started up a wide staircase that led to a gallery. He looked around as the German woman waddled ahead of him. Suits of Tudor armour stood at the foot of the staircase and the panelled walls were hung with pikes, swords and flintlocks. It was a quiet house. The only sounds were the slap of the woman's slippers on the flagstone of the hallway and the clip of Lewis's shoes.

She reached a great door that was carved in relief with flowers entwined with woodland animals, then knocked and opened it.

It led to a vast room with a high ceiling, hung with tapestries and decorated with dark Tudor furniture. In front of a fireplace carved with the intricacy of a medieval cathedral sat two gleaming Doberman Pinschers.

A log fire burned in the hearth. Ernhart was sitting in a large bishop's straightback throne chair. He had been reading a sheaf of papers and as Lewis entered, he threw them onto the fire.

'I hate those bloody shredding machines, don't you?' he said to Lewis, and at that moment Raoul entered one of the window doors from the garden. Immediately the Dobermans got up and began to circle one another in an agitated fashion.

Raoul noticed and made a clicking noise but they ignored him.

'Maybe they're related to the Alsatians, Raoul,' Lewis said lightly. Ernhart looked at him sharply.

'What's that supposed to mean?' he said.

'Just a joke Raoul and I have,' Lewis said easily.

'I don't like jokes I don't understand,' Ernhart said with a sharp edge to his voice.

'If ever I work for you, I'll bear that in mind,' Lewis said coldly.

Immediately, Ernhart became businesslike.

'Listen to this,' he said and walked over to the huge table that ran through the centre of the room.

Near a silver bowl full of long-stemmed red roses was a small tape recorder next to a telephone. Ernhart pushed the start button and the sound of a telephone ringing came to them clearly.

'*Dobri dyen,*' said a man's voice with a heavy Russian accent, and another man spoke in the same language. The conversation continued until Ernhart reached out and snapped off the recorder. Lewis looked at Ernhart expectantly. The big man leaned against the ancient oak table and smiled.

'Do you know who that was?'

Lewis shook his head.

'Our friend Renfrew.'

'Good,' Lewis said. 'But I already knew he could speak Russian.' Ernhart gave a short, barking laugh.

'What you don't know is, that conversation was recorded two hours ago.'

Lewis was impressed.

'Who was he talking to?'

Ernhart shook his head. 'I can't tell you.'

'I suppose you have a good reason.'

Lewis looked up at the intricately carved ceiling and for a moment his mind went to the ruined staircase in the palace in Quatara. He wondered how Ernhart would appreciate two or three hundred rounds of nine-millimetre ammunition pumped into his fine carvings.

Ernhart walked slowly over to the fireplace and the glowing fire reflected on his impassive face.

'I want to be there when you pick them up.'

Lewis shook his head.

'You know I can't do a deal like that.'

Ernhart looked round at him.

'Those are my terms. I will only tell you where they are if you play it my way.'

Lewis folded his arms and watched the heavy figure who had turned back to gaze once again into the flames. He knew he had to believe him.

'All right, Max,' he said with conviction.

Ernhart nodded without turning round.

'Be back here at ten o'clock in the morning.'

Lewis started for the door.

'Raoul, take Captain Horne to London.'

The bodyguard walked with him but in the hallway they found Ernhart's daughter once again.

'I'm going into London,' she said. 'Do you want a lift?'

He glanced at Raoul and nodded. 'As far as Chelsea,' he said.

'That's all right, Raoul,' she said. 'I'll take Mr Horne.'

The big man hesitated for a moment then gave her the car keys.

*

The dark blue Audi dropped him on Cheyne Walk and Lewis watched Sharon drive into Oakley Street before he turned and rang the bell on the red door. After a while the ancient housemaid appeared and looked up enquiringly at Lewis.

'May I speak to Mrs Renfrew, please,' he said and she continued to gaze at him suspiciously.

'I was here the other day,' he said, 'with Mr Mars.'

She peered at him more closely, then she opened the door wider.

'Come in,' she said. 'Wait here.'

He stood in the hallway and watched the black-clad figure as she shuffled away. A few minutes later Claire Renfrew entered the hallway.

'Forgive me for this intrusion, Mrs Renfrew. I was here the other day. My name is Lewis Horne.'

'Yes, Mr Horne,' she said in a quiet voice.

'I would like to look through Mr Renfrew's rooms.'

She nodded. 'Very well. Edna will take you up. If you need anything, please ask her.'

Lewis thanked her and she seemed to drift away from

him. Edna plodded up the staircase with Lewis on her heels. He went into the bedroom and Edna stood at the door with her hands clasped in front of her.

'Don't let me keep you,' Lewis said and he could see that she left the room with the greatest reluctance.

He sat on the neatly made bed and slowly looked around the featureless room.

'There's something here,' he said in a soft voice. 'There always is.' He took the slim penknife from his jacket pocket and started to search the room with slow methodical thoroughness. But after two hours he was ready to give up, defeated. Never before had he found so little trace of a personality.

It was as if Renfrew had refused to leave any clue to the human being that had once inhabited these featureless rooms. His clothes were neatly hung in the wardrobe and folded in the chest of drawers. A desk held nothing but the volumes of his stamp collection. Lewis probed, poked and slit with the razor-edged knife and still found nothing.

Finally, almost wearily, he took each of the records from the shelf and shook the covers. From the seventh, a photograph fluttered to the floor. It was a cheap colour picture taken with an inexpensive camera. Lewis studied it for a long time and then he placed it carefully in his inside pocket.

*

At nine-fifty the following morning, Lewis paid the mini-cab outside Max Ernhart's stately home in Hayes. There was a light drizzle in the air so that he had to button Rene Malle's raincoat to the throat as he pressed the intercom on the gate.

'Yes?' it squawked at him after a moment.

'Lewis Horne,' he said and the gate buzzed until he pushed it open. He walked carefully to avoid the muddy indentations in the gravelled drive and the dense trees wept steadily upon him until he emerged by the lawn before the house.

Ernhart stood at the open door and watched him walk towards the house. When he got to the porch Ernhart said in a conversational tone: 'What did you say to my daughter yesterday?'

'Nothing special. Why?'

Ernhart ushered him into the house.

'She went back to her husband today.'

'I'm delighted to hear it. But you must be disappointed.' Ernhart stopped.

'Disappointed? Me, why?'

'Because he's a no-hoper, non-achiever. In your eyes anyway.'

Ernhart shrugged.

'He's not a bad lad, really. Once he gets all the rubbish about loving humanity out of his system he'll be fine.'

Lewis followed Ernhart into the room they had met in the day before.

'Suppose he remains an idealist,' he asked.

'There's no chance of that, son. He's in constant contact with human beings. You can only remain an idealist if you keep everyone at a distance.'

'But you think individuals can remain loyal to each other?'

Ernhart looked at him without emotion.

'Some have the luck, but it's a random business, like being born with a high IQ or being an albino.' Ernhart looked at him closely. 'Take you. Gone for a soldier. You really believe it, don't you?'

Before Lewis could answer, the telephone buzzed quietly. Swiftly Ernhart crossed the room and lifted the receiver. He listened for some time then hung up.

'I suppose you want to know the identity of the Russian Renfrew was talking to,' Ernhart said.

Lewis nodded.

'Karaskov,' Ernhart said. 'When I learned he was the one who was running Renfrew I had him covered continuously for seventy-two hours. He's got a bolt-hole in Fulham owned by the lady who visited him from the Swedish Girls' Massage Parlour. I put a tap on their phone.'

'What did they say?' Lewis asked.

'Very little,' Ernhart replied. 'Renfrew assured him he was in a safe place and Karaskov told him to call again tomorrow morning at ten o'clock when he would give them an exit route. I have just heard where it is.

'Karaskov has instructed them to make for one of the

tiny Hebridean islands where they are going to be picked up tomorrow morning by a Russian trawler. They put in at those islands all the time, buy supplies and have the odd drink. We've all known about it for years and turned a blind eye.'

Ernhart bent over and scratched one of the Dobermans, though Lewis kept his distance.

'I have a great many arrangements to make before we start on our journey. Is there anything I can do to make your stay prove pleasant?'

'Yes,' Lewis said. 'I wouldn't mind a swim.'

'You'll find bathing suits in the pavilion next to the pool, Captain. Go out through those french windows and it's to your left. I hope you enjoy your dip.'

Despite the awful weather, Lewis looked forward to the exercise. He undressed quickly and put on a pair of bathing trunks from a selection strung on radiators in the changing rooms.

It was a fair size for a private pool. Lewis dived in and swam a length beneath the surface, turned underwater and swam back. When he broke the surface there was the figure of a woman in a bathing suit looking down at him.

At first he took her to be Ernhart's daughter but when he had wiped the water from his eyes he could see that she was older, although of similar build and colouring.

As he looked at her she dived over him into the water and swam lazily to the end of the pool before swimming back to greet him.

She grinned as she came to rest alongside him.

'We must be bloody mad, swimming in this weather,' she said in a pleasant, low voice.

Lewis held out his hand, feeling slightly awkward to be shaking hands in a swimming pool. 'My name is Horne. I'm an associate of your husband's, too.'

They swam for some time in silence and when Lewis had had enough exercise, he showered in the pavilion and dressed once again. Mrs Ernhart had simply put on a large, white towelling robe and a pair of sandals.

As they walked back towards the house, Ernhart came out to greet them wearing an anorak and a tweed fisherman's hat.

His wife put her arm through his and laid her head on his shoulder for a moment. Ernhart looked amused at Lewis's puzzled expression.

'Yes, Captain Horne, the rumours are quite wrong,' he said. 'My wife and I are happily married.'

They walked on for a while. 'Think how vulnerable I would be if people knew I loved her. In this modern world, it sometimes helps to disguise the things you truly care for.'

As he spoke, a chattering sound grew to a shattering climax and a Sikorsky helicopter came down on to the lawn before the house, blowing the trees at the edge of the wood into disorder and throwing leaves into the air. As soon as it settled, the door opened and Charlie Mars came out in a crouch and hurried towards them.

'You'd better get a move on,' he said. 'Our boat is ready at North Uist.'

Raoul came out of the house carrying two large holdalls, Ernhart kissed his wife and climbed aboard the massive helicopter after Charlie, Lewis and Raoul.

'Next stop, Scotland,' Ernhart said as they lifted off.

*

Lewis watched a cormorant weave and dip in the clear sky above him as the twin Merlin engines thrust the boat through water as blue and calm as the Mediterranean. Despite the clear stretch of sea they crossed, there were banks of white, rolling mist that occasionally engulfed them.

Lewis felt uncomfortably hot in his navy blue fisherman's Guernsey. Ernhart, who was at the wheel of the powerful motor boat, seemed unaffected by the heat even though he was wearing a heavy-knit white roll-neck sweater.

'According to my calculations,' Charlie said from his position at a small chart table in the cabin, 'we should see the island to the north-west any time now.'

Lewis looked at his watch. It was eleven-twenty. They were cutting it a bit fine, he thought. Just then, a call from Raoul drew their attention and they could see where patches of the mist cleared to reveal their destination.

Ernhart altered course very slightly and sent the boat surging forward with even greater speed. Eventually, he throttled back and the boat cruised into the little stone-walled harbour.

Keeping their faces away from the direction of the jetty, they found a berth as far from the main harbour steps as they could. Raoul tied up as they pulled on reefer jackets. Each of them wore seaman's boots. To the casual observer they blended into the scenery.

Lewis looked around and realised their task would not be difficult. A narrow street led down to the harbour front. A general store and post office stood at one corner of the lane and a small public house on the other. Next to the store was a ship's chandlery and the rest of the harbour was ringed with tiny flintstone houses.

Charlie walked slowly over to an old seaman who sat by the harbour wall and engaged him in conversation. Raoul entered the ship's chandlery and Lewis, the general store. Ernhart tried the door of the pub but it was closed. He ambled over to the harbour steps and sat down with his hands in the pockets of his reefer jacket.

Lewis came out of the store with a day-old copy of the *Daily Record* and sat down to read in the shadows in front of the store. Raoul left the ship's chandler's and walked over to the harbour wall to gaze down at the water as it lapped pieces of box wood against the stone wall.

Then they heard the buzz of an outboard motor and they could see a cutter entering the harbour mouth.

'Russkies,' Lewis heard Raoul say, and at that moment there was the sound of footsteps coming down the narrow street.

Lewis slipped his hand inside his jacket pocket to grip the butt of his Browning automatic as he watched the three figures pass him and make for the harbour steps. They were quite close when Renfrew made his move.

Instinctively, he reached out with both hands and pushed Jessica and Tania away from him before he reached for the revolver in his waistband. It was a terrible mistake.

Almost casually, Max Ernhart took the Walther from his jacket pocket and shot Renfrew in the chest. Before he collapsed onto the cobblestones, Lewis could see the blood pumping from the wound. Raoul had moved close to Ernhart and as he did so, Jessica Crossley looked down at Renfrew and gave a terrible, keening cry of grief. Then she came at Ernhart in a crouching lunge and Lewis could see she was holding a long-bladed knife in her left hand. Raoul stepped in front of him and blocked her way but he could not deflect the weapon. She drove the blade deep into his solar plexus as he got his stubby, powerful hands around her throat. Such was the strength of the man they could see she was a dead woman.

There was confusion in the Russian cutter. They were about to pull away when Ernhart shouted for them to stop.

Tania was still on her knees where she had fallen. Ernhart walked slowly forward and took her hands to help her to her feet.

They did not speak but nor did they take their eyes from each other until he had led her to the steps and pointed down at the boat. Then he said in German, 'The telephone call in the Kaiserhof. It was you, wasn't it?'

'Yes,' she said, without any emotion in her voice.

'Thank you for that,' Ernhart said as he let go of her hand.

Quickly she walked down to the boat. Ernhart watched her for a few moments more.

Then he turned back to Lewis and the crowd of people who had appeared to look down on the embrace that Raoul and Jessica had achieved in death.

'You knew this girl was the killer, didn't you?' Ernhart said and Lewis nodded. He took the colour photograph he had found in Renfrew's room from the pocket of his jacket and handed it to Ernhart. It showed Jessica and Renfrew together. They were sitting at a table on a terrace somewhere in the sunshine.

'That doesn't seem very strong evidence,' Ernhart said. 'Everyone knew they had known each other for some time.' Lewis nodded.

'When I found this I went to her flat and searched it. She'd kept a diary. Every night when Renfrew left her to cross the river to Chelsea, she wrote what had happened that evening, what they had talked about. She'd even told me about the affair in Paris. Though mentioning no names, of course.'

'Where is it?' Ernhart asked with interest.

'I burned it,' Lewis said.

Ernhart smiled grimly.

'You are a romantic, Captain. It must be the Welsh in you.'

Lewis watched Ernhart who was now looking out to sea.

'Do you think it's over, now?'

Ernhart turned to him.

'We gave them Tania back, but who knows? I might still want you to take poor old Raoul's job.' He looked down at the bodyguard for a moment. 'He was not a particularly nice man, but he was loyal to me.'

Lewis nodded. 'Even unto death,' and then realised that his hand still rested on the butt of his Browning automatic.

Charlie, who had knelt beside Renfrew, came to where they stood as he wiped his bloody hands on the fisherman's sweater. 'He's gone,' he said. 'His last words were in German.'

'What did he say?' Lewis asked. Charlie shrugged.

'He said, "The building is falling upon me." I wonder what it meant?'

*

Once again, Lewis sat outside the Café Flore and watched the waiters perform their morning ritual at the Brasserie Lipp.

On the empty chair beside him was a carrier bag containing Rene's purloined raincoat. Lewis had sent it to the most expensive cleaners in London. He had left the bill inside, hoping it would mollify the owner.

The waiter brought him a *café crème* which he carefully sugared to his liking. As he stirred the coffee, a shadow fell across his table and a familiar polished emblem was placed next to the cup.

He looked up into Hanna's face, she stood over him with her hands in the pockets of a raincoat.

'What is the Geneva Convention covering the treatment of prisoners?' Hanna said.

Lewis took a sip of his coffee.

'Name, rank and serial number must be given. Food and shelter must be provided. And it's every officer's duty to attempt to escape.'

She sat down beside him and slowly their heads came together as they began to talk. A few minutes later, Rene Malle arrived to keep his appointment with Lewis.

After a moment of glancing around at the packed tables, he spotted him, then hesitated.

The couple clearly had no wish to be interrupted.

Rene smiled and walked away. After all, he was a Frenchman.

All Futura Books are available at your bookshop or newsagent, or can be ordered from the following address: Futura Books, Cash Sales Department, P.O. Box 11, Falmouth, Cornwall TR10 9EN.

Please send cheque or postal order (no currency), and allow 60p for postage and packing for the first book plus 25p for the second book and 15p for each additional book ordered up to a maximum charge of £1.90 in U.K.

B.F.P.O. customers please allow 60p for the first book, 25p for the second book plus 15p per copy for the next 7 books, thereafter 9p per book

Overseas customers, including Eire, please allow £1.25 for postage and packing for the first book, 75p for the second book and 28p for each subsequent title ordered.